DOUBLE TAKE

DOUBLE TAKE

JOE HILLEY

RiverOak®

Good News in Fiction

COOK COMMUNICATIONS MINISTRIES
Colorado Springs, Colorado • Paris, Ontario
KINGSWAY COMMUNICATIONS LTD
Eastbourne, England

RiverOak® is an imprint of
Cook Communications Ministries, Colorado Springs, CO 80918
Cook Communications, Paris, Ontario
Kingsway Communications, Eastbourne, England

DOUBLE TAKE
© 2005 by Joseph Hilley

Quotation of John 14:16–17 on page 245 is adapted from the *Revised
Standard Version of the Bible*, copyrighted by the Division of Christian
Education of the National Council of the Churches of Christ in the United
States of America, and is used by permission.

Cover Design: Two Moore Designs/Ray Moore
Cover Photo: ©2005 PhotoSpin®

First Printing, 2005
Printed in United States of America
1 2 3 4 5 6 7 8 9 10 Printing/Year 08 07 06 05

ISBN: 1589190327

For those loyal friends who joined us in
the Fellowship of the Book.

I know I've seen this place before
Lord can't you hear me screaming

"Baltimore"
Lyle Lovett

PROLOGUE

Thick morning dew dripped from the eaves of the house as Steve Ingram opened the back door. He stepped outside onto the deck and found himself smothered in warm, moist air. Without moving at all, his skin became damp and tacky. Somewhere in the distance behind him, the sun crept toward the horizon. Soon it would burst into view, igniting the humid air and spreading a blanket of sweltering heat that would make even the dense shade of the sprawling live oaks unbearably hot. Already in the gray light of dawn, the morning was muggy, sweaty, and miserable.

Ingram's house, a raised two-story Creole cottage, sat along the eastern shore of Mobile Bay in the tiny community of Battles Wharf, a quaint hamlet nestled between a crook of shoreline and the narrow road that ran from Fairhope to Point Clear. A long driveway lined with tall oaks led from the road to the house. Draped with Spanish moss, the trees shielded the house from view. High brick walls down both sides of the property separated it from the neighbors. A fence across the front with a heavy iron gate kept others away, but it was all unnecessary. The houses on either side were summer homes, occupied only on weekends and during an occasional extended summer vacation. Most of the time, no one was around.

Standing in the doorway behind Steve that morning was a young woman clad in a thin cotton T-shirt. Her blond hair stuck out from her head in all directions, and her eyes were swollen and red. Even disheveled and half awake she made him wonder why he was going to work. He pulled her close and kissed her, then sauntered across the deck. She smiled, waved good-bye, and closed the door.

Coffee cup in one hand, a copy of the *Mobile Register* in the other, Steve moved down the steps on the far side of the deck to the driveway. At the bottom step he paused and took a sip of coffee. A gentle breeze tousled his hair. He lingered a moment.

Beyond the deck, the driveway separated the house from a white frame three-car garage. To the left of the garage, a long wooden pier extended several hundred feet into the bay. Weathered and gray, it seemed to float on top of the water in the morning haze. At the end of the pier was a boathouse. Weathered like the pier, it rose above the water like a gray ghost. Its darkened windows looked like eyes, and the gentle motion of the waves made it seem as though it swayed from side to side.

Out past the boathouse a small boat bobbed on the water. Two men, one in either end of the boat, appeared to be fishing. Steve watched for a moment and took another sip of coffee.

Farther to the left, beyond a tiny patch of dark green lawn and the brick wall at the edge of the property, his neighbor's pier stretched into the bay. Midway down the pier was a small bath-house. As Steve sipped from the coffee cup, something near the building caught his eye. He glanced in that direction, scanned along the pier, then turned away.

He sipped from the cup again and watched as seagulls circled overhead. Near the end of the pier, a pelican tucked its wings and dove headlong into the water. Steve smiled to himself, took another sip of coffee, then started across the driveway toward the garage. Holding the newspaper in front of him, he glanced at the sports section between sips as he walked.

In the garage, Steve opened the door to a red BMW and sat down behind the steering wheel. He closed the car door and reached above his head to the sun visor for the garage door opener. His fingers found it without taking his eyes from the newspaper. Mindlessly, he pressed a button on the opener. An electric motor overhead began to hum as it lifted the door. The door rattled and rumbled as it slid along the tracks in the rafters above the car. He took one more sip of coffee and finished reading an article, then tossed the paper onto the seat beside him. He placed the key in the ignition and turned it.

In an instant, the building erupted in a huge explosion. Thick, black smoke billowed into the sky, followed by a giant, rolling fireball. Pieces of the roof shot into the air above the fire and smoke. What remained of the garage was engulfed in flames.

One

ike Connolly sat alone on the hard wooden pew and stared at the stained-glass window behind the altar at the far end of the chancel. St. Pachomius Church had been around almost as long as the city itself. Built in the 1840s, it looked old and felt old, but it had aged well and had a regal aura. Far from being musty and decayed, it was alive with mystery and wonder. Connolly soaked himself in that wonder.

The sanctuary had been dark when he arrived for morning prayers. Dawn came as he knelt with the others to receive the Eucharist. By the time he rose from the altar rail, brilliant sunlight streamed through the stained-glass windows along the walls. One by one, the others had filed out to join the day, but Connolly had lingered, reluctant to trade the quiet, tranquil sanctuary for the demands of another busy morning.

Finally, at a quarter past eight, he rose from the pew and made his way up the aisle to the rear of the church. In the vestibule, he pushed open one of the massive doors and stepped outside to the portico.

St. Pachomius Church was located in the heart of downtown Mobile. The oldest Protestant church in the state, it now found itself surrounded by an expanding courthouse, boxed in on three sides by the sheriff's office, the probate court, and a new high-rise government complex. It was an unusual place, a unique blend of architecture, liturgy, and tradition.

Connolly ambled down the steps from the church to the sidewalk. At fifty-six he was still trim and athletic, but he found it harder to move with agility in the morning.

From the church, he crossed the street to the rear of the courthouse and cut through the first-floor lobby to Government Street on the front side of the building. He crossed Government in the middle of the block and walked up Ferguson Alley to the service entrance at the back of the Warren Building. He checked his watch. No point in hurrying. Mrs. Gordon was already at the office. Plenty of time to grab a cup of coffee before anything important happened.

He exited the building on Dauphin Street and turned left. Port City Diner was in the middle of the second block.

A few yards from the diner, he crossed Dubose Alley. As he strode past the alley, a voice called to him in a raspy whisper.

"Mike."

Startled, Connolly stopped in midstride and turned to see who spoke.

Buildings on either side cast a shadow over the alley, but from the street the morning sun covered the sidewalk with a glare. From where he stood, Connolly could see only the figure of a man standing a few feet down the alley, peering from behind a garbage Dumpster. He stepped to the edge of the sidewalk.

The man behind the Dumpster looked familiar, but Connolly couldn't quite place him. He wore wrinkled blue pants and a gray sweatshirt. The legs of the pants were shiny from wear and the dirt of living on the street. The front of the shirt was stained. The neckband was grimy and black. His hair was oily and clung to his head in strands. His face was covered with a dark, three-day beard. Even from a distance, Connolly could see his hands were filthy, his fingernails caked with dirt.

Shielding his eyes from the morning sun, Connolly crept into the alley. As he drew near the Dumpster, he moved beyond the glare. Engulfed by shadow, he recognized the man.

"Harvey Bosarge. Is that you?"

"Come here," Bosarge insisted. He waved his hand in an urgent gesture.

Connolly lowered his hand from his eyes and moved up the alley.

Harvey Bosarge was a retired detective from the Mobile Police Department, where he had enjoyed a long and distinguished career. When he retired, he moved to Bayou La Batre, a small fishing village in the heart of the low country on the coast at the southern end of the county, his childhood home. He continued to use his detective skills and vast network of friends and connections working as a private investigator for some of the largest law firms in the city. Since Bosarge was always dapper and well groomed, Connolly found his appearance and demeanor that morning disturbing and out of character.

"Harvey, what are you doing here? You look terrible."

Bosarge placed his finger to his lips for silence. He stepped away from the Dumpster and motioned for Connolly to follow. Farther up the alley, Bosarge opened a door to a building on the right and nodded for Connolly to enter. Reluctantly, Connolly stepped through the door.

Inside, the building was dark. The air was heavy and humid. Connolly hesitated. Bosarge nudged him. Connolly moved a few feet from the door. He waited there, hoping his eyes would adjust to the dim light.

Bosarge stepped inside and closed the door. He dug a match from his pocket and struck it against the top of a metal drum that stood nearby. The bright flash lit up the room. From a crack in the wall, he produced a broken piece of candle. He lit it and dripped hot wax onto the top of the drum, then pressed the end of the candle into it to hold it in place. The glow from the candle lit their faces.

Connolly frowned.

"You going to tell me what this is all about?" He glanced at Bosarge's clothes. "You don't look so good, you know."

Bosarge slumped against the door.

"Haven't slept in three days."

"What's wrong?"

"I got trouble. Big trouble. We gotta talk."

"Let's go up to my office," Connolly suggested. "You can get something to eat, maybe clean up a little."

Connolly turned to leave. Bosarge stuck out his arm to stop him.

"No," he snapped. "Can't take the chance of being seen."

Connolly gave him a puzzled look.

"Well, then, what do you propose we do?"

"Where's your car?"

"In front of the office. Down the block."

Bosarge brightened.

"Good. Go get it. Pull it up here in the alley. Make sure the back door is unlocked. We can ride around and talk."

Connolly gave him a sarcastic smile.

"Oh, that'll keep people from suspecting anything. A bum and a guy in a suit going up the alley in a 1959 Chrysler Imperial. They'll never notice us." The smile melted into an amused grin. "Let's just talk here."

"No," Bosarge insisted. "Not here. All kinds of people hang out in these buildings. Never know who's listening. Just go get your car."

Connolly sighed and reached for the door. Bosarge once again stuck out his arm to stop him. Connolly looked exasperated.

"What?"

Bosarge blew out the candle, then withdrew his arm.

Connolly opened the door and stepped outside. Bosarge stuck his head out as Connolly left. He looked up and down the alley, then retreated back inside.

Connolly walked past the Dumpster to the end of the alley. At the street, he turned right and walked back to the Warren Building. Across the street from Bienville Square, his office was on the third floor. Windows near his desk afforded a view of the square and the street below. He glanced up at his windows. Mrs. Gordon would be there by now, wondering where he was, preparing to grill him when he finally arrived. He sighed and turned away.

His car was parked out front. A 1959 Chrysler Imperial. He had taken it years ago as his fee for helping a client settle her husband's estate. It was the one thing in his life that had remained constant. He got in and steered it away from the curb.

One block down the street he turned right onto St. Joseph Street and made the block, coming back to Dauphin at the next corner up. From there, he negotiated through the crowded morning traffic into Dubose Alley and eased the car forward.

Just past the Dumpster, the door to the building flew open. Bosarge darted into the alley, jerked open the rear door of the car, and dove onto the backseat.

"Go!"

Connolly slipped his foot from the brake. The car rolled forward at little more than an idle.

"Let's go!" Bosarge shouted. He banged his fist against the back of the front seat. "We can't hang around here like this. Someone will see me."

"Relax," Connolly grinned, amused at Bosarge's antics. "Stay low in the seat. No one will recognize you. Especially not the way you look."

At Conti Street, Connolly turned right and drove away from downtown. A few blocks beyond Broad Street, he turned onto Springhill Avenue. A mile or so later, he slowed the car and turned through the gates at Visitation Monastery.

"What are we doing here?" Bosarge turned to look over his shoulder, checking to make sure they weren't followed. "Great," he muttered as he faced forward, his voice laden with sarcasm. "We're hiding out with a bunch of nuns. No one will notice us now."

"Relax," Connolly soothed once again. "Nobody will find us here. And if they try, we'll see them before they see us."

Connolly drove the car along a narrow driveway that wound through the grounds toward a cluster of three-story buildings. Made of brick with red tile roofs, they were an imposing contrast to the lush, green landscape. Connolly brought the car to a stop beneath a large oak tree a hundred yards from the entrance. He switched off the engine and turned in the seat to face Bosarge.

"Okay. What's this all about?"

Bosarge looked about nervously.

"You sure no one can find us here?"

"They can't find us."

Bosarge glanced around once more.

"Start talking," Connolly insisted.

Bosarge leaned back and rested his head on the seat. He closed his eyes.

"This is all confidential, right?" His eyes popped open and stared at Connolly. "I mean, can't nobody make you tell what I'm about to say, can they?"

The question struck Connolly as an odd one, coming from a former detective.

"No." He was curious about where this conversation was headed. "Not if I'm your lawyer."

"All right." Bosarge nodded. "You're my lawyer. We need to sign something to make it official?"

"No." Connolly was exasperated. "Look, Harvey. Either tell me or don't. I don't care. But if you're going to talk, get started. I've got a hundred things waiting on me back at the office."

Bosarge took a long, deep breath, then let out a long, loud sigh. He pulled a crumpled cigar from his shirt pocket.

"Mind if I smoke?"

Connolly hesitated. The smell of tobacco smoke irritated his sinuses, but three days on the street without a bath left Harvey smelling rather foul. Cigar smoke was nothing compared to the stench rising from the backseat. He shrugged his shoulders.

"I guess not."

Bosarge shoved the cigar in his mouth and dug a soiled box of matches from his pocket. The match flared a bright orange, but went out. A second match fared no better.

"Forget it," he grumbled.

He snatched the cigar from his mouth and tossed it out the window. He leaned back in the seat once more and closed his eyes.

"You heard about that guy Steve Ingram?"

"Yeah."

"That guy was incinerated." He glanced at Connolly. "Garage went flying across the county."

Connolly raised his eyebrows.

"You were there?"

Bosarge nodded but did not reply. Connolly pressed him for more.

"Doing what?"

"Ingram was seeing a ... a woman ... named Ann Grafton. A waitress at Jake's Social Club out on the causeway. Her husband thought she was fooling around. Hired me to follow her.

I was standing on a pier next door taking pictures of her and Ingram when the garage blew up."

The look on Connolly's face turned to a frown.

"He had a woman with him? Paper didn't say anything about anyone else being killed."

Bosarge shook his head.

"She wasn't in the garage. She was in the house."

"So what's the problem?"

"Somebody must have seen me. Police have been calling. They want to talk to me. Came by the house a couple of times. I wasn't there and I ain't been back, either."

"How do you know they want to talk about Ingram?"

"I made a call." Bosarge smiled at Connolly. "I got a friend down at the city jail."

"Who came to see you?"

"Somebody named Robert Batiste the first time. Second time it was Anthony Hammond. You know him?"

"Yeah. Batiste is a patrolman. I don't know why he'd be coming to your house. How did they find out about you?"

Bosarge glanced away.

"I ... I don't know."

The tone in his voice made Connolly uneasy. Something inside him seemed dissatisfied with what Bosarge had to say. He thought about it a moment, then moved on.

"You know, if Hammond is handling this case, you're going to have to talk to him. Probably sooner rather than later. He's not like some of those other guys they have. He won't just let it drop. Especially not if he has your name."

"I know." Bosarge sighed. "Think you could talk to him? Maybe find out how much he knows about me? What he wants?"

"I'll call him. But he'll want to see you himself. Where have you been staying?"

"On the street."

Connolly shook his head in disbelief.

"It's no fun, either," Bosarge continued. "I don't care what those guys on the park bench say."

Connolly chuckled.

"All right. We need to find a phone. I'll call Anthony. I imagine he'll agree to let you come in instead of having you picked up."

Bosarge turned away again and stared out the window. Connolly hesitated.

"Something you're not telling me, Harvey?"

"Nah."

"I can't do you any good if you don't tell me everything." Connolly's voice was stern and serious. "The advice I give you is based on the information you give me. Understand?"

Bosarge nodded, still looking out the window.

"Yeah." His voice sounded quiet and subdued. "I understand."

Connolly turned around in the seat and started the engine. He drove the car down the driveway and out the front gate. A few blocks toward town, he turned into the parking lot at the Quick Stop convenience store. He parked the car at the edge of the lot as far from the building as possible and switched off the engine. He glanced at Bosarge in the rearview mirror.

"Wait here."

Bosarge looked worried.

"Where you going?"

"To call Hammond. We can't let this wait, and I don't want to talk about it on a cell phone."

Connolly stepped out of the Chrysler and walked across the parking lot to a telephone booth. He inserted two quarters in the pay phone and punched in a number. In a few minutes, he was talking to Hammond.

"I've been hired to represent Harvey Bosarge. I understand you want to talk to him."

"Yeah," Hammond replied. "We've been trying to find him. You know where he is?"

"What do you want to talk to him about?"

"Uhh ... Steve Ingram."

"What about him?"

"I don't think I can ..."

"Come on, Anthony," Connolly interrupted. "You know I'm not going to help you if this is just a fishing expedition."

"I want to talk to him about that explosion over at Point Clear."

"Shouldn't police over there be working on this?"

"Yeah, well, we're helping them out."

"Do you just want to talk, or is he the target of an investigation?"

Hammond was silent for a moment.

"I ... ahh ... can't say."

His voice sounded strained and distant. Once again, Connolly felt uncomfortable with what he was hearing.

"You can't tell me whether my client is a suspect?"

"No."

Connolly felt frustrated and perplexed.

"Anthony, you know I can't let him talk without knowing whether he's a suspect."

"Do whatever you have to."

"If I bring him in like this, he's only going to refuse to talk."

"Like I said ..."

"I would tell him not to ..."

Hammond cut him off.

"Mike, do what you have to do."

Connolly banged his fist against the phone. Hammond had never been this difficult.

"Any chance you and I could meet and discuss this further?"

"I ... ahhh ... can't talk about our investigation while it's still going forward."

Connolly hung up the receiver and walked back to the car. What he heard on the phone was just as unsettling as what he heard from Bosarge. He had dealt with Hammond a long time. He was as eager to make a case as anyone, but he was always straight. If someone was a suspect, he didn't play around. He'd say so up front.

By the time he reached the car, Connolly was sure there was more going on than Bosarge had told him. He opened the door and got in behind the wheel.

"Well?"

Connolly shook his head.

"He wants to talk to you, but he won't tell me whether you're a suspect."

"They think I did it?"

"I don't know. Sounds like they don't know, either."

Bosarge leaned his head against the window.

"So now what?"

"I take you home, and we wait to see what they do."

"Wait?"

"Yeah. Wait." Connolly made it sound more like an order than a suggestion. "Hopefully, they'll call first and give you a chance to come in on your own. If not, don't put up a fight. Let them take you in, and then call me." Connolly started the car. "In the meantime, I'll see what I can find out."

Bosarge sighed and slid low in the seat. Connolly backed the car away and steered it toward the street.

Two

After taking Bosarge home, Connolly returned to Mobile. Instead of going to his office, he drove east through Bankhead Tunnel and onto the causeway that stretched across the northern end of Mobile Bay. When he reached the east side of the bay, he turned south. A mile below Fairhope, he came to Battles Wharf. He had little trouble finding Steve Ingram's house. A strand of yellow crime-scene tape stretched across the drive.

Connolly eased the Chrysler off the road and brought it to a stop. He climbed from the car and unfastened the tape, then drove toward the house. The charred remains of the garage lay ahead of him at the end of the drive.

As the Chrysler moved forward, a patrol officer dressed in a blue uniform appeared at the end of the driveway and motioned for him to stop. Connolly continued past him and turned the car into the parking area behind the house. He turned off the engine and stepped from the car. The officer strode across the drive, his face twisted in an angry scowl.

"Didn't you see me? I told you to stop."

Connolly was indifferent.

"Just need to look around."

"I don't care what you need," the officer growled. "This is a crime scene. The public's not allowed back here."

Connolly took a business card from his pocket and handed it to him.

"I'm not the public."

The officer looked at the card, then slipped it in his pocket. The scowl disappeared from his face.

"All right. But stay out of the way, and don't touch anything."

"Sure," Connolly replied.

The officer sauntered back toward the driveway. Connolly turned toward the garage.

A bed of gray ashes covered what had once been the garage floor. Pieces of metal, twisted from the heat and force of the blast, were scattered about. In the far corner, a few charred boards clung to each other. In the center, two blackened columns rose above the ashes like sentinels, wounded and disfigured by a terrible battle, but still guarding their posts.

Connolly stepped forward. ATF agents were busy sorting through the ashes and rubble. One of them looked up as he approached.

"Don't come any closer," the agent barked. "We're still processing this area."

Connolly stopped a few feet from the edge of the building site.

"Find anything interesting?"

The agent stepped around one of the columns and moved toward Connolly.

"You represent the Ingrams?"

"Not exactly."

A quizzical look appeared on the agent's face.

"You look familiar." He took a rag from his hip pocket and wiped his hands as he spoke. "Haven't I seen you before?"

Connolly shrugged.

"You've probably seen me around the courthouse."

"Yeah." The agent smiled. "You're the guy who had that

apartment on Carondolet Street. Went home one night, opened the door, and the place blew up."

Connolly nodded. The agent continued.

"I knew you looked familiar." He stuck out his hand. "I'm Tom Sinclair. ATF."

They shook hands. Connolly's mind raced as he tried to recall seeing the man.

"Mike Connolly."

"Sure, Mr. Connolly. I remember you, but you were on an ambulance gurney last time I saw you. You're lucky to be alive."

"I believe it took a little more than luck."

"You may be right about that." Sinclair chuckled. "If you'd taken one more step inside that apartment, you'd have been killed."

Connolly pointed toward the rubble around them.

"So any idea what happened here?"

"Yeah. Got a pretty good idea." Sinclair turned toward the remains of the garage. "Found traces of explosives on pieces of the cars."

"Dynamite?"

"No." Sinclair shook his head. "Semtex."

"Semtex?" Connolly looked puzzled. "Never heard of it."

"Don't see much of it in the U.S.," Sinclair explained. "Sort of a C-4 knockoff. Manufactured in Europe. Terrorists use it a good bit. Cheap, but effective."

Sweat dripped from Connolly's forehead. He slipped off his jacket and slung it over his shoulder, then unbuttoned his collar and loosened his tie.

Sinclair glanced toward the sky.

"Hot out here, isn't it?"

"Yeah," Connolly replied. He pointed to the wreckage in front of them. "Sounds like this was a complicated job."

"Not complicated. Just sophisticated. We're pretty sure we've found pieces of the detonators."

Connolly wiped his forehead with the palm of his hand.

"Detonators? There was more than one?"

"Yeah. We've found three so far." Sinclair faced the garage and gestured with his hands as he talked. "There were three cars in the garage. Looks like there was at least one charge in each car. I'd say they wanted to make sure they got him. Made the destruction pretty much complete, too. Not a bad way to cover their tracks." He gave Connolly a confident smile. "But we know how to work these sites. We'll know exactly what happened by the time we're through."

Connolly sighed and shook his head.

"Never knew what hit him."

Sinclair nodded.

"He might have had a moment to realize an explosion was happening, but I doubt he felt much." Sinclair stepped a few feet into the rubble. "He was in a BMW parked here. There was a post supporting the roof on the other side of the car and then two more stalls with cars in them. The blast in the BMW was so strong it blew the car sideways, took out the post, and shoved the BMW and the next car all the way across the garage. Third car in the last stall was blown completely out of the building. We found pieces of it hanging in a tree way down the drive."

Connolly stared at the ashes.

"What triggered it? Ignition on the car?"

"I don't think so. Looks like they used some kind of remote device."

"Remote device?"

"Yeah. Waited until he was in the car. Flipped a switch. Pressed a button."

"So they knew he was in the car?"

"Maybe. We're not sure yet."

Connolly let his eyes pan across the site. As he did, he saw in his mind an image of Steve Ingram sitting in the car. Bright red, shiny. The garage was awash in sunlight. It reflected off the chrome trim on the door and glinted off the glass in the driver's side window. Ingram's head turned to the left as he slipped the key in the ignition on the steering column. Their eyes met. A look of terror swept over his face. Bright orange flames engulfed him. Connolly jumped.

A voice called to him. He looked up. Sinclair was staring at him, a strange look on his face.

"You okay, Mr. Connolly?"

Connolly rubbed his hand over his face, for a moment unsure of where he was.

"Yeah." His voice sounded far away. "I'm all right." He ran his hand through his hair as he collected himself, then pointed over his shoulder. "You mind if I look inside the house?"

"I ... I don't mind." Sinclair hesitated. "Detectives from the sheriff's department were working on that part. I don't know whether they're through or not."

"I just want to look around for a minute. I won't be long." He stepped away, then turned to one side and called over his shoulder. "Thanks for your help."

"Sure thing," Sinclair replied.

Connolly crossed the parking area and stepped onto the deck at the rear of the house. He crossed to the back door and pushed to open it. The door wouldn't budge. He jiggled the doorknob to make sure and tried again. Still, it would not open. He backed away and glanced around. Tiny slivers of wood from the garage were embedded in the siding on the house. The doorframe looked out of alignment with the rest of the house. A window next to it had been knocked out of its frame. He shook his head in disbelief.

"Whoever it was," he mumbled, "they made sure he didn't get away."

He moved back to the door. This time, he leaned his

shoulder against it and pushed with his legs. The door scraped against the floor as it slid open.

Inside, the kitchen was a mess. To the left, the pantry door was ajar. Cans of food were strewn about the floor. To the right, cabinet doors hung open, the shelves stripped bare, the contents shattered on the floor. He picked his way through broken dishes and made his way toward the middle of the house.

In the den, a bookshelf lay on the floor in one direction. Books and other items from the shelves littered the room. A recliner lay on its side in the opposite direction. Connolly glanced around. The rooms downstairs had been damaged by the force of the blast, but most of the mess looked as though it had been done afterward.

He crossed the room to the stairs that led to the second floor. He gave the banister a tug to make sure it was stable, then started up. A few steps from the top he grasped the corner of the wall and leaned around to peer down the hallway. What he saw confirmed what he had suspected. Someone had been in the house searching for something.

Down the hall, a dresser lay on its side. Its drawers were piled on top. The contents had been removed and scattered about the floor. Craning his neck and leaning farther away from the corner, he could see other pieces of furniture lying beyond the dresser. He placed his free hand on the floor to steady himself and moved back from the corner. As his hand touched the floor, he felt it land on something sticky. He took the last step to the hallway and glanced at his hand. A candy wrapper stuck to his palm.

"Tootsie Roll."

He peeled away the wrapper and grimaced at the thought of where it might have been before it landed on the floor. He flipped it aside and slipped around the dresser.

Cautious now, he made his way down the hall, checking

each of the rooms as he went. At the far end, he found the master bedroom. Located on the left side of the house, it was a large room taking up more than a third of the second floor. A window on the wall opposite the door overlooked the driveway and gave a clear view of the second floor of the house next door.

A dresser lay facedown in the middle of the room. The drawers had been removed and tossed aside. A mattress and box springs leaned against the wall beside the door. The bare bed frame sat in its original place, its legs embedded in the carpet. Next to the frame was a small nightstand. Connolly stepped over the rails of the frame for a closer look.

The top of the stand was cluttered with scraps of paper and other items. Another candy wrapper lay on top. Like the dresser, the drawers to the stand were missing. Connolly took a pen from his pocket and sorted through the items, moving them aside as he looked. When he found nothing of interest, he turned away and glanced through the opening in the nightstand where the drawers had been. Through the opening he could see the floor beneath the stand.

Something caught his eye. He knelt and reached through the opening.

Tucked under the edge of the nightstand he found a photo negative. He pulled it out and held it between his fingers. In the dim light of the room, images on the film were hard to see. He stood and moved to the window. In the sunlight he could see the thin strip of film contained three photos. They appeared to be pictures of people at a party. He studied each of the images but didn't recognize any of the faces. After a moment, he slipped the film in his pocket.

Across the room, he checked the walk-in closet. It was bare, its contents thrown in a heap on the closet floor. Connolly raked through the pile with his foot. Most of the items were men's clothing, but near the bottom he found a dress and a woman's silk robe.

A door at the end of the closet led to the bathroom. To the left of the door was a shower large enough for a small party. Next to it was a Jacuzzi. A vanity with double sinks lined the wall opposite the door. Connolly glanced at the items on the countertop. A woman's makeup bag sat to one side.

Leaving the bathroom, he wandered back to the bedroom and moved past the bed toward the door. On the opposite side of the room, he paused and surveyed the room. As he turned to leave, his eyes swept across the ceiling. An air-conditioning vent caught his attention.

On the corner of the vent cover, near one of the screws that held it in place, tiny, bright scratches reflected the light from the window. Connolly started toward the center of the room to get a better look.

"Find anything interesting?"

Startled, Connolly jumped around to see who spoke.

Standing at the door was a man about six feet tall dressed in a dark gray suit. He had a large, round stomach that strained the buttons on his white shirt and a thick neck that rolled over the top of his collar. The floor creaked as he stepped through the doorway from the hall.

"Not much," Connolly replied.

The man moved toward him.

"What are you doing here?"

"Who wants to know?"

The man stood in front of Connolly just a few feet away, glowering at him. He was huffing as if he'd climbed the stairs in a hurry, and his breath smelled of cigarette smoke and coffee.

"This is private property. You're not supposed to be here."

"You work for the Ingrams?"

The man took a step back and gestured toward the door.

"Let's go."

Connolly didn't move.

"I haven't finished looking around."

"Yes, you have." The man gestured again. "Let's go."

Connolly hesitated, then thought better of it. He crossed the room and stepped into the hall. The man ushered him to the stairway and followed him downstairs. At the bottom of the steps, the man guided Connolly across the den and through the kitchen to the back door.

"Don't come around here again." His voice was stern and threatening. He jerked open the door and pointed outside. "If I find you here again, you'll be arrested."

Connolly stepped onto the deck outside and walked to the Chrysler. The man followed him to the driveway. Connolly backed the car away from the house and started down the drive. He glanced in the rearview mirror and saw the man standing in the drive behind him, arms folded across his chest.

Three

*F*rom Battles Wharf, Connolly retraced the route to Mobile. He lowered the windows in the Chrysler and let the warm breeze circulate through the car. The smell of salt from the bay filled the air. With nothing for company but the wind in his hair and the smooth sound of the Chrysler's engine, his mind began to wander. Soon, he was daydreaming about what life must have been like for Steve Ingram.

Steve was the middle son of Joseph Cathcart Ingram, president and majority owner of Ingram Shipbuilding Company. The Ingrams were an old Mobile family, members of society's inner circle in a town where society meant everything. Estimated by several financial magazines to be worth almost a billion dollars, most of the family fortune was held in company stock owned by Joseph and his brothers, Leon and Herschel. Cousins and in-laws claiming kinship through each of the three brothers owned smaller interests in the business. Control, however, resided with Joseph, now seventy-five years old. Leon and Herschel, both several years older, took no interest in the business other than to spend their share of the profits and stir up trouble. The three brothers had not spoken to each other in years. Theirs was a deeply divided family, one whose numerous disputes were frequent fodder for the society pages and gossip columns.

Frank, Joseph's oldest son, held an MBA from Harvard

and a law degree from Columbia University. He found success as an investment banker on Wall Street and enjoyed the posh style of the Upper East Side in Manhattan. But as Joseph grew older, he pressured Frank to take over the family business. Forced to return home, Frank proved to be a capable executive and broadened the company's contacts, but he chafed at the quaint rituals and slow pace of life in Mobile. He was brilliant at negotiating contracts and putting together big deals, but he made no secret of his disdain for almost everyone around him.

Joey, the youngest son, decided at a young age not to pursue the family business. Like Frank, he went to law school. But unlike him, he opted to attend the University of Alabama rather than a prestigious East Coast school, much to Frank's chagrin. After graduation, he went to work at Hager, Litton, and Lynch, a large Mobile law firm that represented Ingram Shipbuilding.

Though Frank and Joey were very different, neither was an embarrassment to their father. Steve was a different matter.

Against his father's advice, Steve spent well over a million dollars building the house at Battles Wharf. He filled the garage with a new BMW, a 1956 Corvette, and a 1960 MG roadster. To entertain his frequent guests, he purchased a large, very fast boat. He had a reputation for partying most nights and wasn't often seen at the shipyard before lunch. Wherever he went, a crowd of unsavory friends followed in his wake. Money flowed from his bank account as if it had no end.

Perpetually tanned, he wore shiny knit shirts that were always one size too tight and unbuttoned one button too low. He combed his hair straight back from his forehead and held it in place with heavy applications of styling mousse. Two gold chains hung around his neck, and he wore a diamond-studded ring on his little finger. He looked like a cross between a television evangelist and a redneck pimp.

Connolly knew the lifestyle well. He'd seen his share of bars and clubs, and more than once he'd awakened to a breakfast served from the bottom of a gin bottle. Thinking of Steve took him to a place he had tried hard to forget. The stale smell of a bar at closing time, the musky fragrance of a dancer looking for a ride home, all blended together in his mind, reminding him of who he had been not so long ago and a lifestyle that had cost him everything.

He ran his fingers through his hair and tilted his head out the window, catching the breeze full in his face. The blast of warm air seemed to drive the thoughts from his mind.

Connolly crossed the causeway and drove back through Bankhead Tunnel, emerging on Government Street near the courthouse. Instead of turning toward Dauphin Street and the office, he turned left and made his way to Texas Street a few blocks south of the house where his daughter, Rachel, lived. He turned right and drove toward the house. A block away, he could see it sitting on the corner.

Three cars were parked in the side yard. A crumpled metal garbage can sat by the side door. Nearby was a child's plastic three-wheeler. Next to it was a small swing. He slowed the Chrysler to an idle. Hoping to see Rachel emerge from the house. Hoping for a chance to see Elizabeth, his granddaughter.

Rachel had her own problems. About the time she graduated from high school, Connolly's marriage to her mother, Barbara, reached an end. By then, he was drinking a quart of gin a day just to function and spending most nights at the office slumped over his desk. The divorce proved acrimonious. Rachel escaped to college.

In the middle of her second semester she dropped out and moved in with Dave, a bartender at the Brown Pelican Bar in the Essex Hotel not far from Connolly's office. Twice her age, he was married and had three children. When Rachel became pregnant two months later, Dave returned to his wife.

Unwilling to go home, Rachel moved into the house on Texas Street with Craig and Mark, two friends she met in college.

She had rebuffed Connolly's previous attempts to help and had refused to allow him to see Elizabeth, Connolly's only grandchild. Even now, she was reluctant to allow him close enough to hold the baby.

When Connolly reached the corner, he brought the car to a stop and sat there a moment opposite the house, watching. Just as he was about to leave, he caught a glimpse of Rachel as she passed an upstairs window. A moment later she passed the window again, this time carrying Elizabeth wrapped in a towel. In that fleeting instant he could see Elizabeth's hair was wet. She must have just finished a bath. A smile stretched across his face. He imagined what she might be saying. The sound of a child's laughter danced across his mind.

Suddenly, the blare of a car horn jerked him back to reality. He glanced in the mirror to see a car sitting behind him, the driver shouting something and flaying the air with his hands.

Connolly pressed the gas pedal. The Chrysler started forward. Deep loneliness settled over him as the car rolled past the house. Tears came to his eyes. More than ever before, he wanted a drink.

Four

The following day, Connolly arrived at the office in the middle of the morning. Myrtice Gordon, Connolly's secretary, was seated at her desk near the front door when he entered. At seventy-five years of age she was often dour and cantankerous, but she was the only secretary he had ever had, and she did her best to keep him out of trouble.

"Finally decide to come to work?"

"Good morning, Mrs. Gordon," Connolly replied, ignoring the tone in her voice. "Any calls?"

"A few." She handed him a stack of phone messages. "Harry Giles called twice."

Connolly stood at her desk and sorted through the messages. Mrs. Gordon glanced up at him.

"You know Harry Giles very well?"

"Met him a few times."

"I wouldn't trust him with my neighbor's dog."

Connolly chuckled at the tone of her voice. He stuffed the messages in the pocket of his jacket and turned to leave.

"That's pretty strong, coming from you." Something on the floor caught his eye. He stooped to pick it up. "What's this?"

He stood, dangling a key from a piece of ribbon.

"Oh," Mrs. Gordon exclaimed. "My office key. It must have fallen off." She slid her chair over and leaned around the edge of her desk, searching the floor.

Connolly squatted and felt under the edge of the desk.

"This what you're looking for?"

He stood, this time holding a small silver spoon. The end of the handle had been bent to form a loop.

"Yes," Mrs. Gordon replied. She took the spoon from his hand. "Thank you."

"What is it?"

"A spoon."

"I can see that. What's it for?"

"A key chain," she replied. She threaded the ribbon through the loop in the spoon handle and tied it. She held the spoon up to show him. The key dangled on the ribbon.

"Whatever," he mumbled.

He turned aside and walked down the hall to his office. He tossed the messages on his desk, then removed his jacket and hung it on the coatrack by the door. Mrs. Gordon left her desk and walked down the hallway toward him.

"He's a snake."

She leaned against the doorframe. Connolly moved around his desk and took a seat.

"Who?"

"Harry Giles."

"An old boyfriend?"

Mrs. Gordon blushed.

"We ... ahh ... I never ..."

She took a deep breath to collect herself. Connolly chuckled. Mrs. Gordon was not amused.

"How you can take so much pleasure from my discomfort is beyond me."

Connolly chuckled again.

"If you could see the look on your face, you'd laugh, too."

Her cold glare softened. The corners of her mouth lifted in a faint smile. Connolly forced himself to take a more serious tone.

"Was he a handsome young man?"

"Yes." Her voice became quiet, almost wistful. "He was."

A grin broke across his face. "Must have been a torrid affair."

She straightened herself and turned away. "Just keep your eye on him."

She disappeared up the hall toward her desk. Connolly called to her.

"Mrs. Gordon."

She returned to the doorway, hands on hips, an impatient look on her face. Connolly left his chair and retrieved the negative he found in Steve's bedroom from his jacket.

"Could you have some prints made from this?"

He handed her the film. She held it up in the light to look at it.

"Yes," she replied. "Which photo do you want? Looks like there are three on here."

"One of each," he replied. "Can you get them this afternoon?"

She lowered the negative and cocked her head toward him. The corners of her mouth turned down in a frown.

"I think I can handle it," she sniped.

"Good."

He crossed the room to the desk and around to the chair. In one move, he threw his feet on the desktop, leaned back in the chair, and rested his head against the wall.

"Close the door on your way ..."

The sound of the front door opening interrupted him. A man appeared in the hallway behind Mrs. Gordon. She turned to see who it was. Connolly leaned around the corner of the desk to look down the hall.

Slender and not very tall, he wore a dark gray suit with a white shirt and a paisley tie. His jacket lay smoothly along his shoulders and followed the contours of his slim torso as if he were the perfect mannequin wearing the perfect size. The cuffs of his jacket sleeves fell at the base of his thumb, revealing a quarter of an inch of shirt sleeve cuff and no more. His trousers touched the tops of his shoes with only a hint of a break in the razor-sharp crease. His shoes shone as if they'd been rubbed by hand only minutes before, the edge of the soles black, the bottoms as clean as new.

"Hope I'm not interrupting."

He had a pleasant smile as he moved down the hall toward them. As the man drew closer, Connolly could see the skin of his face was smooth—as if he'd shaved just before he appeared—and almost transparent. His body was lean, taut, and too perfect to be real. And yet, he was curiously disarming.

"Not at all," Connolly replied, still seated at his desk. "How could I help you?"

The man was at the doorway now.

"I'm Greg Drummond."

He said it as if they should recognize his name. Mrs. Gordon stepped aside to let him pass. He acknowledged her with a nod as he stepped toward the middle of the room. Connolly stood.

"Mr. Drummond, I don't believe we've met. I'm Mike Connolly."

They shook hands.

"I believe you know my boss," Drummond replied. "Hogan Smith."

A knowing smile broke across Connolly's face.

"Ah yes. Senator Smith."

"I'm his chief of staff."

Connolly pointed to a chair in front of the desk.

"Have a seat."

Behind them, Mrs. Gordon rolled her eyes at Connolly and closed the door. Drummond and Connolly took a seat.

"How is the good senator these days?"

"He's doing quite well," Drummond replied. "But he's a little concerned about the Ingrams. I understand you represent Harvey Bosarge."

"Word gets around."

"Well, we make it our business to stay on top of things. Especially down here. The Ingrams and Senator Smith are good friends. And, in light of the nature of their business, we just want to make sure we stay ahead of the political curve on this."

"The political curve?"

"A man in Senator Smith's position can't afford any surprises."

"I see."

"Find anything at the house yesterday?"

Connolly gave him a puzzled look.

"Whose house?"

Drummond smiled.

"Steve Ingram's."

"Who said I was over there?"

"Like you say, word gets around."

Connolly pushed his chair back from the desk and crossed his legs.

"Looked like someone had been in there ahead of me. I imagine all the interesting stuff was gone before the fire was out."

"Perhaps."

"I'm sure you must know Harry Giles. He's in charge of security at Ingram Shipbuilding. You talk to him?"

"Harry and I work together on several projects."

"He probably knows more about this case than the police."

Drummond looked away, crossed his legs, and straightened the crease of his pants.

"I just want to make sure you understand, Senator Smith is concerned about this matter. The Ingrams are his friends. I understand ... he understands you have a client to represent, but Steve's death was a personal loss for him. He wants to know how this happened, and he wants to be able to take whatever measures he can to help the family."

"I understand," Connolly replied. "But I'm sure you know way more about what's going on than I do."

Drummond gave him a smug smile. He slid forward in his chair.

"Listen, I'm not asking you to do anything that compromises your client. But if you find anything ... interesting, I'd appreciate it if you'd give me a call." He slipped a business card from his pocket and handed it to Connolly. "I'm staying at the Essex Hotel. Phone number's on the back. Feel free to call me anytime. I like to receive important news immediately."

Drummond stood. Connolly came from behind the desk and opened the office door.

"If I find out something I think might interest you, I'll give you a call."

"Good," Drummond replied.

They shook hands. Drummond stepped through the doorway and started up the hall. Connolly returned to the desk, propped his feet on the desktop, and closed his eyes. A moment later, Mrs. Gordon came to the door.

"What was that all about?"

"I have no idea," Connolly replied, his eyes still closed.

"Did you call Harry Giles back?"

"In a little while."

Mrs. Gordon turned away and closed the door. Connolly was soon asleep.

Five

*H*arry Giles' office was located in the basement of the administrative building at Ingram's primary yard near the south end of Water Street. Connolly guided the Chrysler through the narrow, cluttered streets and turned in at the main gate. A security guard instructed him to park in a lot near the front of the building.

Inside, another guard sat at a desk in the center of the lobby. Unlike the sleepy, disinterested guards in many offices, this one was alert, intense, and armed. He stood as Connolly entered.

"May I help you, sir?"

"I'm here to see Harry Giles," Connolly replied.

"Your name?"

"Mike Connolly."

The guard picked up a clipboard with a list of preapproved appointments for the day. He found Connolly's name at the bottom.

"Very well, sir." He laid the clipboard on the desk in front of Connolly, offered him a pen, and pointed to a blank line next to his name. "Sign in here and surrender your driver's license, please, sir."

"My driver's license?"

"Yes, sir. Everyone entering the building without prior DOD security clearance must surrender their driver's license."

"DOD?"

"Department of Defense."

"What if I don't have a driver's license?"

"Can't enter the building, sir," the guard smiled.

Connolly removed his wallet from the inside pocket of his jacket and took out his driver's license. He hesitated, then handed it to the guard.

"Have it right here for you when you're ready to leave," the guard assured him.

The guard took a building pass from a desk drawer and handed it to Connolly.

"Wear this at all times," he instructed. "Turn it in when you leave."

Connolly nodded.

"Mr. Giles' office is in the basement. Take the elevator around the corner," he gestured over his shoulder.

Connolly walked past the desk and found the elevator. He stepped inside and pressed a button for the basement. Moments later, the elevator doors opened into a broad corridor. Signs indicated Giles' office was to the right. Connolly followed the hallway around the corner to a set of double doors. As he approached, one of the doors opened automatically.

Beyond the doors was a small reception area. A secretary sat at a desk to the far right. She smiled as Connolly entered.

"Good afternoon, Mr. Connolly."

He was taken aback that she knew who he was. She nodded toward the door.

"Go on in. He's waiting for you."

Through the open doorway he saw Giles seated at his desk, talking on the telephone. Giles waved for him to enter.

Harry Giles was sixty-five years old, but lean and hard as a rock. Six feet tall, he had gray hair cut close to the scalp and a ramrod-straight back. In spite of his age, he ran six miles every morning and spent an hour in the weight room each evening. A former colonel in the Marine Corps, he served a tour of duty in Korea and two in Vietnam. When he retired from the marines, the CIA recruited him. Finally, at the age of sixty, a friend in the navy helped him get a job with Ingram Shipbuilding as the director of security, a job he had held for the past five years. He was intense, professional, and well versed in the art of protecting secrets and maintaining security.

Connolly stepped a few feet inside Giles' office and paused. Giles motioned for him to take a seat in a chair opposite the desk. Connolly sat down and waited while Giles finished his phone conversation and hung up.

"Navy," he growled. "Been calling me a hundred times a day since they heard about Steve. They act like I just got in this business yesterday."

He stood and offered Connolly his hand.

"How you doing, Mike?"

Connolly rose partway out of his seat.

"I'm doing well," he replied.

They shook hands. Giles returned to his seat. Connolly slipped back into the chair.

"I understand you met one of my men yesterday."

"Yeah," Connolly replied. "A rather unpleasant fellow."

"David Daniels. Being unpleasant is part of his job." Giles shifted in his seat. "So ... you're representing Harvey Bosarge?"

"Word travels fast."

Giles smiled.

"I know things about people." His smile grew broader, stretching across his face. His eyes twinkled. "It's my business." He paused for effect. "Next time you want to look around Steve's place, call me. I'll see that you don't have any trouble."

Connolly nodded.

"Any idea who might have wanted Steve dead?"

"Not really," Giles replied. "I mean, he's had an affair with every woman he's ever met. I imagine there are plenty of husbands with motive to do most anything. Whether that'd be enough to do something like this, I don't know."

Connolly nodded thoughtfully.

"Who's running the investigation?"

Giles shook his head in disgust.

"It's a regular three-ring circus. Mobile police have part of it. Anthony Hammond's handling their end ..." He gave Connolly a knowing smile before continuing. "But you already know that. Battles Wharf is over in Baldwin County. The sheriff over there wants to be in on whatever's happening. ATF and state fire marshal's office are investigating the actual explosion site."

"And the FBI?"

"Yeah. The FBI, too." They exchanged looks. "We do a lot of work for the navy. They sent a team from Naval Intelligence the day it happened. Defense Intelligence Agency. We've got more federal agents around here than we have employees."

"Anyone trying to coordinate things?"

"Not really. Nobody wants to give up their own piece of the pie."

"Sounds like a mess."

"It is. You find anything interesting yet?"

"Not much," Connolly replied. "I understand there was a woman at the house with Steve when the explosion occurred. Anybody talk to her?"

Giles shook his head.

"Can't find her. Bosarge ought to know where she is. He's been following her for a month."

"Yeah," Connolly chuckled. "I guess he should."

Giles leaned forward in his chair and rested his elbows on the desktop.

"Listen, this case is big. I have a lot of nervous people to deal with. A lot rides on how this comes out. I have no problem with you doing what you have to do to represent your client. I always liked Harvey. And I never thought you were the drunken bum everyone said you were, either."

Connolly nodded and gave a tight-lipped smile in response. The thought of those days made something inside him cringe. He waited for Giles to continue.

"So I tell you what I'll do. I'll share with you what I know, but I'm expecting you to do the same."

Connolly gave no reply.

"I want to know what you know before the police or any of these other hundred government agents running around here find out about it. Understand?"

"Yeah." Connolly sighed. "I understand."

"I've got a lot of business to protect here," Giles continued. "Hundreds of jobs, millions of dollars in contracts, and a whole lot of folks getting more nervous by the minute." Giles leaned back in his seat. "Got clients so spooked they're afraid to come around."

"Making you earn your pay."

"Yeah. Every penny of it." Giles stood and moved around the desk. "That's why I need your help. You give me a call as soon as you hear something. I'll do the same for you."

Connolly rose, and together they stepped toward the door. Giles paused there and thrust his hand toward Connolly. Connolly grasped it.

"There is one thing you could help me with."

Giles arched his eyebrows in anticipation of the request.

"What's that?"

"I'd like to talk to Frank Ingram. Think you could set that up?"

Giles thought for a moment.

"Not this week. I'll see what I can do next week. After everybody has a little time to calm down."

He guided Connolly through the door and walked with him as far as the elevator. They shook hands once more, and then Connolly stepped into the elevator and rode to the lobby. At the desk, he handed the guard his building pass, retrieved his driver's license, and walked outside to the Chrysler.

The parking lot was surrounded on three sides by the shipyard, separated by a ten-foot chain-link fence with concertina wire across the top. Beyond the fence, giant steel hulls rested along the banks of the river. Cranes towered in the late afternoon sky, casting long shadows over the boatyard. Connolly felt uneasy.

Drummond's conversation earlier that day had seemed innocuous at the time. Just a political operative trying to keep his boss out of trouble. But Giles had just told him the same thing. Both worked for people who were nervous about this case, and both wanted to know what he knew before he told anyone else. That left Connolly wondering what there was about this case that had everyone so interested in him. Steve's death was a horrible tragedy. Giles' interest in finding out what happened to him was understandable. Ingram Shipbuilding did work for the navy; an extensive investigation could be expected. Hogan Smith was a senator; his aides were paid to keep him ahead of the news. But Connolly didn't represent Ingram or Hogan Smith, and he wasn't involved with the navy or the companies that dealt with the shipyard. He represented Harvey Bosarge, a retired policeman living in a remote fishing village, hired by a jealous husband to follow a capricious wife.

"Everyone has something to hide," he whispered.

Six

*F*rom the shipyard on Water Street, Connolly drove south toward Fowl River. The afternoon was almost gone as he passed Mary's Place, a restaurant specializing in Creole cuisine. Housed in a low country cottage, it sat a few hundred yards from the banks of West Fowl River, surrounded by towering pines and a sea of marsh grass.

Connolly lifted his foot from the gas pedal. The Chrysler rumbled across the wooden-plank bridge spanning the river. Across the bridge, he turned onto a narrow paved road. Marsh grass and ty ty bushes encroached on the shoulders of the road. A mile farther he left the pavement and turned onto a freshly graded dirt road. Red dust rolled through the air behind the car as it glided deeper and deeper into the brown sea of marsh grass known to the locals as Mon Louis Island.

Two miles down the road he slowed the car and turned left again, this time onto a muddy two-rut trail. The car rocked from side to side as it wallowed through the mud, sliding past the pines and cypress that dotted the marsh. He drove with one foot on the accelerator and one on the brake, pressing the car for momentum, then fighting to keep the front wheels ahead of the rear.

Finally, the trail reached the high ground along Garon's Bayou, a narrow, winding inlet that meandered through the marsh and into the river. The trail became hard and firm.

Connolly relaxed his grip on the steering wheel and slipped his foot off the brake pedal.

Ahead, a tar-paper shack came into view. Nestled in a clump of scrub oaks and pines, it sat only a few yards from the bayou. A rickety pier led from the back of the cabin to the water. By then, the sun was a giant orange ball sinking below the horizon in the west behind him.

Hollis Toombs' pickup truck was parked out front when Connolly arrived. Hollis, a survivor of three tours in Vietnam, inherited the shack and a few hundred acres of marsh from his uncle, a fact that rankled several of Hollis' cousins. They contested the will, which is how Hollis and Connolly came to be acquainted.

As Connolly approached, he could see the hood was up on the pickup. Hollis was bent over the front fender, his head buried somewhere beneath the hood. A single light bulb dangled at the end of an extension chord looped over the hood latch. Connolly brought the Chrysler to a stop beside the truck and stepped from the car.

"Truck quit running?"

Hollis glanced at Connolly but did not reply. His hands were busy working on the engine, while his jaw worked on a thick wad of tobacco. Connolly walked around to the front of the truck and leaned over the radiator for a better view.

"What year is this thing anyway?"

"Sixty-two," Hollis replied.

"This thing was worn out thirty years ago," Connolly chided.

Hollis raised up from beneath the hood, cocked his head to one side, and spit a stream of tobacco juice against the front tire of the Chrysler. The brown glob spattered against the tire and hubcap.

"You're a fine one to talk about somebody's vehicle." Hollis turned back to the truck and ducked beneath the hood. "If you came for supper, you're out of luck. I ate early tonight."

Connolly shook his head.

"Didn't come for supper."

Hollis heaved a heavy sigh.

"In that case, you must need some help. I think I squared things with you last time."

"I don't know if we're square or not. But I need some help."

Hollis picked up a wrench that was lying on top of the air cleaner. He slipped it over a bolt on the front of the engine and continued to work.

"Doing what?"

Connolly leaned away from the radiator and folded his arms across his chest.

"You hear about that guy who was killed over at Point Clear a few days ago?"

"Man who got fragged in his own garage?"

"Yeah."

"I heard about it. Rich guy. Rich guys always go out in a blaze of glory. Poor guy gets hit in the head with a hammer. Nobody ever hears about it."

"I need to go over to his house tonight."

Hollis laid the wrench on the radiator and raised himself from beneath the hood once again. He picked up a rag from the fender and wiped his hands.

"What's happening over there?"

"Nothing. I just want to look around."

"You want to break into this dead rich man's house?"

"Sort of."

"Sort of?"

"Explosion tore up the back of the house pretty bad. I don't think we'll have any trouble getting the door open."

Hollis shook his head.

"What you looking for that's so important?"

Connolly looked away, avoiding the question.

"You willing to help?"

Hollis continued to wipe his hands on the rag.

"What you want me to do?"

Connolly turned toward Hollis.

"Go with me."

"Why? You afraid of the dark?"

"Not sure what I'll run into," Connolly replied. "And ... you're the only person I know who could do something like this and not talk about it."

For the first time in a long time a smile broke across Hollis' face. He looked at the sky and scanned the horizon. "Be pitch dark by the time we get there." He tossed the rag on the radiator and stepped away from the truck. "Let's go."

Connolly smiled.

"Don't you want to finish what you were doing?"

Hollis was already to the far side of the Chrysler.

"Nah," he replied, as he jerked open the door. "It'll be right there tomorrow."

Connolly and Hollis drove north from Fowl River to Mobile and crossed the bay. By the time they reached Battles Wharf, Steve Ingram's house was shrouded in darkness. The Chrysler slowed to an idle as they neared the driveway. Yellow crime-scene tape still stretched across the entrance. Connolly brought the car to a stop a few feet off the road and reached for the door handle.

Hollis looked alarmed.

"What are you doing?"

"Going to untie the tape."

"Untie the tape? You mean you plan to just ride up to the house?"

"Yeah."

"Are you out of your mind?" Hollis pointed toward the road. "Ride on down that way."

"What for?"

"Just do what I say, and maybe we can stay out of trouble."

Connolly steered the Chrysler back onto the pavement and drove away. Hollis watched the passing houses out the window. A mile or so down the road, he turned to Connolly.

"Okay, drive back toward the house, but turn in the driveway next door."

Connolly turned the car around. As they neared Steve's house once again, he slowed the car.

"This one or the one on the other side?"

"This one."

Connolly turned the car into the driveway.

"Hope no one's at home."

"They aren't," Hollis replied.

"How do you know?"

"No lights. Grass ain't been cut. Bushes haven't been trimmed in over a year. Leaves all over the driveway. Turn off the headlights."

Connolly switched off the lights. They continued up the driveway in the dark and came to a stop behind the house. Connolly reached across Hollis to the glove box and took out a small flashlight. He felt under the seat and found a screwdriver, then opened the car door. Hollis stepped out on the other side and eased the car door closed.

A high brick wall ran along the property line from the water's edge to the road, separating the neighbor's yard from Steve's. Connolly followed Hollis across a small patch of grass to the end of the wall near the water. There, Hollis crouched and peered around the corner. Connolly knelt beside him.

"See anything?" he whispered.

"Nah," Hollis replied, shaking his head. He shifted to one side for a wider view of the house. "Any idea how they did it?"

Connolly moved behind him and looked over his shoulder.

"Used something called Semtex."

"Semtex?"

"That's what the ATF guy said. There were three cars in the garage. They put a charge in all three of them. Used some kind of electronic detonator."

Hollis glanced at Connolly, a curious look on his face.

"Electronic detonator?"

"Yeah. That's what they said."

Hollis scanned the shoreline.

"They were here when it happened."

"What do you mean?"

"They were here," Hollis repeated. "Next door." He pointed toward the water. "Out there in a boat. In a car at the end of the driveway. Somewhere close, watching."

"Why do you think that?"

"If they did it like you said, they wanted to make sure they got him. Most car bombs are wired to the ignition. Start the car, the car blows up. Wrong person happens to start the car, the whole deal falls apart. What you're talking about is different. Somebody watched and made sure he was in the car. Then they pressed a button on a remote that set off the charges."

Both men fell silent for a moment. Finally, Connolly stepped past Hollis and moved around the end of the wall.

"Come on. Let's get inside."

Connolly led the way across the yard to the deck and the back door. He leaned against the door and shoved it open, then switched on the flashlight. Hollis followed him into the kitchen and pushed the door closed.

"You know what you're looking for?"

"Yeah," Connolly replied. "Upstairs."

They crossed the den to the staircase and made their way upstairs. Furniture was still piled in the hallway. The contents of drawers and closets littered the floor. They picked their way around it to the master bedroom on the far side of the house. Connolly shone the flashlight on the ceiling and located the air-conditioning duct.

"I wouldn't shine that light around too much," Hollis warned. "Neighbors on this side are home."

Connolly glanced out the window. Unlike the house where they parked the Chrysler, the one on this side was well lit. Connolly could see people moving about inside. Hollis took the flashlight from Connolly and turned it off.

"Work in the dark. Your eyes will adjust."

Connolly found a small table in the hallway and carried it into the bedroom. Hollis eyed him with curiosity.

"What you going to do with that?"

"Climb on top of it," Connolly replied. "Hold it steady."

Connolly set the table astride the rail at the foot of the bed frame underneath the air-conditioner vent. Hollis steadied it as Connolly climbed on top. Using the screwdriver, he pried the cover from the duct and reached inside. Hollis stared in amazement.

"What are you doing?"

"Yep." Connolly grinned. "Just like I thought."

"What?"

"A video camera."

"A video camera?" Even at a whisper Hollis sounded incredulous. "What's a video camera doing in the air-conditioner duct?"

"Making videos."

Hollis glanced around the room, then back at Connolly.

"Of the bed?"

"Among other things."

"You think they were filming themselves?"

"They were filming something."

Carefully, Connolly pried the camera loose from its mounting bracket and eased it out of the duct. Connolly held the camera, which was not much larger than a videotape cassette, in one hand for Hollis to see. Hollis shook his head. Connolly smiled as he climbed down from the tabletop.

Suddenly, headlights from a car washed across the room. They both dropped to the floor. Connolly felt his heart rate quicken.

Hollis crawled to a window and eased up to the ledge.

"Looks like someone's untying the tape."

Connolly's heart pounded against his chest.

"Let's get downstairs." He turned to leave. "Maybe we can get out the front door."

"No, wait a minute." Hollis continued to look out the window. He gestured with his hand for Connolly to wait. "Let's see who it is."

Lying on the floor, Connolly heard the car as it started forward.

"What kind of car is it?"

"Looks like a big one," Hollis replied. "I can't really tell. It's behind the trees."

Connolly crawled to the corner of the window beside Hollis and raised himself up for a look. He watched as the man from the car retied the tape across the driveway and returned to the car.

"Mercedes," Hollis whispered.

He moved away from the window. Connolly followed him to the hall. At the top of the stairs, Hollis stopped and leaned against the wall. Headlights from the car moved across the downstairs as the car turned behind the house.

"Too late," he whispered. "We can't get out the front without being heard."

Connolly hurried to a bedroom at the far end of the hall. From a window at the back of the house, he looked down on the deck and parking area. The Mercedes was parked beneath him. As he watched, the driver's door opened. The interior light came on, illuminating the driver's face. Connolly hurried back to the hall.

"It's Frank."

"Frank?"

"Frank Ingram," Connolly explained. "Steve's brother."

Hollis rolled his eyes.

"Why's he here?"

Connolly shrugged his shoulders.

"I don't know."

In a moment, the back door opened. Connolly stepped away from the stairs and retreated down the hall to the bedroom at the rear of the house. Below him, he heard Frank moving around in the kitchen. Hollis lingered a moment longer, listening, then moved down the hall to the bedroom with Connolly.

"What's he doing?"

"Sounds like he's looking for something," Hollis replied.

"What could he be looking for? This place has been searched and ransacked a dozen times."

Hollis did not respond.

"Any idea what we're going to do?"

"Jump," Hollis replied.

"Jump?"

"Yeah. Jump. It ain't that far."

The stairs creaked, interrupting their conversation. Connolly felt his heart skip a beat.

They listened as Frank reached the top of the stairs, holding their breath as they waited to see which way he turned. When Frank's footsteps indicated he had moved down the hall toward the master bedroom, Hollis started toward the door. He motioned with his hand for Connolly to follow.

Hollis led the way as they crept up the hall and down the steps. As they reached the bottom of the stairway, one of the steps creaked. The noise in the bedroom upstairs stopped. Connolly and Hollis froze.

After what seemed like an eternity, they heard Frank moving around the bedroom once again. Hollis tapped Connolly on the chest and gestured for him to follow. They moved across the den to the kitchen and out the back door.

With Connolly hard on Hollis' heels, the two men ran across the backyard and around the end of the brick wall. Once on the other side, they hurried to the Chrysler. Hollis opened the car door and slid in on the passenger side. Connolly tossed the video camera onto the backseat and slid in behind the wheel. He started the Chrysler, turned it around, and drove down the drive toward the road.

At the end of the driveway, Connolly turned the car south and pressed the throttle. He glanced over at Hollis. A broad grin stretched across Hollis' face.

"I haven't done anything like that in a long time."

"You like that kind of stuff?"

"They used to drop us into North Vietnam way up past where anybody was supposed to be. We'd sit for days under a tree and watch Vietcong going by. So close we could have touched them. I loved it."

"You want something else to do?"

Hollis looked curious.

"Like what?"

"Footwork, mostly."

"What kind of footwork?"

"Well, you could begin by checking out your idea."

"What idea?"

"That whoever did this was around here when it happened."

"That was just a hunch."

"Yeah, but the ATF guy said pretty much the same thing. Think you could check it out?"

"I don't know. Maybe. What'd you have in mind?"

"Ask around. See if you can find somebody who knows something. Maybe somebody saw a car that was out of place. A stranger. If they used a boat, there's not that many places to launch one. Somebody might have seen something."

Hollis did not reply. Connolly knew what he was waiting to hear.

"I could pay you a little something. Wouldn't be much."

Hollis' eyes danced.

"Pay me in cash?"

"Yeah," Connolly smiled. "Cash."

Seven

onnolly drove Hollis to his shack on Fowl River. It was well past midnight when he returned to Mobile. Though it was late, he drove to Mrs. Gordon's house.

Mrs. Gordon lived on Houston Street in midtown. Her house, a two-bedroom 1920s bungalow, sat close to the street. It had white clapboard siding, a tiny patch of grass in front, and a narrow driveway on one side.

The house was dark when Connolly arrived. He parked in the drive and climbed the steps to the front porch. He rang the doorbell, waited a moment, then rang it again. A light came on inside. Then he heard Mrs. Gordon's voice.

"Who is it?"

"Mike."

"Mike?"

"Yeah. Mike Connolly. Come on. Open up."

A rattle came from inside as she unlocked the door. She stood behind the door as it came open and peered around at him.

"What are you doing here this time of night?"

"Don't you have a VCR?"

She looked perplexed. "Can't this wait until tomorrow?"

Connolly stepped inside. "Not really."

Mrs. Gordon sighed and closed the door. She was dressed in a nightgown and a bulky housecoat. Her face looked pale, her eyes were tired. She ran one hand self-consciously through her gray hair.

"You want some popcorn to go with your movie?"

The sarcastic tone in her voice left little room for doubt how she felt about the intrusion.

"It's not that kind of tape," he replied. "Where's the VCR?"

"In the den." She started in the opposite direction down the hall toward her bedroom. "Lock the door when you leave."

"I want you to see it, too," Connolly insisted.

She answered him without turning around.

"I don't think so."

Connolly was already in the den.

"It came from Steve Ingram's bedroom," he called.

He heard her footsteps in the hall come to a stop.

"His bedroom?"

"Yeah. Somebody had a camera in the air-conditioning vent above the bed."

"I'm not into that kind of stuff."

Connolly found the VCR underneath the television. He turned on the television and pushed the tape into the player. An image of a bed appeared on the screen. The camera looked down on it from the ceiling.

Mrs. Gordon entered the den behind him.

"Oh. Now that's interesting."

"Any way to make it play faster?"

"Press the button marked 'fast-forward,'" she said.

Connolly pressed the button. The image on the screen flickered as the tape sped through the VCR. In a moment, the image grew darker. Connolly looked at the remote control, then leaned closer to the set.

"What's happening to it?"

"I imagine it's getting dark," Mrs. Gordon replied.

"I can see that. But why?"

"Nighttime," Mrs. Gordon said. "It gets dark at night."

"Oh."

A little longer and the screen was totally black. Then, someone switched on a light. Connolly pressed the play button. The sound of laughter could be heard. Connolly looked surprised.

"This thing has sound?"

"Sounds like it."

A woman flopped backward on the bed. She wore a man's white shirt and nothing else. Steve Ingram appeared, wearing only boxer shorts. He leaned over her and pulled the woman's shirt open.

Mrs. Gordon shifted positions and wrapped her arms around herself.

"Are you really going to watch them?"

"That must be Ann Grafton."

"You can fast-forward past this."

Connolly pressed the button on the remote. Mrs. Gordon turned away. Images on the screen flew past. When the scene changed, Connolly pressed the remote. The picture slowed to normal speed. Steve and Ann lay in bed. The image was lighter. Morning had arrived.

They watched as Steve rolled over and laid his arm around Ann. He pulled her close. The sheet slipped away. Mrs. Gordon cleared her throat. Connolly pressed the fast-forward button again. The machine began to whir.

Images of Steve and Ann flashed by on the screen. Soon, they were gone. The screen showed only the empty bed and the area in the center of the room. Connolly and Mrs. Gordon stared at the television. Connolly pushed play on the remote to watch in real time.

Then, the picture jumped and shook, followed by a loud, rumbling roar. Dust filled the air. Mrs. Gordon gasped.

"That was the explosion," she exclaimed. "When the garage blew up. Where did you get this?"

Connolly grinned.

"Apparently, Ingram liked to watch tapes of his bedroom performances."

"How did you find it?"

Connolly shook his head.

"Trick of the trade."

On the screen, the camera still pointed down at the bed. Connolly pressed the fast-forward button. As they watched, the image on the television screen flickered. Connolly pressed the remote and pointed to the screen.

"What was that?" He glanced at the remote. "Can you make this thing go backward?"

"Press rewind."

Mrs. Gordon sounded impatient. Connolly found the rewind button and pressed it. The tape played backward.

"There," he said, pointing.

"Press play," she said.

Connolly pressed the play button and watched as the tape played at normal speed. A shadow moved across the floor.

"Somebody's in the room."

In the upper-left corner, a man appeared near the night-stand. He wore a red T-shirt, blue jeans, and canvas high-top tennis shoes. Atop his head was a baseball cap with a red A on the front. He was tall, well over six feet. Slim and wiry, he looked like someone who had fought his way out of more than one barroom brawl.

As they watched, he lifted the mattress and stood it on one edge. A second man, just out of the picture to the right, grabbed the mattress and leaned it against the wall. The first man picked up the box spring and flipped it off the frame. The second man propped it against the mattress.

"Check the drawers," a voice said.

The first man turned to the nightstand. With one hand, he pulled the top drawer out of the nightstand and turned it upside down. The contents fell on the floor. He kicked through it with the toe of his shoe. When he found nothing of interest, he tossed the empty drawer across the room and took out the second one. He did the same with it and with the third.

"Check inside the frame," a voice said.

The man knelt and slipped his hand inside the nightstand. He turned to the right and grinned.

"Here it is." He raised his hand from inside the nightstand, holding an envelope. "Taped under the top."

He tore open the envelope. Inside was a stack of photographs. The second man stepped closer and was now visible on the screen. Short and slender, he wore a dark brown shirt, blue jeans, and tan work boots. His brown hair was thick and hung almost to his shoulders.

The taller one flipped through the photographs with his thumb.

"How'd he know where they were?"

"I don't know," the shorter one answered. "Where's the negatives?"

The taller man squatted and ran his hands through the pile on the floor, scattering the contents of the drawers in front of him.

"Ain't none here."

"All right," the shorter one said. "Let's go."

They moved off the screen. The room was quiet.

Connolly pressed the rewind button.

"What did he say?"

Mrs. Gordon did not reply.

Connolly turned up the volume on the television set and pressed the play button.

"Let's go," the short one said.

Connolly let the videotape run. Once the men were out of the room, there was only the image of the bed frame and the bare floor beneath it. Connolly pressed the fast-forward button. The tape sped through the VCR.

Mrs. Gordon turned away.

"I don't think there's anything else on it." She started out of the room. "Lock the door when you leave."

Connolly stepped toward the tape player.

"How do you get the tape out?"

"Just turn it off," Mrs. Gordon said. "The tape will pop out."

Connolly found the switch and removed the tape.

"You think there's somebody who could make some photographs from this video?"

She stopped and turned toward him.

"I think they do it all the time."

He handed her the tape.

"Will you take care of that for me?"

"Will you go if I say 'yes'?"

Connolly smiled.

"Sorry to bother you so late." He started toward the front door. "Take care of that tape."

"Guard it with my life."

Connolly stepped outside. She closed the door behind him. He heard the bolt slide into place as he made his way down the steps.

Eight

*C*onnolly started the Chrysler and pulled away from the curb in front of Mrs. Gordon's house. The day had been long. He felt very tired. He drove across midtown to Government Street. At Tuttle Street, he turned right. A few blocks later he steered the Chrysler into the driveway at the Pleiades. He was looking forward to a hot shower and bed.

A four-story mansion built in 1901, the Pleiades was one of a number of large homes built by Mobile's wealthy families at a time when midtown was the place to live. Constructed by Elijah Huntley, a broker who made a fortune importing bananas from Costa Rica, the house was an architectural marvel for its day. Dumbwaiters moved food from the kitchen on the first floor to the dining room on the second. Electric lights made the rooms glow, and forced-air heat kept them evenly heated during Mobile's short, mild winters. But the most astounding aspect of the place was its air conditioner. While the rest of Mobile sweltered in heat and humidity, the Pleiades was cooled by a crude but efficient air-conditioning system that employed water from an artesian well and a cluster of electric fans. Ornate trim work, enormous rooms, a grand entrance, and a spiral staircase combined with technological gadgets to make the house a showplace.

Behind the main house was a swimming pool. A tennis court sat next to it. Behind the pool was a large ornamental garden, and beyond the garden was the guest house, built as an afterthought at the insistence of Huntley's third wife. With three bedrooms, the guest house was larger than many suburban homes and had its own kitchen and wine cellar.

Now in the hands of Huntley's great-great-granddaughter, Lois Crump, the house and grounds still evoked wonder and awe, but it was not a practical house. Upkeep was expensive. Heating and cooling costs were high. The grounds required a full-time gardener. By the time the house passed to Lois, she was living in Birmingham and had little time and even less money to devote to maintenance. To make the place more affordable, she rented out the guest house. Connolly was the latest in a succession of tenants.

Lights in the main house, timed to make it appear as though someone actually lived there, were already out when he arrived home that evening. The place was dark and quiet. Up the drive, the headlights on the Chrysler fell on a red Trans Am parked near the front door of the guest house. Connolly felt his heart jump.

As he drew closer, the driver's door opened and Marisa stepped out. Dressed for work, she wore red spandex pants, a gold top that accentuated her ample breasts, and six-inch heels. Once out of the car, she ran her fingers through her blond hair and struck a pose, smiling at Connolly. He brought the Chrysler to a stop alongside the Trans Am.

Marisa's real name was Linda Marie Mayhew. Connolly first met her when she worked as a barmaid at the Imperial Palace, a club on the Alabama-Mississippi line thirty miles west of Mobile. Newly divorced, Connolly was a regular customer there. They started seeing each other over breakfast after she got off work. Not long after that, she moved in with him in an apartment on Carondolet Street. Two months later, she convinced him to pay for cosmetic surgery that transformed her into a buxom beauty. Just as quickly, she moved from barmaid to exotic dancer and began calling herself Marisa.

A few months into her new career, Connolly came home to find she had moved out. A note on the kitchen table said she was moving to Florida with Frank, a banker from Panama City. That lasted until Frank's wife found her in the family's beach condo, and then Marisa was back. She stayed a while but left again when Connolly quit drinking and began spending more time at St. Pachomius. He knew she was bad news, but he found it difficult to ignore the way she made him feel.

He stepped from the Chrysler and moved toward the back of the car.

"Didn't expect to see you here."

He stopped near the bumper and leaned against the fender. Still smiling, Marisa stepped toward him. Connolly struggled to keep his eyes from wandering over her. When she was just a few feet away, he folded his arms across his chest. She stopped in front of him and leaned against the fender of the Trans Am.

"Thought you'd be a little happier to see me."

"On your way home from work?"

"Yes. Want to come home with me?"

"Afraid not," he said.

"Be like old times."

"Not interested in old times."

He moved around her and stepped toward the door.

"I guess you're still at the Imperial Palace?"

"For now." She followed behind him and waited while he unlocked the door. "Mind if I come in for a minute?"

"Suit yourself."

He opened the door and stepped inside. She moved behind him to the left toward the living room. "Heard you had some trouble after I left."

Connolly stood in the doorway to the kitchen.

"Yeah. A little."

"I saw it on the news. You're lucky to be alive."

Connolly nodded. She gave him a playful smile.

"Think the same people who blew up your apartment blew up that guy over at Point Clear?"

The comment caught Connolly by surprise. Until then, he had not considered the possibility the two incidents were connected.

"I don't know. Never thought about it."

Her smile spread to a grin. "Maybe my stopping by helped you out."

"Helped me out?"

"Yeah. Aren't you interested in figuring out who tried to kill you?"

"No. Not really. Long as they don't come back again."

She shrugged in response and glanced around the room.

"Whatever. Got anything to drink?"

"Water. Coca-Cola. Milk."

She shook her head. "Never mind. Okay if I use the phone?"

"Go ahead." He pointed across the room. "It's on a table over there by the television."

She crossed the room to the table. With her back to him, Connolly let his eyes follow the smooth curve of her hips. At the table, she leaned over to dial the number. Her spandex pants, already skin tight, stretched even tighter over her hips and buttocks. His eyes ran over every inch, then down her long legs. For a moment, he imagined what it would be like to be with her for the evening.

Then, angry with himself for it, he turned away. As he did, his eye caught the yellow cover of a telephone directory lying on the floor just under the edge of the couch beside Marisa's foot. He stared at the book, trying to remember when he used it last and wondering why it wasn't on the table beside the phone.

Marisa glanced over her shoulder at him and smiled, as if she knew he would be watching her. He turned away and stepped into the kitchen. In a few minutes she appeared at the kitchen doorway.

"Well, I guess I better get on home." She stretched her arms above her head, then sighed as she dropped them to her side. "Sure you won't come with me?"

Connolly smiled at her. "No. Better not."

They looked at each other a moment.

"Why did you stop by here?"

"Needed to use the phone," she giggled. She paused, then turned her head away. The smile disappeared. Her voice became soft. "Wanted to see if you were doing all right."

"How'd you know where I live?"

"You aren't hard to find," she replied.

Connolly chuckled in response. Marisa turned to leave. He moved around her and opened the door. She kissed him on the cheek.

"See ya."

He watched from the door as she slipped into the Trans Am and backed away from the house.

When she was gone, he crossed the room to the telephone table and picked up the directory. The heavy scent of her cheap perfume hung in the air. With it came a flood of memories. He took his time returning the book to its place on the table. As he lingered there, thinking of her, smelling her scent, his gaze fell past the table to the wall. A fine powdery dust lay along the top edge of the baseboard behind the table.

He knelt and wiped his finger through the dust. Rubbing it between his fingers he was sure it was dust from the wallboard around the telephone outlet. He took a dime from his pocket and placed it in the slot of the screw securing the outlet cover. With a twist, he loosened the screw and slipped off the cover.

Behind the cover, wires for the telephone were attached to either side of a plastic outlet block. On the left side, however, a single black wire ran up the wall from the outlet block toward the ceiling. Connolly carefully replaced the cover over the outlet and screwed it in place.

From the living room, he walked down the hall to the bedroom. An access passage to the attic was located in the ceiling of the bedroom closet. He opened the closet door and slid a chair beneath the panel covering the passage. Standing on the chair, he pushed the panel back and stuck his head through the opening. The attic was too dark to see.

He stepped from the chair and hurried to the kitchen for a flashlight. He returned to the chair and poked his head through the opening. Grasping a ceiling joist with one hand, he hauled himself into the attic and switched on the flashlight.

A few feet away, the light fell on a small black box. A shiny antenna protruded from the top. Wires connected to the box snaked across the attic. Connolly switched off the flashlight and slid his feet through the opening to the chair below.

He turned off the bedroom light and stepped to the window. Standing to one side, he peered out into the night. In front, fifty yards away, was the main house. Beyond it was the street, another fifty yards farther. Connolly didn't know much about electronics, but he felt certain the transmitter in the attic wasn't very powerful. Whoever was listening to him had to be somewhere nearby.

From the bedroom, he walked down the hall to the front door and slipped outside. He crossed the garden that lay between the guest house and the pool. A fountain in the middle gurgled as he passed. At the far end of the garden behind several large bushes was the gardener's shed. From the shed, a row of large azalea bushes ran toward the street, separating the property around the main house from the neighbors. Connolly slipped out of sight past the shed and crept along the bushes toward the street. Twenty yards from the curb, he crouched and watched.

To the left, the street was empty. Looking through the bushes to the right, he saw only one vehicle, a late-model pickup truck parked in front of the house three doors down.

"They have to be around here somewhere," he whispered to himself.

After a moment, he scurried from the street back along the row of azaleas to the gardener's shed. From there, he walked to the guest house and entered through the front door.

Inside, the once-friendly guest house now seemed eerie and still. Knowing someone was listening to him left him feeling as though they were actually present, lurking behind a door, looking over his shoulder. He thought more than once about disconnecting the transmitter, but each time he rejected the notion. If he was patient and gave no indication he knew it was there, he was certain he could find out who was behind it. But it made for an uncomfortable existence.

In the bedroom, he took a .38-caliber revolver from the sock drawer of the dresser. He checked to make certain it was loaded and slipped it under the pillow on the bed.

Nine

*C*onnolly arrived at the office before sunrise the following morning. In the gray light of dawn, he squatted behind Mrs. Gordon's desk and located the wall jack for the telephone. He unscrewed the cover and checked the wires. Finding nothing suspicious there, he took a seat at her desk. He unplugged the cord from the phone to the receiver, then unscrewed the cover from the mouthpiece. He saw nothing suspicious there, either.

He repeated the same process with the telephone in the break room and the one at his desk. Satisfied that no one had tampered with them, he checked each of the electrical outlets.

"Why would someone bug the house and not the office?"

Connolly knew he wasn't technically qualified to perform a security check, but he was sure he could locate the listening devices anyone he dealt with might try to install. Most of his clients were thieves and prostitutes, none of whom had any measure of sophisticated technical expertise.

He spent thirty minutes checking as many places in the office as he could think of where someone might install eavesdropping equipment. The light fixtures, the baseboards, the legs of the desks, wherever there was room to tuck something out of the way. As he looked, he began to think.

Since taking on Harvey Bosarge as a client, he'd had a

visit from a senator's aide and a meeting with the security chief for the city's wealthiest family, both of whom were keenly interested in what he knew about Steve Ingram's death. He had been accosted by an Ingram employee, found a video camera in Steve's house, and watched an interesting video of the last hours of a man's life. Now, his own residence was bugged, and here he was crawling on the floor in his office checking under the furniture for electronic gadgets he knew nothing about.

By the time he'd looked in every place he could think of, he was convinced he needed to hire a professional to do a thorough sweep. The only problem was, Mobile wasn't that large a place. If he wasn't careful, the person he hired to check his office might just be the same person who installed listening devices in it.

He took one last look around the office and checked his watch. It wasn't yet seven. Right then, there was nothing else to do but walk up the street to the Port City Diner for doughnuts and coffee. He stepped into the corridor and locked the door.

As he turned to leave, his eye fell on the large access panel for the building telephone system located across the corridor from the office door. He stepped to the panel and pulled on the handle. The door was locked.

He unlocked the office door and moved around to Mrs. Gordon's desk. In the top drawer he found a small metal fingernail file. He returned with it to the access panel. Using the file, he jimmied open the panel door. Inside, he found a tangle of red, white, and blue wires running in and out of a three-foot connection block. Draped across the tangle of colored wires were two black wires clipped from one side of the block to the other.

Each of the connections on the block bore a small white tag identifying the office to which the connection was assigned. He followed the black wire to the right and found it connected at a point identified as 329.

"Three twenty-nine. That's my office."

Connolly was waiting in the lobby when Mrs. Gordon arrived. He put his arm around her and pulled her aside.

"What are you—"

Connolly put his finger to his lips, gesturing for her to be quiet. He led her out the service entrance to Ferguson's Alley behind the building. Once outside he turned toward her, his arm still around her shoulder, his lips almost touching her ear. He felt her body stiffen.

"I have to tell you something," he whispered. "Don't say a word. You hear me?"

Mrs. Gordon nodded.

"The guest house is bugged."

She jerked her head away and looked at him in disbelief. He pulled her close again.

"Every room. Every phone. I think the phones in the office are, too."

He relaxed his grip on her shoulder. She slipped away.

"What are we going to do?"

"I'm going to find somebody to check out the phones," he replied. "See if there's a way around it."

"Why would someone tap our phones?"

"I don't know, and that's what bothers me most."

A frown wrinkled Mrs. Gordon's forehead. She stared at him, trying to make sense of what he had told her.

Connolly opened the service door to the lobby and nodded for her to enter. They walked together as far as the elevator. The doors opened as they approached, and several people stepped off. She turned to get in, then stopped.

"Here." She handed him an envelope. "I picked these up for you on the way in."

Connolly looked puzzled as he took the envelope from her. "What's this?"

"Pictures from those negatives you gave me."

She stepped inside the elevator. The doors closed. Connolly stuffed the envelope into the pocket of his jacket and crossed the lobby to the main entrance.

On the street outside, he walked to the Chrysler and got in. He slipped the key in the ignition, then remembered the photographs in his pocket. He took out the envelope and opened it. Inside he found three photographs. The first was a picture of Frank Ingram standing next to a man who appeared to be from somewhere in Asia. Connolly couldn't tell which country. The photograph was taken at a party. Both men had drinks in their hand, and other people could be seen in the background, smiling and laughing. Connolly studied it a moment, then slipped it back into the envelope and took out the second one.

Like the first, it was a picture of Frank at a party. Standing beside him was Greg Drummond. Connolly looked at it a moment, then took out the third. A man at the same party stood alone near a grand piano. The expression on the man's face looked as if the photographer caught him by surprise. Connolly glanced at it briefly, then slid all three photos into the inside pocket of his jacket and turned the key in the ignition switch. The Chrysler's engine came to life.

From the office, Connolly drove across town to Eight Mile, a small community on the northern edge of Mobile. There, he made his way to the home of Peyton Russo.

He and Peyton had been friends since high school, but after graduation their paths had gone in separate directions. Connolly went to college and law school; Peyton went to work for a fledgling company named International Electronic Processors. Several years later, IEP merged with another company to become part of TRW. In the process, Peyton became an expert in digital technology. He would have had a long and profitable career, but he had a stroke at the age of forty-five. After two years of physical therapy, he retired and opened an electronics repair shop in an abandoned service station across the road from his house. He was one of the few childhood friends with whom Connolly maintained contact.

Connolly parked the Chrysler in front of the shop and got out. Through a grimy window he saw a single light near the back. Connolly pushed the door open and stepped inside.

"Peyton," he called. "You in here?"

He waited, hearing nothing at first. Then the sound of shuffling feet came toward him as Peyton made his way to the front. Connolly smiled at the sight of his old friend. Peyton acknowledged Connolly with a look and motioned for him to follow. They walked through the cluttered shop to a workbench in the back. Peyton glanced over his shoulder at Connolly.

"Want some coffee?"

"Sure."

A coffeepot sat to one side of the bench. Peyton found a mug under a stack of unopened mail and wiped it out with his shirt sleeve. He filled it with coffee and handed it to Connolly.

"So," he said, pausing to sip from his own cup, "what brings you all the way out here?"

"Got a problem at the office."

"You still got that same secretary?"

"Yeah," Connolly nodded, smiling. "It's not that kind of problem. I think my phones are tapped."

Peyton cocked his head to one side, as if the notion intrigued him.

"What makes you think that?"

"Found one on the phone at my house. Phone jack is wired to a transmitter in the attic."

"Find the same thing in your office?"

"No. Didn't find anything in the office. But when I checked the panel in the hall, I found a couple of wires clipped to the connection for my office."

Peyton gave him a knowing smile.

"Amateurs."

"Think so?"

"Yeah." He paused to take another sip of coffee. "Of course, it could be somebody else trying to make you think they're amateurs. What do you want from me?"

"I need somebody to check the office and make sure there's nothing more than a phone tap. And I need somebody to figure out a way to keep them from hearing what I say on the phone, without them knowing they can't hear."

"Blanket the tap?"

"I don't know what you call it," Connolly shrugged. "I don't know anything about this kind of stuff. I just don't want them to know I know they're listening. And I don't want them to be able to hear me."

"So why'd you come to me?"

"I trust you," Connolly replied. "Can you do it?"

Peyton gave him a smile.

"Yeah. I can do it."

Connolly returned to the office with Peyton before lunch. Peyton set up a monitor on Connolly's desk designed to detect the presence of electronic signals. He turned several knobs on the box. Each time he adjusted it, a needle on the front moved back and forth. Connolly sat in a chair near the door and watched.

After a while, Peyton brought out a second device that looked like a standard voltage meter. Wires with clamps extended from one end. He attached one of the wires to the wire from the telephone and turned a knob on the meter.

A few minutes later, he unhooked the phone wire from the meter and turned off the other machine.

"This room is clean." He unplugged the machine and gathered up the cord. "There aren't any signals in here that aren't supposed to be here. And I can't find anything that indicates a passive listening device. But you're right about the phone. It's tapped. Show me the service panel."

Connolly led Peyton to the corridor outside. Peyton smiled when he saw the tangled wires.

"That's it." He pointed to the black wires. "Got you crossed over to this connection here." He pointed to a connection on the opposite side of the block.

Connolly checked the tag on the connection.

"Is that where they are?"

"Nah." Peyton shook his head. "Just got you jumped to that side. That the tag for another office?"

"Yeah. Eighth floor."

"Probably got a tape recorder in the service box for that floor. That way they can check it without you seeing them. Come in at night. Maybe come in during the day dressed like they work for the phone company. Something like that."

"What can we do?"

"You could pull the crossover off, but they'll know it. Probably send somebody down here to put it back. You said that tag is for an office on the eighth floor?"

"Yeah."

"Let's go up there and have a look."

Peyton closed the panel door and turned to leave. Connolly hesitated.

"Ahh ... maybe you should go without me. If somebody sees me up there ..."

"All right," Peyton replied. "I'll be back in a minute."

Peyton disappeared around the corner. Connolly returned

to his office. He took a seat at his desk, propped his feet on the desktop, and closed his eyes.

Sometime later, he felt someone shaking his foot. He opened his eyes to see Peyton standing in front of the desk.

"Find anything?"

"Yeah," Peyton said. "Got it wired to a recording unit in a broom closet up there. Downloads everything to a floppy disk. Looks like something out of a catalog. Not very sophisticated."

"So, what can we do about it?"

"I took care of it."

"Took care of it? What did you do?"

"You got a second connection block out there that comes to this office. Somebody who had this place before had a second line in here, or maybe it was two offices."

"We have three lines."

"No. You got three numbers. They're all coming in on one line."

Connolly looked perplexed.

"Trust me," Peyton said. "You got one line servicing this office. But there's a second one wired from this office to the box, but it's not hooked to the phone company's line." He paused. "Well ... it wasn't before."

"I'm afraid I—"

"Don't worry about it. I wired your phones through the back of the panel to the second block. Wired the first block, the one they're tapping off, to the pay phone on the street out front. If they send the same amateurs that wired it over here to check on it, they'll never figure it out."

"And if they do?"

"If they take their tap off the block it's on now, the pay phone won't work."

"You sure?"

"Positive."

Connolly looked skeptical.

"Hey." Peyton tossed up his hands. "Best I can do on short notice. Just tell your secretary to check the pay phone before she comes up every morning. If you don't get a dial tone, call me."

Ten

The next morning, Connolly left the guest house and drove from midtown through the suburban clutter that sprawled along the western edge of the city. At Irvington, he turned south and descended into the low country, a broad band of savannah marsh twenty miles wide that lay along the coast below Mobile. Thirty minutes later, he reached Bayou La Batre.

A rough-and-tumble fishing town, Bayou La Batre was home to a large fleet of shrimp boats and a dwindling oyster business. Tucked along a broad bayou, the town lay hidden beneath towering cypress and sprawling oaks, concealed from view and shielded from the ravages of time. Life there was an odd and intriguing mixture of Catholic ritual, Cajun superstition, and Acadian debauchery.

Connolly drove through town and turned onto Front Street, a narrow road that bordered the bayou. A mile or two south of town the road made a sharp left turn, crossed through a sea of swamp grass, and emerged on the shore of San Souci Beach, a narrow strip of sand on the shallow bay between the mouth of the bayou and Coden, another fishing village a few miles to the east. Harvey Bosarge's house sat a short way down the road, facing the beach and the water beyond.

The house was a rambling white two-story wood-frame structure built in 1902 as a summer home for a wealthy Mobile family. They used it until the hurricane of 1906 blew off the roof. It sat empty and in disrepair until Harvey's grandfather won it in a poker game. He restored it and moved in. Bosarges have lived in it ever since.

Connolly turned off the road and let the Chrysler roll across the grass to the house. He brought the car to a stop beneath a large oak tree near the front steps. Harvey sat on the porch in a rocking chair, rocking back and forth. A cloud of smoke from the Cuban cigar in his mouth drifted above his head. He watched as Connolly stepped from the car.

"We got trouble?"

"No," Connolly replied. "Just thought we'd talk some more."

Connolly made his way up the steps and took a seat on the porch next to Bosarge.

"Anything new happen?"

"No," Connolly replied. "Not really. Went over to Steve Ingram's house."

"Find anything?"

"ATF agent says whoever set the explosives knew exactly what they were doing. Pretty sophisticated job. Used something called Semtex. Plastic explosive."

Bosarge rolled his eyes.

"Great. Now I'm not worried about the police, just some radical extremist creeping up behind me."

"I don't think we have any radical extremists around here," Connolly replied. "At least not the foreign variety." He paused a moment. "Talked to Harry Giles."

Bosarge looked concerned.

"Think that was a good idea?"

"I don't know." Connolly crossed his legs. "Didn't think it would hurt. Why?"

"I don't trust him. He talks a good game, but whatever he's telling you is only half the story. The half he wants you to know about. What did he tell you?"

"Told me there were a lot of agencies involved in this investigation. Police, sheriff, ATF, fire marshal, FBI, DIA, the navy."

"Like we didn't already know that. What else?"

"The navy's pretty nervous. FBI is interviewing everybody remotely connected to Ingram Shipbuilding. They're talking about spies and secrets and all that."

Bosarge smiled. "Like I said, radical extremists. If the FBI is worried, I'm worried." He took a puff from the cigar. "I still have some friends around, you know. They tell me Anthony Hammond isn't calling the shots on this case. They tell me if it was up to Hammond, they wouldn't be interested in me, whether I was there or not."

A cloud of cigar smoke drifted past Connolly. He waved his hand in front of his face, trying to clear it from around his nose.

"Who are your friends?"

Bosarge smiled and shook his head.

"You may be my lawyer, but there are some things I don't tell anyone." He puffed again on the cigar. "This case is way too weird. I'm not putting those guys in jeopardy any more than they already are."

Connolly waved the smoke away once again. His face wrinkled in response to the stinging in his nostrils.

"So who do your friends think is running the investigation?"

"Nobody seems to know." Bosarge puffed once more on the cigar, then noticed the look on Connolly's face. "This smoke bothering you?"

"My sinuses." Connolly pointed to his nose. "It drives my sinuses crazy."

Bosarge stubbed the cigar out on the arm of the rocking chair. He leaned forward and tossed what was left of it across the porch railing into the yard.

"Sorry. Keeps the mosquitoes away." He settled into the chair once again. "They said when you called Hammond that first time, that day I stopped you in the alley, they said there was a guy standing right there by him when he took the call. That's why he sounded so strange."

Connolly nodded.

"Any idea where Ann Grafton's husband is?"

Bosarge's eyes darted away. He shifted positions in the chair and leaned against the armrest on the side away from Connolly.

"No. He ... ahhh ... works offshore on an oil rig. Sometimes I don't hear from him for weeks at a time."

"What's his name?"

"Tommy. Tommy Grafton."

"Think he had anything to do with this?"

"I ..." Bosarge paused, his eyes fixed on some imaginary point in the distance. "You never can tell about people. He could have. I guess anything's possible. He didn't seem like the type to me, though."

"Any idea where Ann is?"

"Not really. They lived in a little house in Tillman's Corner. She worked at Jake's, out on the causeway. I told you that." He glanced at Connolly. "Didn't I tell you that?"

"Yeah," Connolly replied.

"I called Jake's yesterday." Bosarge continued before Connolly could respond. "They said they hadn't seen her in several days. I guess she's laying low someplace."

"Any idea where?"

Bosarge shook his head.

"I don't know. Could be anywhere. She has a sister, but I'm not real sure where she lives."

"How long had you been following her and Steve?"

Bosarge thought a moment before answering.

"Couple of weeks, maybe a month."

"Keep a log of where you went?"

"No."

"Where'd they go?"

"Mostly to clubs around here and to his house."

"What clubs?"

"Usual places. Florabama in Orange Beach. Roy Bean's in Daphne. I kept notes of the dates and times. I just didn't keep a formal logbook."

"Still got the notes?"

"Uh ... I'm not sure. I can look and see. Maybe try to find them."

Connolly found Bosarge's answers troubling.

"Go anywhere else? Out of town? Some place out of the ordinary?"

"Nah. Not really."

"Got any pictures?"

Bosarge chuckled and gave Connolly a sarcastic look.

"Do you think I have pictures?"

"I need one or two of Ann."

Bosarge rose from his chair and disappeared inside the house. He returned with a handful of photographs and dropped them in Connolly's lap.

"Those are the best ones of them together."

Most of the photos were taken from a distance with a long lens. The images were fuzzy and grainy. Connolly shuffled through the stack without paying much attention. Then, one caught his attention. Sharper than the others, it was a view of Steve Ingram lying in bed with a woman. The picture was taken from above the bed. Connolly glanced at Bosarge to see if he was watching. Bosarge was staring across the lawn toward the bay, his eyes fixed on that imaginary point out beyond the horizon. Connolly flipped through several more photos.

"Anybody try to talk to you about Steve and Ann before the explosion?"

"No."

"Giles didn't ask you about them?"

Bosarge jerked his head around to face Connolly.

"Did he tell you he did?"

"No. I didn't ask. Did he?"

"No. I haven't talked to Harry in ... years."

Connolly took two pictures from the stack in his lap and handed the rest to Bosarge.

"Here."

Bosarge took the pictures. They sat in silence for a moment. The morning was hot and humid. Sweat formed on Connolly's forehead.

"Well, I need to get back to the office. You need anything?"

"Nah," Bosarge replied, his eyes still fixed in a stare out toward the bay. "I'm all right."

Connolly rose from the chair and moved across the porch toward the steps.

"I'll let you know what I find."

"All right," Bosarge mumbled.

Connolly started down the steps.

"Oh," Bosarge exclaimed. "I almost forget this."

He took an envelope from his pocket and handed it to Connolly. It wasn't sealed. Connolly could see cash inside.

"What's this?"

"Retainer. I want to make sure you're really my lawyer."

Connolly shoved the envelope in his pocket.

"Thanks."

Bosarge acknowledged him with a nod. Connolly stepped from the porch and walked to the Chrysler. He opened the car door, laid the pictures on the front seat, and slid inside. He tossed a wave out the window as he drove away. When he glanced in the rearview mirror, the porch was empty. Bosarge was gone.

Eleven

From Bosarge's house, Connolly returned to Front Street and drove along the bayou. To the left, rows of shrimp boats lined the docks at the fish houses up and down the meandering, murky stream. Lashed together three and four deep, they left only a narrow passage near the middle of the bayou for boat traffic. As he drove he thought about the photograph he had seen. The picture had been taken from videotape shot by the camera he found above the bed. That meant the camera was Bosarge's, not Steve's, and that Bosarge had been in the house. He found that disturbing enough, but something else bothered him. For someone hired to follow an unfaithful spouse, Bosarge knew surprisingly little about Ann Grafton. He didn't seem to know much about her husband, either.

In the middle of town he crossed the drawbridge to the other side of the bayou and turned south. Two miles down the bayou he came to a large mailbox that dangled from a rotting wooden post at the side of the road. A driveway paved with oyster shells ran from the road at the mailbox to a house surrounded by a grove of pecan trees.

Made of concrete blocks and painted white, the house had jalousie windows shaded by large awnings. Once painted green and white, the awnings now were a patchwork of faded green, dirty yellow, and shiny gray aluminum. Below the windows, unkempt azalea bushes sprawled in every direction, their branches scratching against the windows and leaving dark stains on the wall beneath.

Connolly turned the Chrysler onto the driveway. The shells crunched beneath the tires as the car rolled toward the house. He brought the car to a stop near a picnic table ten yards to the right of the side door. He slid out of the Chrysler and made his way up the steps.

At the top of the steps, he peered through the screen door at the kitchen inside. A metal table with a red Formica top and four matching Naugahyde chairs sat to the left. Beyond the table near the door to the hallway was a gas stove. To the right of the stove was a refrigerator. Cabinets covered the wall to the right, with a window in the middle and a large porcelain sink below it.

Connolly pulled open the screen door and stepped inside. He made his way across the kitchen and down a short hall. A few feet beyond the kitchen was an archway that opened to the left into the living room. A sofa sat along the wall to the right. Two chairs sat beneath a large picture window on the wall opposite the archway. At the end of the room to the far left was a recliner, and in it sat Connolly's uncle, Guy Poiroux.

At eighty-five, he now spent most of the day napping, a luxury he had only recently allowed himself to indulge. He dropped out of school in the sixth grade to work an oyster skiff, laboring from dawn to dark. It was backbreaking work, lowering the tongs, raking them full of shells, hauling them aboard, then shucking them for the meat while he rested, and all for mere pennies. At the age of fifteen, he left the skiff and took a job as a deckhand on a shrimp boat. By the age of twenty-one, he was a boat captain and spent the next fifty years piloting shrimp boats, first on weeklong runs south of town, then later on trips far out into the gulf, lasting months at a time. It was a hard life, but he enjoyed working, and it was a life that favored him.

When Connolly was ten years old, his father died. His

mother turned to alcohol to escape the worries of raising two children alone. Often in a drunken stupor, she was frequently gone for days at a time. Then, she met a man at a truck stop in Loxley and left altogether. It was years before Connolly saw her again. Left to fend for themselves, Connolly and his younger brother crammed what they could in a pillowcase and hitchhiked to Bayou La Batre. Guy and his wife, Ruby, raised them as their own. It was Guy who paid for Connolly to attend college, and Guy who pointed him toward law school.

Connolly tiptoed across the room to the recliner. He laid his hand on Guy's shoulder and spoke with a soft voice.

"Uncle Guy."

The old man opened his eyes.

"Hey." He had a startled look on his face. "Didn't expect to see you today." He rubbed his face and smiled at Connolly. "You want some lunch?"

"Sure," Connolly replied.

Guy pushed himself up from the chair and padded across the living room. Connolly followed him to the kitchen. From the refrigerator, Guy took out a stockpot and set it on the stove. Connolly sat at the table and watched.

"Made some gumbo last night." Guy turned a knob on the stove. A blue flame appeared on the burner under the pot. "Pretty good, too."

While the pot heated on the stove, he poured two cups of coffee. He set one in front of Connolly and took a seat on the opposite side of the table.

"So. What brings you down here?"

Connolly took a sip of coffee. Guy stared him in the eye and waited for a reply. Connolly took another sip.

"Had to see a client."

"Anybody I know?"

"Yeah."

"Interesting case?"

"You hear about that big explosion over near Fairhope?"

"Heard *about* it? I heard it."

"You heard the explosion?"

"Yes. Rattled the dishes in the cabinet. Your client had something to do with that?"

"Police seem to think he did."

"That was quite an explosion. Take a lot of dynamite to do something like that."

Guy stood and walked to the stove to stir the gumbo.

"ATF thinks it wasn't dynamite," Connolly replied. "They think whoever did it used a plastic explosive. Something called Semtex."

"Never heard of it. Your client a professional bomber?"

"No," Connolly smiled. "He's not even an unprofessional bomber."

"Sounds interesting." Guy crossed the room to a cupboard over the sink. He took down two bowls, then opened a nearby drawer and took out two spoons. "So why does all this bring you down here?"

Connolly hesitated. Guy leaned against the sink. The look on his face said he was waiting for Connolly to respond.

"You can't tell anyone," Connolly said.

Guy grimaced at the comment.

"You ain't got to tell me that."

He turned away and moved to the stove. He lifted the lid on the pot of gumbo and filled the bowls. Connolly took a sip of coffee.

"My client is Harvey Bosarge."

Guy crossed the room with the two bowls of gumbo and set them on the table. He lumbered back across the room to the sink to retrieve the spoons. At the table, he dropped into his chair.

"Harvey Bosarge," he muttered. "He couldn't blow his nose without directions. He don't know nothing about what you're talking about."

Connolly smiled. Guy continued talking.

"He was always good at putting on a show up in Mobile. I think they loved him up there. Of course, you notice he never worked around here."

"Maybe he just wanted something different."

"Huh. He tried to hire on with the police down here. They turned him down."

"I thought his daddy would have fixed that."

"He could have taken care of it, but he didn't. That ought to tell you something about Harvey right there. His own daddy wouldn't even help."

They ate in silence for a few moments. Finally, Connolly spoke.

"You think there might be somebody around here who knows about this sort of thing?"

"Harvey? Everybody knows about Harvey."

"Not Harvey," Connolly replied. "Explosives."

Guy glanced over at him.

"Explosives? You think somebody else around here had something to do with it?"

"Not really. But this is a ... different kind of place."

"You mean strange." Guy took another spoonful of gumbo. "It's a strange place."

"Well ... yes, it is strange. Lot of people in and out of here. I just thought there might be someone around who knows about this sort of thing, or knows someone."

Guy rested his spoon on the rim of the soup bowl and looked at Connolly.

"Are you asking for help?"

Connolly looked over at him.

"Yes. I need some help with this case."

Guy smiled. The thought of helping Connolly with a case seemed to please him. He picked up his spoon.

"I'll see what I can find out."

Twelve

That afternoon Connolly walked from his office to the Tidewater Bank building on Royal Street. Forty stories of bright, gleaming glass and steel, it was the newest and tallest office building in the city.

He entered the lobby and took the elevator to the offices of Hager, Litton, and Lynch on the fourteenth floor. The city's largest and oldest law firm, Hager Litton employed seventy-five lawyers and a support staff of hundreds. The firm's practice was diverse, but most of its revenue came from defending claims for insurance companies and in representing the city's largest businesses. Ingram Shipbuilding was one of the firm's biggest clients. Joey Ingram was one of Hager Litton's senior associates.

When Joey, the youngest of the three Ingram brothers, graduated from law school, the firm offered him a job. Now in his fifth year as an associate, he had proved to be more than the son of a wealthy client. He worked hard, studied the profession, and did his best to develop skills necessary to make him a successful trial attorney. Connolly knew him, though not well. He had seen Joey around the courthouse a number of times, and they knew each other by name.

Connolly stepped from the elevator to the receptionist's desk. A petite young blonde greeted him.

"Good afternoon," she smiled. "May I help you?"

"I would like to see Joey Ingram," Connolly said. "If it's not too much trouble."

"And you are ...?"

He took a business card from his pocket and handed it to her.

"Mike Connolly," he replied. "He'll know what it's about."

The receptionist glanced at the card and reached for the telephone. "Just a minute. Let me check."

Connolly stepped away from the desk. The room was furnished with antique-reproduction furniture. A camelback sofa sat against the wall to the far left. Matching wingback chairs sat at either end. A low coffee table sat between the chairs in front of the sofa. A reproduction Monet hung on the wall.

"Sir," the receptionist called.

Connolly turned toward her.

"Mr. Ingram will be with you in a few minutes," she said. "You may have a seat if you like."

"Thank you," Connolly replied.

He stepped around the coffee table to the sofa and sat down. The upholstery was soft, smooth, and comfortable. He laid his legal pad in his lap and folded his hands on top of it. Soon, his eyes were shut. His chin dropped against his chest.

Sometime later, he felt someone tapping him on the shoulder.

"Mr. Connolly," a voice said.

He opened his eyes and blinked away the sleepy haze. Joey Ingram stood in front of him, dressed in gray wool slacks with leather suspenders and a white shirt. His tie was loosened at the collar, and the top button of his shirt was undone.

"Mr. Connolly," he repeated. "You wanted to see me?"

Connolly smiled, embarrassed.

"You want to talk here, or in my office?"

Connolly stood.

"Your office," he replied.

Joey led him down the hallway to a small conference room. "How about in here," he suggested. "My office is a mess."

Connolly followed him into the room. Joey took a seat at one end of the conference table. Connolly took a seat on the side nearest the door.

"I guess you're here to talk about Steve. Aren't you representing Harvey Bosarge?"

"Yes."

Joey shook his head. "Everybody knows Bosarge didn't have anything to do with Steve's death."

"You know him?"

"Yeah. Use him all the time on insurance cases. He's a good investigator."

Connolly gave him a sober look. "Any idea who killed Steve?"

"No. I've spent a lot of time trying to figure it out. But I have no idea who or why."

"Think Frank knows anything about it?"

Joey looked away, avoiding eye contact with Connolly.

"I don't know," he sighed. "Frank isn't much interested in anyone but Frank these days."

"I understand he and Steve had some rather heated arguments."

"Yeah," Joey replied, returning his gaze to Connolly once again. "They got into it a lot."

"What about?"

"Anything. Everything."

"Like what?"

"Toward the end it was mostly over business. The company."

"The company?"

"Yeah. Frank did some deals Steve didn't like."

"What kind of deals?"

"Ships. He and Frank saw everything in completely opposite extremes. Frank saw money. Steve saw ... principle, though you'd have to understand his definition of that word."

Connolly reached into the inside pocket of his jacket and took out the photographs from the film he found on the floor at Steve's house. The top photograph was one of Frank standing next to a man of Asian descent. He handed the photograph to Joey.

"Any idea who the man next to Frank is?"

Joey glanced at the picture. "Where'd you get this?"

"Uhhh ... part of my investigation," Connolly replied.

"Man in the background is Greg Drummond."

"He and Frank were friends?"

"I don't think Frank has any friends," Joey replied. He handed the photograph back to Connolly. "He knows a lot of people, though. He and Greg work together a lot. You know, lots of government regulations to maneuver through. Agency approvals, that sort of thing." Joey leaned back in his chair and smiled. "I always wondered how Smith avoided getting into trouble over that Attaway case you handled. You seemed to stop right before proving he was involved."

"Ahhh ... you know." Connolly smiled and shrugged his shoulders. "My client got off. Smith's a senator. Seemed like a good time to shut up and go home."

Joey laughed. "Can't say that I blame you."

"Besides," Connolly continued, "with Albritton and Attaway both dead, there wasn't much way to connect Smith to any of it. Though I suspect most people made the same connection you did."

"It was rather obvious he was the one who got Agostino appointed to the federal bench. What do you think they'll do to him?"

"Agostino?"

"Yeah," Joey nodded.

"Probably send him off to a minimum-security prison some place. Let him play golf all day. I imagine his friend the senator will see he gets the best of everything."

Joey laughed again. Connolly pointed to the third photograph, the one of the man standing beside the piano.

"Any idea who he is?"

Joey leaned forward and looked at it.

"That's Perry Loper. These pictures were taken at his house in New Orleans."

"New Orleans?"

"Yeah. Perry has a house off St. Charles Avenue." He looked at the photo again. "That's Perry's piano."

"What does Perry Loper do?"

"He's a shipping agent. He and my father are good friends."

"He lives in New Orleans?"

"Yeah."

Connolly slipped the photographs into his pocket.

"Sure you don't have any idea who would have killed your brother?"

Joey slouched in his chair and folded his hands in his lap.

"Nah," he said. "Not really. I mean, there are plenty of possibilities. He loved women. Most of them were married. I imagine he had a lot of husbands mad at him. But I don't think they would do something like this."

"What about ..." Connolly hesitated. Joey gave him a look to continue. "I hate to bring up the subject, but I don't have much choice. What about drugs?"

"No," Joey snapped. An angry frown furrowed his brow. "Somebody suggest drugs had something to do with it?"

"Well ..."

"That had to come from Frank," Joey retorted, cutting him off. "That's just Frank talking. You talk to Frank?"

"Not yet."

"Well ... that's just Frank talking, whoever told you. Steve didn't use drugs, and he didn't sell drugs. I saw him almost every day. If he'd been into something like that, I'd have known about it." He still looked angry. "He drank like a fish, but he had nothing to do with drugs."

The question touched a nerve. Connolly waited a moment to give Joey a chance to calm down, then changed the subject.

"Did you know the woman Steve was seeing?"

"Ahh ... no."

Once again, Joey glanced away, avoiding eye contact with Connolly.

"Ever see her with Steve?"

Joey looked uncomfortable. He sat up straight in the chair.

"No. I don't think so. You talk to her?"

"No. Haven't been able to locate her."

"Probably scared." There was an intense look in Joey's eyes. "I would be. Think you can find her?"

The look on his face made Connolly uneasy.

"Yeah. I think so. Might take a little time."

Connolly wasn't sure how far to pursue the issue of Ann. Each time he brought her up in the conversation, Joey seemed to get uncomfortable. But the look on his face made Connolly very curious.

"Think anyone else in your family knows her or knows where she is?"

"I ... ahh ... I don't see how they would," Joey replied. He glanced at Connolly. "Somebody say they did?"

Connolly deflected the question with a shrug.

"It was just a thought," he replied. He stood and extended his hand. "Well, I've taken up enough of your time. I appreciate you seeing me. I know this is difficult for you to talk about."

Joey rose from his chair. The two men shook hands.

"Hope I was of some help." Joey moved in front of Connolly to open the door. "Listen, if you find her ... the woman ... let me know if she needs anything. Place to stay. Whatever."

"Yeah," he replied. "Sure. I'll let you know."

He looked away.

"It's just that she was important to Steve," Joey continued. "I wouldn't want to leave her in a bad spot."

Connolly smiled.

"Sure," he said. "I'll let her know."

Thirteen

*T*he next day, Connolly drove to Jake's Social Club on the causeway at the north end of Mobile Bay. A simple concrete block building only a few feet from the water's edge, it was a dank, musty place. The drive from Connolly's office took less than ten minutes.

Two cars were parked out front when he arrived. He brought the Chrysler to a stop near the door and went inside.

A bar ran along the back wall opposite the entrance. Tables sat between the door and the bar. The room was dark, cool, and humid. The stale smell of cigarette smoke and beer hung in the air. Brightly labeled bottles lined the shelves behind the bar. Connolly let his eyes run down the row, noting each label as he went. His taste buds screamed for a Gibson.

Three people sat at the bar, watching a baseball game on a black-and-white television that sat on a shelf above the cash register between the rows of bottles behind the bar. A burly, middle-aged man tended the bar. He had long, greasy black hair that was pulled behind his head in a ponytail, and he wore a white T-shirt that was one size too small. Tattoos covered his right arm.

The place had a familiar feel.

Just one, he thought. *Just one little sip.* He forced the thought aside and stepped to the bar. The bartender moved down the bar toward him.

"What could I get you?"

"Nothing," Connolly replied. "I just need to ask you a couple of questions."

The bartender nodded for him to continue.

"I'm trying to locate a woman who used to work here named Ann Grafton. Any idea where I could find her?"

The bartender shook his head.

"You're about the tenth person who's asked about her. I ain't seen her in a week. Maybe more."

"Any idea where I could find her?"

The bartender glanced down the bar at the customers watching the television, then nodded for Connolly to move in the opposite direction. Connolly followed the man down the bar.

"Who are you?"

"Mike Connolly. I'm a lawyer."

"Who you represent? Her husband?"

"No. I'm working on a criminal case. Doesn't have much to do with her."

"Criminal case? What kind of trouble is she in?"

"She's not in trouble," Connolly said. "I just need to talk to her about something."

The bartender looked skeptical.

"Really," Connolly insisted. "She's not in trouble. I don't have any papers to serve. I just want to ask her a couple of questions."

Again, the bartender glanced toward the three men at the bar.

"She used to live in Tillman's Corner," he said, lowering his voice. "That's all I know."

"When was the last time you saw her?"

"Like I said, it's been about a week." There was an edge to his voice. "Maybe a little longer."

"You saw her here?"

"Yeah. She came to work. Went home that night. Ain't seen her since."

"She leave with anybody?"

The bartender glanced away again, then moved still farther down the bar. This time, he didn't gesture for Connolly to follow. He picked up two empty glasses and carried them to a sink under the bar. Connolly waited for him to return.

"Who's been looking for her besides me?"

"A couple of detectives. And a couple of guys who didn't say who they were."

"Her husband?"

The man's face turned hard and angry.

"He knows better than to come in here."

Connolly nodded.

"What about a friend? Maybe a coworker? Somebody like that she might be staying with."

"I don't know." He glanced around nervously. "Look, I've told you everything I know about the woman."

He moved down the bar to the sink and began washing the glasses. Connolly turned away and walked toward the door. As he crossed the room, he glanced at the three men at the bar. One of them turned to look at him over his shoulder. Their eyes met. The man stared at him a moment, then turned casually back to watch the ball game. Connolly felt a chill run down his spine. He opened the door and stepped outside.

When he reached the Chrysler, the bartender emerged from the far corner of the building. He motioned for Connolly to wait as he approached.

"Listen, I didn't want to say too much in there." His voice was low and quite. "You're the man that represented that ... black man. The one they tried to pin with that lawyer's murder, aren't you? His name was Thompson, or something like that."

"Yes."

"My brother worked with him. Thought a lot of him."

Connolly nodded in response.

"Well, look, Ann has a sister," the bartender continued. "Jean Weaver. Lives in a trailer out at Irvington. I don't know exactly where it is. Ann used to stay with her some. She might be out there."

"Thanks," Connolly replied.

The bartender turned away and disappeared around the corner of the building. Connolly opened the car door and got in behind the steering wheel. He glanced at the entrance to the bar.

In his mind, he could hear the tinkling sound as the ice hit the bottom of the glass. He could feel the burning taste of gin on the back of his tongue as it slid toward his throat.

Just one drink. Just one.

He slapped the steering wheel in anger and shoved the key in the ignition switch. With a quick turn of the key, the Chrysler came to life. He backed away from the building, jammed the car in gear, and pressed the accelerator. A spray of dust and gravel billowed from behind the car as it shot out of the parking lot and onto the highway.

Fourteen

From the causeway, Connolly drove to Irvington. A rural community fifteen miles west of Mobile, it consisted of two abandoned service stations and one Handy Pak convenience store. Connolly eased the Chrysler off the highway and brought it to a stop at the far end of the parking lot in front of the Handy Pak. He switched off the engine and went inside.

To the left of the door was a counter. On it sat a manual cash register, all but obscured by displays of trinkets, candy, and a rack of betting sheets for the dog track. At the far end of the counter sat a glass cabinet with hot dogs turning on a rotisserie inside. Beyond the hot dogs was a gallon-size glass jar full of pickles. A coffee machine sat beside the pickles. At the end of the counter was a door to the stockroom. The door was open. Connolly could hear someone moving boxes around inside.

A woman greeted Connolly from behind the cash register. "May I help you?"

"I'm trying to find someone named Jean Weaver," he said. "Any idea where she lives?"

The woman looked askance.

"You with the police?"

"No." Connolly smiled. "Just a lawyer."

"Uh," she grunted. "That's worse."

"Do you know where she lives?"

"I'd ... I'd rather not say," she replied.

A man stepped from the stockroom and came around the coffee machine.

"I'll tell you where she lives," he said. "Go down here about a mile—"

"Paul," the woman interrupted, "just stay out of it."

"Whatever trouble she's in, she deserves it," the man snapped. "She never should have married him in the first place."

He turned to Connolly again.

"If you go down here about a mile, there's a race track on the left." He pointed over his shoulder. "Across the street is Webster's Motel. Just before you get to Webster's, there's a road turns off to the right. Take that right and go about two miles. You'll see a dirt road to the left. Can't miss it. There's a spot there where folks been dumping trash. Couple of washin' machines, an old 'frigerator, stuff like that piled up there by the road. Turn there and it's the first trailer on the right."

"I appreciate it," Connolly said.

"Her husband's name is Ted," the man continued, "but everybody around here calls him Catfish. He's my first cousin. He's all right. I don't care too much for him, though. He ain't never been nothing but trouble."

"I appreciate it," Connolly repeated.

From the store, Connolly drove west. He found the race track and the motel, just as the man said. He took the road to the right, and a little way down the road he found the pile of rubbish. He turned left onto a narrow dirt road. Half a mile later he saw the mobile home.

A double-wide trailer, it sat in a clump of towering pine trees fifty yards from the road. Supported by concrete blocks, it rested two feet off the ground. A dog lay in the shade under the edge near the front steps.

Tire tracks worn through the grass led from the road across the yard. Two cars were parked near the door. Children's toys were scattered between them. In back, a dilapidated pickup slumped against a pine tree, its wheels missing, the doors hanging open. A clothesline stretched from the trailer to the pine tree beside the old truck.

Connolly turned the Chrysler off the road and followed the tire tracks. He parked behind the two cars and stepped out. Almost immediately, the door opened and a woman appeared, wearing shorts and a loose-fitting shirt. He recognized her from the photographs Bosarge had given him. She was Ann Grafton.

"My name is Mike Connolly." He walked toward the steps as he talked. "I'm an attorney. I represent—"

She turned away and tried to close the door. Connolly took two quick steps and grabbed the door to stop her.

"Wait," he said. "I just want to ask you some questions."

"What about?"

"I represent a man who's been accused of murdering Steve Ingram."

Her face turned white. For a moment, she looked as if she was going to faint.

Suddenly, a man appeared behind her. Bare to the waist, he wore only a pair of faded blue jeans with torn pockets and a rip in one knee. His hair was tangled as if he had been asleep, but he had a beer can in one hand. He glared at Connolly.

"What do you want?"

His voice was rough and demanding.

"You must be Catfish," Connolly said.

"What's it to you?"

"Paul down at the store said you might be up here."

Catfish seemed to find satisfaction in the comment. He grinned, took a sip from the can of beer, and drifted away.

Ann stepped outside and closed the door. Connolly backed away. She moved down the steps.

"Don't say anything about him being here. My sister don't know he's here. He's supposed to be at work."

Connolly nodded.

"I need to ask you some questions about Steve Ingram," he began.

She leaned against the fender of one of the cars in front of the trailer and folded her arms across her chest.

"What you want to know?"

"You were at the house the morning he died."

She sighed, as if the question required a painful answer, but Connolly couldn't tell whether she was bothered by the memory of that morning or the realization that someone knew she was there.

"Yes," she said. The word seemed to ooze out.

"What happened?"

"Garage blew up."

Her tone was curt, dismissive, almost irritated. Connolly smiled.

"I mean, tell me what happened that morning," he explained. "Walk me through it. You woke up. And then what?"

She sighed and glanced away, then reluctantly began to talk.

"We woke up early. Sometime around five thirty. Actually," she smiled, "he woke me up."

Connolly waited for her to continue.

"We ... ahh ... fooled around in bed awhile and then took a shower. Steve made coffee. We had a cup in the bedroom. He had another in the kitchen. And then he left."

"You were standing at the back door."

She stared at him, as if wondering how he knew that.

"Yeah." She let the word slide out as she thought about it some more, then let the moment pass. "We were in the kitchen. He walked out. I kissed him. And then he started toward the garage. I went back inside and went upstairs. About the time I got to the top of the stairs, it was like ... the whole world was coming down around me. There was this awful sound. Hurt my ears. I couldn't hear much for a couple days. And the house shook. I thought the whole place was going to fall apart."

"What did you do?"

"I fell on the floor. Covered my head with my hands. Then, when the house didn't fall apart, I could see smoke in the back, so I ran to the bedroom and looked out. The garage was on fire, and I seen the cars in there, and I knew Steve was dead. So I run downstairs to the den. My clothes was down there. And I got dressed and run to the front door."

"Your clothes were downstairs?"

As soon as he said it, he knew it was an unnecessary question.

"Yes." She smiled, almost embarrassed. "That's where we left them when we came in the night before."

"All right," he said. "So what happened after that?"

"When I got to the door, fire trucks and a police car was coming up the driveway. I waited until they got past, then I slipped outside. People was pulling off the road and running up the driveway, and I just went right through them and walked away."

"How did you get home?"

"There's a little store up the road from his house. I walked up there and called my sister. She come and got me."

"How long had you been seeing Steve?"

"Seven or eight months. Might have been a little longer. Wasn't quite a year, though."

"Do you know why he was killed?"

"No," she said. Once again letting the words slide out with a sigh.

"What do you mean?"

"Well, when we first started dating, Frank, Steve's older brother, came by the house one day. I was over there. He and Steve got into an argument. They was in the kitchen, so I went upstairs."

"What were they arguing about?"

"Most of the time I didn't know what they was arguing about. That time, they argued about me."

"About you?"

"Yeah."

"Why?"

"Well, Frank didn't like me." She gave him an odd smile. "Told Steve I wasn't nothing but a slut. Which I always found amusing."

"Did you and Steve go anywhere unusual?"

"No. Not really. I mean we went to bars and stuff, but mostly just around here. Went down to Orange Beach a time or two. We went down to New Orleans a couple of months ago. I thought we were going down there to party, but Steve got a phone call. Now that's something interesting." She wagged her finger as she spoke and had a look on her face as if she'd thought of something Connolly might think important. "He started carrying this cell phone with him everywhere he went." Her hands dropped to her hips. She shook her head, grinning. "I thought it was weird. He wasn't much on technology, and here he has this cell phone in his pocket. Anyway, he got this call, and we go rushing off down that street that has the street car on it ..."

"St. Charles."

"Yeah." She nodded her head and waved her arms for emphasis. "He turned up some little alley in between these big, fancy houses. And then he stops the car and tells me to wait while he goes off through the bushes behind this house. Left me there, by myself. Didn't even lock the car door."

"Did he say what he was doing?"

"Well, he took a camera with him. And that's something else." She interrupted herself. "Always had a camera with him in the car. Nikon something or other. Cell phone and a camera. I told him next thing I'd see was a pager."

She laughed, amused at what she'd said. Connolly prompted her.

"So he ran through the bushes with the camera."

"Yeah. And when he came back, he came jogging down the alley and jumped in the car. I seen him coming. He was grinning from ear to ear. Jumped in the car and said, 'I got him.' He was like a little kid. 'I got him.'" She repeated the phrase, moving an arm and hand across her body in a clinching gesture. "I'd never seen him so excited. Went back to the hotel and ..." The uneasy smile returned. "Well ... it was an exciting night."

"Did he tell you what he saw?"

"No. I assumed it had something to do with his brother. But he never said."

"Did you see the pictures?"

"No."

"What happened to them?"

"I don't know."

"See anybody suspicious around the house?"

"No."

"Steve had a younger brother, Joe. Ever see him?"

"I heard about Joey, but I never saw him. Now, I wasn't with Steve all the time, you understand. I had a job during the day, and nights my husband was home I went home to him after work. So he might have come around some I didn't know about. But I never met him."

"Go anywhere else out of the ordinary?"

"No. Like I said, just the usual places. He'd come to Jake's a couple times during the week. Watched me work."

"Didn't meet anybody strange?"

"All Steve's friends are strange. But no, we didn't meet anybody too weird."

Connolly reached inside his coat pocket and took out one of the pictures from the negative he found on the floor in the bedroom. The picture showed Frank Ingram standing next to the Asian man. He handed the picture to Ann.

"Ever see that man before?"

She glanced at it.

"No." She shook her head. "Never seen him."

"You sure?"

"Yeah."

She handed the picture back to Connolly.

"Do you have any idea where your husband is?"

"I ain't seen Tommy since before Steve died."

"Somebody said he works offshore. Do you know where?"

"No. He leaves out of some place over in Louisiana. At least that's what he told me. I ain't never been there, and I ain't never seen no paycheck from him, neither. Always came home with a big wad of cash. No telling where he is."

"Think he had anything to do with Steve's death?"

"Tommy?" She sounded surprised. "Tommy'd get mad at me if he knew I was over there, but he wouldn't get mad at Steve."

Connolly thought for a moment, then decided it was time to leave.

"Mrs. Grafton, I appreciate your time."

She smiled at him.

"No problem. And, like I said, don't mention you saw Catfish today to nobody. He's supposed to be at work, and if my sister found out he was here with me all day, we'd both be in big trouble."

Connolly nodded. He stepped toward the Chrysler. Ann moved up the stairs. She stopped at the door to the trailer and called to him.

"How'd you find me, anyway?"

"You have lots of friends."

He waved in her direction and slipped behind the wheel of the Chrysler.

Fifteen

A crowd stood outside the office building when Connolly arrived the next morning. Three television trucks occupied the spot out front where he normally parked. He drove past them and parked the Chrysler up the street near the Port City Diner. As he walked back toward the building, someone in the crowd turned toward him and began pointing in his direction. The crowd surged around him. Bright klieg lights came on above the television cameras. Microphones were suddenly thrust in his face.

"Do you have a comment on your client's arrest, Mr. Connolly?"

Before he could respond, someone else shouted another question.

"Have you spoken to him yet?"

Connolly was bewildered.

"I ... I have no ... I have no comment," he managed to say.

He had no idea what they were talking about.

"When will he appear in court? Do you have a trial date yet?"

Connolly pushed his way toward the building entrance. The crowd followed him, swarming around him, all of them talking at once. He managed to reach the door and pull it open. As he slipped inside, a reporter next to him asked one last question.

"Do you think Harvey Bosarge will be found guilty?"

Only then did Connolly realize Harvey had been arrested.

The telephone was ringing as he entered the office. Mrs. Gordon held up her hand to stop him as he passed her desk.

"All right, Mr. Bosarge. Just a minute." There was an urgent tone in her voice. "He just walked through the door. Hold on just a minute."

She placed the call on hold, then turned to Connolly.

"This is Harvey Bosarge. He's calling from the jail. It's the third time he's called this morning."

"When did they arrest him?"

"Early this morning. First time he called he was in a holding cell. Now, they have him upstairs in a cell. He's pretty upset."

"I'll take it in my office."

Connolly walked down the hall to his office. He removed his jacket and hung it on the coatrack, then took a seat behind the desk. As he reached for the receiver he hesitated. He called out to Mrs. Gordon.

"Did you check the pay phone?"

"Yes," she replied, irritated. "I checked it."

"Still working?"

"Was when I came in."

He lifted the phone from the cradle.

"Harvey, are you all right?"

"I don't know. They arrested me this morning."

"What time did they pick you up?"

"Sometime before sunup. You gotta get me out of here."

"Who came for you?"

"Hammond and a couple of patrolmen." Bosarge sounded nervous. "They got me charged with capital murder. You got to get me out of this place."

"Capital murder? They set a bond?"

"No. Said the judge refused to because it's a capital case."

"All right," Connolly replied. "I'll go see Judge Cahill and see if he'll set a bond. Try to stay calm. I'm on my way."

Connolly took the elevator to the lobby. He glanced toward the front doors. The crowd was still gathered out front. Instead of facing them once more, he turned the opposite way and went out the service door to Ferguson's Alley behind the building. He hurried down the alley to Government Street and crossed it in the middle of the block. He managed to reach the courthouse before any of the reporters in front of the office knew he was gone.

When he reached Judge Cahill's courtroom, he was surprised to find it empty. He walked past the bailiff's desk to the right of the bench and through a door to the judge's chambers. Judge Cahill stood near the windows on the wall opposite the door, drinking a cup of coffee.

"Mike Connolly," he called with a smile. "What brings you to our courtroom this morning?"

"Aren't you hearing a docket today?"

"Sure," Cahill replied. "But not until nine o'clock." He glanced at his watch. "It's only five after eight right now."

"Oh," Connolly replied. "I didn't realize it was this early."

"What can I do for you?"

"Anthony Hammond arrested Harvey Bosarge this morning. Charged him with capital murder on that Steve Ingram case."

"I heard about that," Cahill chuckled. "Walter told me they had to roll him out of bed to get the cuffs on him."

Judge Cahill stopped grinning long enough to take another sip of coffee. Walter, the bailiff, entered with a box of doughnuts.

"Walter," Cahill called. "Perfect timing. Bring those nice, hot Krispy Kremes over here. I need one with my coffee. You want one, Mike?"

Connolly stood in the middle of the room, one hand on his hip, the other gripping a legal pad. His jaw was set, his lips stretched tight, and a frown across his forehead so deep it forced his eyebrows down on top of his eyelids.

"Oh, don't look so serious," Cahill said. "We'll get the file up here in a minute and see what we can do. Have a doughnut and some coffee."

Connolly hesitated.

"Come on." Cahill took an empty cup from the window ledge and handed it to Connolly. "Have some coffee."

Connolly took the cup and moved across the room. Judge Cahill sat in a nearby chair, coffee in one hand, doughnut in the other.

"Now this is the way to start a morning," he grinned. "Take a seat, Mike."

Connolly drew a cup of coffee from the urn on a shelf under the window, picked up a doughnut, and took a seat in a chair a few feet from Cahill.

"I wondered how long it was going to be before they arrested Harvey," Cahill said.

"Why's that?"

"Hammond came in here a couple of days ago with a search warrant he wanted me to sign."

"For Harvey's place?"

"Yeah. I guess they found what they were looking for."

"I didn't know anything about a search. Did they bring you the return?"

"Yeah. But I don't remember what they found."

Connolly looked perplexed.

"Walter," Cahill called.

Walter appeared from one of the offices.

"Run down to the clerk's office and get the file on Harvey Bosarge. They arrested him this morning. If they don't have a file made up yet, get whatever they have and bring it up here."

"Yes, sir," Walter replied. He strode to the window and took a doughnut from the box. "Need one for the walk," he smiled.

Later that morning, Henry McNamara, an assistant district attorney, arrived in Judge Cahill's courtroom, carrying a cardboard box filled with files for the day's cases. Not long after he arrived, a door near the back of the courtroom opened, and a deputy appeared, leading a string of prisoners handcuffed and shackled together. Their chains made an odd jingling sound as they moved in procession across the courtroom to the jury box, where they were seated for the morning docket.

When everyone was ready, Judge Cahill came from his chambers. He bounded up the steps to the judge's bench and took a seat. From his perch above the courtroom, he surveyed the group of prisoners, then leaned over the bench to Walter, who was seated at his desk to the right.

"You tell them to bring over Harvey Bosarge?"

"Yes, Judge. They said they'd get him over here later. He wasn't on the list for court this morning, so they didn't have him ready with the others."

"Very well," Cahill replied. He turned to Connolly. "Find a comfortable place to sit, Mike. We'll get Harvey over here in a little while." He turned to McNamara. "Henry, you got your file on Harvey Bosarge?"

McNamara stood.

"No, Your Honor. He's not on the docket for this morning."

"Better call somebody and have them bring the file up. We're going to have a bond hearing this morning."

"Judge," McNamara protested, "that's a capital case. We haven't had any notice of a hearing."

"I'm giving you notice now," Cahill replied. "I don't think your argument will change whether you have five minutes or five hours to read the file. Will it?"

McNamara sighed and stepped from behind the counsel table. Cahill pointed over his shoulder in the direction of his office.

"Use the phone in the back."

McNamara disappeared through the door behind Walter's desk.

Shortly after eleven that morning a sheriff's deputy led Harvey Bosarge into the courtroom. He was seated with the other prisoners in the jury box. Connolly moved across the room and took a seat next to him. Harvey looked worried.

"What's going on?"

"Relax," Connolly replied. "Judge Cahill has agreed to hear our motion to set a bond for you."

"Oh."

"Did anybody come out to your house with a search warrant the last few days?"

"Not while I was there. Why?"

"Cahill said Hammond came to him a few days ago to get a search warrant for your place."

Bosarge looked stricken but did not respond.

"Said they came back with the return later," Connolly continued. "Sounds like they found something."

Connolly retreated from the jury box and took a seat on a bench behind the counsel tables. A few minutes later, Anthony Hammond entered the courtroom. He brushed past Connolly and took a seat beside McNamara. The two of them huddled together over Hammond's file. Then, Judge Cahill caught Connolly's eye.

"You ready, Mike?"

Connolly stood.

"Yes, Your Honor."

McNamara looked up as they spoke. Cahill turned to him.

"You ready, Henry?"

"Yes, Your Honor. We'd just note for the record that we object to—"

"You have your objection," Cahill interrupted him. He glanced at the court reporter. "You got that?"

The court reporter nodded in response. Judge Cahill glanced at the file on the desk in front of him and then began.

"We are here today on case number 41195, State of Alabama versus Harvey Bosarge. And we are here today on the defendant's oral motion to set bond. The defendant is represented by Mr. Mike Connolly. The state is represented by Mr. Henry McNamara. Mr. Connolly, you may proceed."

McNamara took a seat.

"Thank you, Your Honor," Connolly began. "Sometime before dawn this morning, my client, Mr. Harvey Bosarge, was rousted from his bed in Bayou La Batre. He was handcuffed, placed under arrest, and charged with capital murder in the death of one Steve Ingram. Mr. Bosarge is a retired member of the City of Mobile Police Department, where he served a long and distinguished career as both a patrolman and detective. His reputation in this county is beyond reproach. He owns a home and other property here. His children and other family members live here. He has, Your Honor, significant and substantial ties to this community. We assert that the state has not one shred of evidence implicating this defendant with the crime as charged, and we would respectfully ask this court to set a bond in a reasonable amount."

When Connolly concluded, he took a seat. Cahill nodded to McNamara. McNamara stood.

"Your Honor, the defendant is charged with capital murder. But this was not a mere killing. It was an annihilation. Mr. Ingram was blown apart in his own garage, while seated in his own car, in a deliberate and heinous act. Contrary to Mr. Connolly's belief, we have evidence that directly links the defendant to this crime. As this court is aware, two days ago

Detective Hammond and other law-enforcement officers executed a search warrant at Mr. Bosarge's residence." He flipped
open a file on the desk and glanced at the top page. "In the
garage, they found a small quantity of C-4, which is a plastic
explosive, and a bag containing small devices used to detonate
explosives from a remote distance, all of which were of the
type used in killing Mr. Ingram. In addition, police found Mr.
Bosarge's prints in the victim's house, and we have an eyewit-
ness who can place him at the scene on the morning of the
explosion. Your Honor, we object to the setting of any bond for
this defendant and ask that he be held without bond until this
case goes to trial."

Judge Cahill turned to Connolly.

"Mr. Connolly, you know anything about this plastic
explosive?"

Connolly stood.

"No, Your Honor, I don't. But it doesn't have much to do
with the issue before this court. Almost every person in this
room knows Harvey Bosarge. And every one of them knows
that when we finally get to the bottom of this, it will be obvious Harvey Bosarge had nothing to do with Steve Ingram's
murder. Now I don't know how that stuff got in Harvey's
garage, and I don't know how Detective Hammond knew right
where to look for it—"

Anthony Hammond leaped to his feet.

"Now wait just a minute. You can't—"

McNamara tried to guide Hammond back to his seat.
Judge Cahill banged his gavel hard on the desk.

"Order," he shouted. "Order in the court." Judge Cahill's
face was red. The veins in his neck pulsed. "Mr. Hammond,
you will conduct yourself with dignity and order in this courtroom, or I will have you placed under arrest for contempt. Is
that clear?"

"Yes, Your Honor."

Cahill took a deep breath and tried to relax. McNamara and Hammond sat. Cahill turned to Connolly.

"Mike, I hope you have some basis in fact for that accusation."

"Your Honor, I'd be glad to put Mr. Hammond on the stand."

Before Cahill could respond, Hammond grabbed the file from the desk and started toward the witness stand in an angry jaunt. It was exactly the reaction Connolly had hoped for.

Cahill turned to McNamara.

"You have any objection?"

McNamara looked over at Hammond, then down at the file.

"No, Your Honor." There was a hint of resignation in his voice. "I have no objection."

"Very well," Cahill replied. "Raise your right hand, Detective."

Cahill administered the oath, and Hammond took a seat in the witness box. Cahill nodded to Connolly.

"All right, Mr. Connolly, you may proceed."

Connolly moved from the counsel table and stood in front of Hammond.

"Detective Hammond, you executed a search warrant on Mr. Bosarge's residence, did you not?"

"Yes, we did."

"What day was that?"

"Day before yesterday."

"And do you have a copy of that warrant with you?"

"Yes, I do."

"Would you show that to me, please, sir?"

Hammond removed a copy of the search warrant from the file folder in his lap and handed it to Connolly. Connolly scanned over it, then offered it back to Hammond.

"Detective, I'd like for you to read the last line of this paragraph right here."

He pointed to a paragraph in the middle of the page.

"This warrant—"

"Don't read it all," Connolly interrupted. "Just read the line I showed you."

McNamara jumped to his feet.

"Objection, Your Honor. We're entitled to have the entire document introduced."

Connolly turned to Judge Cahill.

"Mr. McNamara can introduce anything he likes, Your Honor. I don't have to introduce the entire document if I don't want to."

"Overruled."

Connolly turned back to Hammond.

"Read the line, please, sir."

"... to search the entire premises, including house, garage, outbuildings, and the like."

"This warrant authorized you to search the entire premises?"

"Yes."

"The garage?"

"Yes."

"Any storage buildings?"

"Yes."

"You could dig up the garden?"

"Yes."

"Search the house?"

"Yes."

"Did you dig up the garden?"

"No."

"Did you search any storage buildings other than the garage?"

"No."

"Did you search the house?"

"No."

"The first and only place you looked was the garage."

Hammond shifted in his seat.

"Yes."

"And the only thing you found were the items Mr. McNamara alluded to earlier."

"Yes."

"Where were they?"

"On a workbench in the garage."

"And where was that workbench?"

"Near the door."

"The same door where you came in?"

"Yes. There's only one door."

"Didn't have to look too hard to find it, did you?"

"No."

"Did you look anywhere else?"

"No."

"Didn't go into the house?"

"No."

"If this was a search in a drug case and you found drugs in the garage, wouldn't you search the house?"

Once again, McNamara jumped to his feet.

"Objection, Your Honor."

"Overruled."

"Wouldn't you have searched the house?"

"Yes, probably."

"What led you to Mr. Bosarge's garage?"

"We had a tip."

"From whom?"

"An informant."

"This informant contacted you?"

"No. Not me."

"Who did this informant contact?"

"The FBI."

"So the FBI came to you and said they had a tip?"

"Yes."

"They came to you to get you to conduct a search?"

"Yes."

"Didn't that strike you as odd?"

"No. We cooperate on many cases."

"But why didn't the FBI get their own warrant and conduct their own search?"

"You'd have to ask them."

"Did they accompany you on the search?"

"Yes."

"Who was in charge at the scene during this search?"

"I was."

"Who located these items we've been discussing?"

"One of the FBI agents."

"What's his name?"

"I can't remember his name."

"Do you have the names of these agents recorded somewhere?"

"I have some notes back at the office. They aren't in the file I brought with me. I think I have their names."

"Now, after the FBI agent found these things, the C-4 and the other things, did you suggest searching the house?"

"Yes."

"And what prevented you?"

"The agent said he didn't think it was worth the time and that we should leave before anyone came home."

Judge Cahill leaned forward in his seat.

"All right. I've heard enough."

Connolly paused and turned toward the bench, waiting to see what Cahill would do.

"Mr. Bosarge," Cahill called.

Harvey rose from his seat in the jury box.

"Mr. Bosarge, I'm going to set your bond at $50,000."

McNamara scrambled to his feet.

"Judge, this is a capital case," he protested. "You'd set a higher bond than that in a straight murder."

Judge Cahill scribbled an order in the file and handed it to Walter. He turned to McNamara.

"Fifty thousand, Henry," he glared. "Keep talking, and I'll let him sign his own bond."

Hammond slid from his seat in the witness box.

"Detective," Cahill said.

Hammond stopped and faced the judge.

"Yes, Your Honor."

"Make sure you give Mr. Connolly the names of those FBI agents."

"Yes, sir."

"You sure they were FBI agents?"

"Yes, Your Honor."

"All right. Make sure you give Mike their names."

Sixteen

*T*he next day, Connolly drove to Hammond's office at police headquarters. He parked the Chrysler in a spot near the front door reserved for detectives and went inside to the receptionist's desk.

"I'd like to see Anthony Hammond," Connolly said.

"Is he expecting you?"

"He ought to be, but I don't have an appointment."

The receptionist paused a moment, her face expressionless, as though weighing whether to allow him past. As she looked at him, she rolled a wad of chewing gum around in her mouth.

A faint smile appeared.

"Top of the stairs, turn right."

Connolly walked up the stairs. He had been there many times before. He knew where to find Hammond.

Most of the second floor was one large room filled with desks, filing cabinets, and clutter. Detectives moved about the room, shuffling papers, interviewing witnesses, waiting for something to happen. The room was crowded and noisy. When Connolly emerged on the second floor, he turned right. Hammond's desk was near the center of the room.

A knowing grin spread across Hammond's face as Connolly approached. Connolly pulled a chair up to Hammond's desk and sat down. Without a word, Hammond took a file from his desk and opened it.

"John Lockwood and Bill Deer," he said, in a matter-of-fact tone.

Connolly took a pen from the inside pocket of his jacket. He tore a page from a notepad on Hammond's desk and jotted down the names.

"Are they local?"

"No." Hammond paused a moment. A smug look replaced the smile. "They're from Washington, D.C."

"Still in the area?"

"Far as I know."

"Yesterday you said you knew they were FBI agents. How did you know that?"

"Dave Brenner told me they were coming to see me."

Brenner was the special agent in charge of the Mobile FBI office. Connolly wondered why they would bring agents all the way from Washington, but he let it pass. Hammond probably didn't know, and even if he did, he wouldn't tell.

"Didn't it strike you as strange that they found C-4 in the garage, when the stuff used to kill Ingram was Semtex?"

Hammond closed the file on his desk with a loud slap. The room fell silent.

"Listen to me," he said, his voice low, his face tense. "I gave you the names of those two agents only because Judge Cahill ordered me to. Now, I don't have to answer any more of your questions." He paused and took a deep breath. "I think it's time for you to leave."

Connolly slipped the pen back in his coat pocket. He and Hammond glared at each other. Connolly folded his arms across his chest.

"This would all go a lot easier for both of us if you'd just tell me what's going on."

"I've told you what's going on," Hammond replied.

"Who put that stuff in Harvey's garage?"

"I have no idea."

Connolly looked skeptical.

"Anthony?"

Hammond threw his hands in the air in frustration.

"Look, they came to see me. Said they had a tip from an informant. I asked who it was. They wouldn't tell me. They wanted me to get a search warrant. I asked them why they didn't get one themselves. They said they didn't want anyone to know they were involved in the case."

Connolly tipped his head to one side, reinforcing the skeptical look on his face.

"Honest," Hammond insisted. "That's how it happened. I'm just totin' water for two white guys from Washington."

"Come on, Anthony. The FBI's all over this case. They're interviewing everybody in town. Why wouldn't they want someone to know they were ..." Connolly stopped. His eyes widened. "Unless they aren't investigating Ingram's death."

Hammond slid low in his seat. He looked away.

"I can't help you there."

"Were they already investigating Ingram?"

Hammond did not respond.

"Or Harvey? Were they investigating Harvey?"

"I don't know anything except what I've told you. Didn't I tell you to leave already?"

"Didn't you think something was wrong when they found this stuff and then didn't want to search any further?"

Hammond leaned back in his chair and covered his face with his hands.

"Somebody get this guy out of here," he groaned. Suddenly, he leaned forward and propped his arms on top of the desk. "You think the FBI put Bosarge's fingerprints inside Ingram's house?"

"I don't know."

"Try explaining that one so easily."

"Where were they?"

"Kitchen, den, upstairs. He was in and out of there so much he probably had his own bedroom."

"Who found them?"

"One of the Baldwin County deputies," Hammond replied. "They dusted the house the day of the explosion. FBI wasn't anywhere near the house, if that's what you're getting at. Deer and Lockwood didn't show up until sometime the next day."

Connolly thought for a moment.

"You got anything else on this case?"

Hammond sighed and leaned back in his chair.

"Fire marshal's report. ATF report."

"What does the fire marshal say?"

"Nothing you don't already know."

"When did you get those reports?"

"Couple of days ago."

Connolly looked suddenly alert.

"Wait a minute. You had the fire marshal's report and the ATF report a few days ago?"

"Yeah."

"Then you knew the stuff you found wasn't used to kill Steve Ingram when you did the search. You knew that yesterday when you were in court."

Hammond stood.

"Time for you to go."

"No way," Connolly protested. "This search was nothing but a pretext. Who would think of something like this? Didn't your FBI guys know they were planting the wrong stuff?"

Hammond scrambled around the desk and grabbed Connolly by the shoulder. He lifted him from the chair and started across the room. Connolly stumbled trying to keep up.

"Come in here," Hammond growled.

A door opposite his desk led to an interrogation room. Holding a fistful of Connolly's jacket, Hammond guided him by the shoulder toward the room. When he reached the door, he kicked it open with his foot and shoved Connolly inside. He slammed the door shut behind them.

"Sit down," he ordered.

Connolly took a seat at a small table in the center of the room. Hammond leaned over the table toward Connolly, their faces only inches apart.

"I'm going to tell you this, and you're going to keep quiet about it," he snarled. "Understood?"

"Yeah," Connolly replied.

He was offended by the rough treatment, but he wanted to hear what Hammond had to say. Hammond glared at him a moment, then continued.

"You're right. I lied in court. We didn't find that stuff on the workbench. We found it under the hood of your client's car."

Connolly was taken aback.

"Under the hood?"

"Wired to the ignition coil. One turn of the key and your buddy Bosarge would have been in as many pieces as Ingram."

"But it was the wrong stuff, Anthony. They didn't use—"

"It wasn't C-4." Hammond cut him off. "McNamara's an idiot."

"How did you know ..."

Hammond leaned away from Connolly's face.

"I'm not telling you any more," he snapped.

"The FBI knew it was there? They knew right where to look?"

"I'm not saying anything more about this. Probably shouldn't have said anything at all, but I don't want you running off at the mouth about how I set somebody up on a bogus search warrant."

"So if the FBI knew Harvey was in trouble, didn't they know Ingram was, too?"

In one step, Hammond moved from the table to the door and jerked it open.

"Leave," he ordered.

Connolly slid the chair back from the table and stood. He started toward the door, then paused.

"Can I get a copy of those reports?"

Hammond was caught off guard by the question.

"What?"

"The reports," Connolly grinned. "Fire Marshal. ATF. Can I get a copy?"

Hammond looked deflated. His shoulders sagged. His head drooped.

"If I give you a copy, will you leave?"

"Sure." Connolly smiled. "For now."

Hammond started across the room toward the desk. Connolly followed him.

"You're a real piece of work, you know that? I'm going to give you a copy of those reports, and you're going to leave." Hammond slipped a pair of handcuffs from a clip on his belt and waved them for Connolly to see. "One way or the other."

Connolly left police headquarters shortly before noon. He drove downtown and parked the Chrysler in front of the Port City Diner. Inside, the lunch crowd filled the tables. Connolly found an empty place at the far end of the counter near the back. A waiter set a glass of ice water in front of him.

"What will you have today, Mr. Connolly?"

"Turkey sandwich," Connolly replied.

"Your usual?"

"Yeah," Connolly smiled. "My usual."

The waiter scribbled the order on a notepad and moved away. As he did, a man in a gray suit took a seat on the stool next to Connolly. He slipped a business card from his pocket and slid it in front of the water glass near Connolly's hand.

The card identified him as Dave Brenner. Connolly glanced at the card, then looked at Brenner.

"Why don't you get that sandwich to go," Brenner said. The tone in his voice left little doubt it was more than a suggestion. "We need to talk."

He slipped from the stool and walked through a doorway at the back of the dining area. Connolly waited while the waiter wrapped his sandwich, and then followed Brenner.

Beyond the door, a narrow hallway led to a pantry off the kitchen. Past the pantry, a door opened to the alley that ran alongside the diner. Connolly pushed open the door and looked out. Brenner moved a few steps up the alley and motioned for him to follow. Connolly stepped outside and moved alongside him.

"I understand Hammond gave you the names of two of our agents," Brenner said.

He continued moving down the alley, away from the street as they talked.

"Yeah," Connolly replied. He glanced around, making sure they were alone. "He didn't have much choice. Cahill would put him in jail if he didn't."

"I need you to forget about them."

"I can't really do that," Connolly replied.

"Why not?"

"I have a client to defend. Those agents searched his property. Looks to me like the whole thing was a pretense, and a pretty obvious one at that. I can't just forget about it."

Brenner stopped abruptly and faced Connolly.

"Look, people's lives are at stake here. I have agents working on something that goes way beyond what you are concerned with. I can't let you expose them."

"Can't let me?" Connolly bristled at the tone in Brenner's voice. "Since when do I have to ask your permission to do anything?"

"I can't let you expose them," Brenner repeated, his voice tense and measured. "I won't let it happen."

"What are you saying?"

"I'm saying, if you try to contact them, I'll take whatever measures are necessary to stop you."

Brenner glanced down the alley. The look in his eye told Connolly he had seen something. Connolly jerked his head around in time to see someone disappear around the corner of the building near the street.

"All right," Brenner turned back to Connolly. "I have to go now. Go back inside the diner. Wait a few minutes; then leave out the front as if nothing has happened."

Connolly hesitated.

"Go now," Brenner ordered.

Connolly turned away and stepped toward the door at the rear of the diner. As he opened it, a car turned into the alley and drove toward them. Connolly moved inside the building and pulled the door closed, leaving a narrow crack through which he could see the alley outside. He watched as the car came to a stop alongside Brenner. Through the narrow opening he could see Hammond seated in the driver's seat behind the steering wheel. Brenner opened the rear door of the car and sat inside. The car drove away. When it was out of sight, Connolly pushed the door closed and made his way past the pantry to the dining area.

Seventeen

*L*ate that afternoon, Connolly received a call from Harry Giles.

"You still interested in talking to Frank?"

"Yes."

"I can get you five minutes," Giles said.

"When?"

"Now."

Connolly hurried downstairs to the Chrysler and sped down Dauphin Street. In a matter of minutes he reached the shipyard and came to a stop at the guard station outside the main gate. As before, the guard assigned a vehicle pass for the Chrysler and instructed him where to park. He drove to the administration building and parked the car near the front entrance. At the lobby desk inside he surrendered his driver's license and was issued a visitor's pass.

"Know where you're going?"

"Yes," Connolly replied. "I've been here before."

He walked past the desk and around the corner to the elevators. He rode to the basement and entered Giles' office. Giles was on the phone. When he saw Connolly approaching, he cut the conversation short and hung up.

"Are we meeting down here?"

"No," Giles shook his head. "Upstairs. Frank's in his office." He took his jacket from the coatrack and slipped it on. "Come on. He's waiting for us."

They rode the elevator to the top floor. When the doors opened, they stepped into a reception area outside Frank's office. Decorated with antique furniture and oriental rugs, it looked more like a living room than an executive suite.

Beyond the reception area, a secretary sat at a large mahogany desk that faced the elevator doors. To the left of the desk was the door to Frank's office. Giles whisked Connolly past the secretary and through the door.

The office was enormous, occupying two-thirds of the top floor. Windows lined the three exterior walls, flooding the room with light and affording a commanding view of the shipyard below. In the distance, the blue water of Mobile Bay shimmered in the afternoon sun.

A desk and credenza sat opposite the door. With the windows and view behind it, the desk seemed to float in midair. The desktop was bare and shined to a high gloss that reflected light from the windows. The credenza behind the desk was slightly lower than the desktop in a way that removed it from the view of anyone seated in front of the desk.

Frank sat in a chair behind the desk, dressed in a charcoal gray suit with a white shirt starched stiff enough to stand by itself. Gold cuff links held the sleeves in place, leaving just a hint of white fabric showing from underneath the cuff of his suit jacket sleeves. His silk tie bore a subdued, multicolored pattern that accented the suit perfectly. It was tied in a long, elegant knot tucked neatly under the edges of his shirt collar.

He rose from his chair as they approached. Tall, slender, and athletic, even at fifty-five he looked like someone from the cover of a fashion magazine.

"Frank," Giles said, "this is Mike Connolly."

They shook hands.

"I'm pleased to meet you," Frank said.

"Thank you for agreeing to see me," Connolly replied.

Frank gestured to a chair in front of his desk.

"Have a seat."

Connolly took a seat to the right. Giles sat to the left. Frank wasted no time directing the conversation.

"I understand you represent the man who killed my brother," he began. His voice was even and unemotional, but his words came at Connolly with the precise thrusts of an expert swordsman.

"No," Connolly countered. "I represent a man the police have accused."

Frank's lips drew taut in a thin, tight smile. He propped his elbows on the armrests of the chair and laced his fingers together in his lap.

"Well, there's no need to quibble over semantics." He cocked his head to one side in a dismissive manner. "What can I do for you?"

Connolly crossed his legs.

"I was wondering if you had any idea who would have wanted your brother killed?"

"That is the question, isn't it? Who? And, perhaps, why?" There was a hint of arrogance in Frank's voice. "Are you interested in the 'why' also, Mr. Connolly?"

"I'm not trying to be difficult." Connolly was bored with their verbal jousting. "From what I've heard, your brother was a ... lady's man. He liked to party. He wasn't particularly interested in the kind of attention to detail required to run a business like this. But nothing about him would suggest he was a candidate for execution."

"I suppose the obvious suspect might be a jealous husband."

"I'm sure you've seen all the forensics reports on your brother's death. Not too many jealous husbands have access to the kind of material used to kill him. A shotgun, yes. A few sticks of dynamite or a fire while everyone was asleep, perhaps. But four electronically controlled charges of plastic explosives, I doubt it."

"Maybe this time he happened upon a woman with a sophisticated husband. I understand he was with a woman at the time. A woman who was married, I believe. Have you checked into that?"

"How well did you get along with Steve?"

Frank shot a look at Giles. Giles shifted uncomfortably in his chair.

"We got along," Frank replied.

"I have a witness who was present when you and your brother got into a heated argument. Was that common?"

"We were brothers, Mr. Connolly. Brothers sometimes bump into each other. Steve lived a very unsavory lifestyle. We exchanged unpleasant words about it from time to time."

"Is that the only thing you argued about?"

"Yes."

"You never argued about business? About Ingram Shipbuilding?"

"Mr. Connolly, as you obviously are aware, neither of my brothers is involved with the business decisions here. My youngest brother, Joey, is a lawyer. I'm sure you know him. He's a good kid. Steve was a drunk, a drug dealer, and a lover of other men's wives. How could we have possibly argued over the business of Ingram Shipbuilding?"

"Any of those arguments ever come to blows?"

Frank glared at Connolly from across the desk. Connolly pressed the issue.

"Ever get into a fight with your brother?"

Frank leaned forward and rested his arms on the desktop.

"Mr. Connolly," his words came in a slow, firm voice, "it's no secret I didn't care for my brother. And he didn't care for me. But if you're implying I had something to do with his death, you are out of your mind. I didn't socialize with him.

We didn't see each other on holidays. I didn't allow him to come near my house or family, and I attended his funeral only out of some archaic sense of family duty. But I assure you, I had nothing to do with his death." He took a deep breath and stood. "Now, if you don't mind, I have other people waiting."

Giles stood. Connolly did as well. Frank came from behind the desk and ushered them both toward the door.

As he turned to leave, Connolly noticed the wall near the door was lined with photographs—most of them were of ships. Instead of walking toward the door, he moved to the right and wandered along the wall, studying the pictures. He glanced over his shoulder in Frank's direction.

"These all ships y'all built?"

"Yes," Frank replied, a hint of impatience in his voice.

"Submarines," Connolly noted, pointing to one of the pictures. "You make submarines here?"

"No." Frank sounded more irritated by the moment. "We don't build them. We just overhaul them."

"'Just overhaul them,'" Connolly repeated, chuckling to himself. "Like saying 'We just do brain surgery.'"

"Yes." Frank acknowledged the comment with another thin, tight smile. "It's a rather complicated process."

Connolly moved farther down the wall. He pointed to a picture of a ship being launched. A red flag was draped over the bow of the ship. Almost hidden in the folds of one corner of the flag were a golden crescent moon and two gold stars.

"You build ships for other countries?"

"Yes," Frank replied. "We do now."

Connolly pointed to the flag on the bow of the ship in the picture.

"That looks like a Chinese flag."

"Yes," Frank sighed. "I really must be going," he insisted. "I have another appointment."

Connolly stepped away from the picture and moved toward the door.

"China. The People's Republic of China?"

"Yes."

"Not Taiwan?"

"No. Not Taiwan."

"I had no idea you were building ships for them. Right here in Mobile."

Frank guided him closer to the door.

"Yes. Right here in Mobile." He held out his hand to direct Connolly through the door. "I'd love to chat, Mr. Connolly, but I have other people waiting."

As Connolly was about to step through the door, a picture on the opposite side of the doorway caught his eye. It was a picture of Frank standing beside the same Asian man from the photograph he made with the negative from Steve's house. Connolly stopped and pointed to it.

"Who is that?"

"Excuse me?"

Connolly brushed past Frank and moved in front of the picture.

"Who is this?"

He pointed to the man in the picture.

"His name is Wu Yi." Frank sounded exasperated. "Mr. Connolly, I have no time for this sort of thing. I must get to—"

"Wu Yi," Connolly repeated, interrupting him. "He's Chinese. Those his boats you're building?"

He gestured with his thumb over his shoulder toward the pictures on the other side of the door, all the while avoiding Frank's glare by staring at the picture.

"Yes!" Frank snapped. Suddenly, the tightly constrained façade came undone. "Yes, yes, yes!" His words fired in rapid succession, propelled from his lips by the pent-up frustration.

His head bobbed up and down with each word. His clinched fists pounded the air. "He's Chinese. He's a charming man. He lives in Dallas with his wife and two children. He's a vice president with China Overseas Investment Corporation. We're building ships for them. We also build ships for companies in Denmark, Sweden, and Singapore. I can't remember who else we build for, but I'll find out if you will just leave!" His voice rose in pitch as he spoke. By the time he finished, it was shrill and loud.

Connolly smiled and extended his hand. Frank grasped it.

"Thank you for your time." Connolly's voice was a calm and polite contrast to Frank's. "I know this is a difficult subject for you to talk about. I'm sorry you lost your brother."

Frank sighed. His shoulders slumped, the energy drained from his body. He managed a smile.

"I'm sorry I couldn't be of more help to you."

Connolly nodded and turned away. Giles led him past the secretary's desk and through the reception area toward the elevator. Frank closed the office door.

Giles was silent as they entered the elevator. He stood next to Connolly and pressed a button to send them to the lobby. When the doors closed, he turned to Connolly.

"What was that all about?"

"He's a cool customer."

"I thought you had something specific you wanted to talk to him about."

"I did."

"Well, what was it?"

"Frank Ingram."

"What?"

"I wanted to talk to Frank about Frank."

"You think he had something to do with this?"

"I don't know, but I think he has something to hide."

"Something to hide?"

"Yeah."

Giles shook his head.

"I have no idea what you're talking about."

Connolly gave him a look.

"I mean it," Giles said. "I can't help you if you don't let me in on what you're up to."

"Right," Connolly smiled.

The elevator opened in the lobby. Connolly stepped through the door and was gone.

Eighteen

Connolly was at the office the following morning when Mrs. Gordon arrived. She came down the hall and stood at the door to his office. Connolly was seated at his desk, working behind a stack of books and files when she appeared.

"You're here mighty early," she said.

"Trying to make up for lost time."

He didn't bother to look up as he spoke.

"You never told me how your meeting went with Harry Giles the other day."

Connolly glanced at her, irritated by the interruption. The curious look on her face made him pause. He relaxed and leaned his chair away from the desk.

"It was ... interesting."

"Did he have much to say?"

"He was friendly," Connolly replied. "I'm not real sure why he wanted to talk. But he was friendly."

Mrs. Gordon nodded.

"He can be very charming when he wants to."

Connolly folded his arms behind his head and rested the back of the chair against the wall.

"How do you know him?"

Mrs. Gordon blushed. She pushed herself away from the doorframe and stood up straight.

"I ... I can't really talk about that."

"Mrs. Gordon," Connolly urged.

She lowered her head and looked at the floor a moment.

"He was—"

Just then, the telephone rang. She hurried up the hallway to her desk to answer it. A moment later, she called to him.

"Uncle Guy's on the phone."

Connolly reached for the receiver.

"I think I found someone who can help," Guy said.

Connolly hung up the phone and took his jacket from the coatrack. He walked up the hall toward the front door. He paused as he passed Mrs. Gordon's desk.

"You were about to tell me how you know Harry Giles."

Mrs. Gordon shook her head.

"Not today," she replied.

"You're leaving way too much to my imagination," Connolly grinned.

Mrs. Gordon looked up from the papers on her desk.

"You better get going."

The grin on Connolly's face grew wider.

"Okay. But you're going to tell me about you and Harry."

"Someday," Mrs. Gordon replied.

Connolly opened the door and stepped into the corridor.

The drive to Bayou La Batre took forty-five minutes. Guy was standing in the kitchen, dressed and waiting when Connolly arrived.

"Come on," Guy said, brushing past him.

Connolly grinned, amused by the old man's enthusiasm. He followed him to the Chrysler.

"Which way?"

"Toward town," Guy replied.

At the end of the driveway, Connolly turned left and followed the road along the bayou.

"Where are we going?"

"Landry's Seafood."

Two miles from the house, they reached the first of the many fish houses that lined the northern end of the bayou.

"I think it's the third one," Guy said. "Should be a sign out front. Built so many of these things in here I can't keep up with them anymore."

As they drew closer, Guy spotted the sign.

"There it is."

Connolly leaned over the steering wheel and squinted his eyes. Ahead was a sea of buildings and signs.

"Where?"

"Fourth one on the right."

Connolly slowed the Chrysler, still looking. Finally, he saw it. A sheet of plywood painted white with purple block letters leaned against a telephone pole near the road. He turned the Chrysler onto the parking lot paved with small white oyster shells.

Landry's Seafood was housed in a plain white building made of concrete blocks. A loading dock ran across the front of the building. Two trailer trucks were parked there. Workmen were busy loading boxes of frozen seafood. The doors to the building were open. Vapor from the cold air inside billowed out to form a white cloud around the back of the truck.

To the right of the loading dock was a door that led to a small office in the corner of the building. Beside the building was a large compressor unit that operated the quick-freeze processor used to prepare seafood for shipment. Behind the building was a pier that jutted into the bayou.

"Park on the side," Guy instructed.

Connolly did as he was told and brought the car to a stop near the compressor unit. Guy opened the door and climbed out.

"Wait here."

Connolly watched as the old man made his way past the trucks and went inside.

In a few minutes, Guy returned. Behind him came a young man dressed in dirty blue jeans and a white T-shirt. Over his clothes he wore a white rubber apron and on his feet were white rubber boots. Guy waved for Connolly to join them.

He climbed from the Chrysler and joined them behind the building near the pier.

"Mike," Guy began, "this is David Landry."

Connolly extended his hand.

"You don't want to shake my hand," Landry warned, holding up his hands. "You'll smell like fish all day."

Connolly smiled.

"Go ahead, Mike," Guy prompted. "Ask him whatever it is you're wanting to know about."

"I suppose you heard about that guy that was killed over near Fairhope the other day," Connolly said. "Big explosion in his garage."

"Yeah," Landry said. "I heard about it. Mr. Poiroux said you were looking for someone who knew something about explosives."

In spite of his appearance, Landry was educated and intelligent. He spoke with an ease and fluency that struck Connolly as a stark contrast to their surroundings.

"Yes, I am," Connolly said. "I have a client who is being investigated by the police. They think he had something to do with it. I'm looking for somebody who might know something about that sort of thing."

Landry had a cautious, inquisitive look on his face.

"Dynamite, or what?"

"Not dynamite." Connolly shook his head. "This was a little more sophisticated. Plastic explosives."

Landry folded his arms across his chest and looked away.

"Motivation to do it wouldn't be a problem. Any number of people around here would be willing to do something like that." He turned toward Connolly. "I mean, we got all kinds around here. But not with what you're talking about. What I know about plastic explosives I learned in the army. Powerful stuff, but it's illegal. Hard to get. Even harder to get the detonators you'd need."

Connolly nodded. He waited for Landry to continue.

"Though, I guess anything can be had. Lot of things happen around here that folks don't know about." He gestured with a wave of his hand toward the boats moored along the bayou. "Some of these boats go as far as Venezuela. Stay out a month at a time. Come back right here to this dock. Never see a customs agent or Coast Guard or anybody. Anything you want, you could probably get."

Connolly nodded again.

"Ever hear anybody talking about this sort of thing?"

Landry shook his head.

"No. Not personally. There's folks around here like that, though." He looked Connolly in the eye. "But if you could find them, you wouldn't want to know them."

Connolly smiled and nodded his head.

"Probably not, but I don't have much choice."

Landry sighed.

"I have a cousin, lives over at Bayou Heron. You know where that is?"

"Yeah," Connolly nodded.

"His name is Stamm Guidry. He might not know the people you're looking for by name, but he can tell you where to find them."

Landry turned away and stepped toward the building.

"Thanks," Connolly called after him. "I appreciate your help."

Landry opened the door and stepped inside without reply-
ing. Connolly turned to Guy.

"Who is he?"

"He's Gerald's boy." Guy started toward the car. "Come on.
Let's go down to the Catalina. I'll let you buy me lunch."

Nineteen

After lunch, Connolly took Uncle Guy home and then drove west along the coast toward Bayou Heron and Stamm Guidry. Beyond Grand Bay, the highway made a broad, sweeping curve as it approached the Alabama-Mississippi state line. As the car entered the curve, a building came into view.

"Frank's," he whispered.

Frank's Place was the first of a string of bars and cafés that crowded the highway on both sides of the state line. Beer joints. Crumbling, rotten buildings that reeked of stale cigarette smoke and beer. Connolly knew them well, and for an instant the sight of that first building felt like greeting an old friend after a long absence.

He took a deep breath and did his best to focus on the highway.

Just keep driving, he thought.

The car moved past Frank's to the right. The Pink Pony went by on the left. A sign caught his eye. A memory flashed through his mind. Another sign. Another memory. Buildings moved by on either side. The Ala-Miss Lounge. The Painted Lady. Sea Horse. Images from the past whirled through his mind.

Then from the midst of the clutter he saw it.

The Imperial Palace.

From the side it looked like nothing more than an enormous

metal warehouse, but it had a brick façade on the front, with a gleaming white portico that extended into the parking lot. Painted gold, the building was outlined in purple and green neon lights that made it impossible to avoid. Just to make sure, spotlights near the highway were trained on an oversized billboard sign that sat twenty feet in the air. The sign depicted a scantily clad, voluptuous woman, reclining on a chaise lounge. She had a come-on smile, and one of her eyes winked every few seconds. At night, the glow from the neon and billboard lights lit up the sky for miles around.

As he drew nearer, Connolly could see the parking lot. He glanced at his watch. The afternoon crowd was there now. Marisa was, too.

His foot lifted from the gas pedal. The car slowed. Connolly stared out the window across the parking lot. His foot shifted to the brake pedal, hesitated, then moved back to the gas. He forced his head to turn away. He pressed his foot against the pedal. The engine responded. The car picked up speed.

At the last moment, he glanced out the window for one more look. His eyes scanned the lot on the far side of the building. Marisa's Trans Am was parked near the back. His heart skipped a beat. He pressed the gas pedal harder. The Chrysler whisked him down the highway.

Beyond the state line, Connolly turned left onto a narrow paved road that led through the marsh toward the coast. The road rose and sank with the gooey black mud beneath and made the Chrysler buck and bounce with each dip.

A mile or two farther, the road became even narrower as it entered a grove of cypress trees. Ditches along both sides of the road grew wider, deeper, darker. Large cypress trees, their trunks bigger than one man could reach around, towered above, their limbs forming a canopy that cast a dark, cool shadow over the roadway. Spanish moss dangled just above the roof of the car. A little farther and the ditch to the right was now a bayou.

The road curved gently to the right and crossed over the bayou on a one-lane wooden bridge. The boards rattled and rumbled beneath the wheels as the Chrysler rolled across. The bayou, now to the left, was lined with oyster boats tethered bow and stern to the knobby roots of the cypress trees that stood at the water's edge.

The road came to an end and spilled into a large parking area paved with oyster shells. Around it, the savannah swamp spread out in a sea of brown marsh grass. Beyond the grass lay the blue water of the gulf.

To the right of the parking lot sat a low one-story wooden building, weathered and gray from the salt air and constant humidity. A faded Dr Pepper sign tacked on the wall outside identified it as Bayou Heron Fish Camp. Beside it, a muddy trail led to three houses located behind the building. As weathered and gray as the fish camp, they were all but hidden in a cluster of cypress trees.

Not much above the high-tide mark, the place was damp and musty. The pungent, sour odor of the marsh stung Connolly's nose.

He parked near the fish camp and stepped out of the car. A gentle breeze whispered through the treetops high above his head. Out on the marsh, a seagull croaked a lonely cry. But there wasn't another sound. No motors, no cars, no voices.

To the right of the car near the Dr Pepper sign was a screen door. Nothing marked it as the entrance, but it was the only door on the front side of the building. Connolly pushed it open and stepped inside.

Inside, the building was dark and hot. A counter ran from the right side of the door to the far wall, dividing the building. A single lightbulb dangled from the ceiling above the counter, providing the only light in the room. Behind the counter were rows of shelves containing canned goods, fishing gear, and other items. To the left was a potbellied stove used to warm the building in the winter. Several cane-bottom chairs sat in a circle around the stove. Along the wall to the far left was a live bait tank. In the middle of the room, by the stove, sat a dirty, dusty box fan that stirred the air. A fly buzzed around Connolly's head. Sweat formed on his forehead. He slipped his jacket off and slung it over his shoulder.

A man emerged from the rows of shelves behind the counter. Tall and slender, he wore a white shirt tucked neatly into cotton trousers. Sweat stains ringed both sides of the shirt beneath his arms. The pants were spotted with bits of dirt and shrimp shell. He let his eyes run down Connolly, then back up.

"Something I can help you with?"

"I'm looking for a man named Stamm Guidry," Connolly replied.

The man stared at Connolly for what seemed like an eternity before he finally spoke.

"What for?"

"I need to talk to him about a case I have."

The man's eyebrows lifted, and his eyes grew a little wider.

"A case? You the law?"

"No," Connolly replied, shaking his head and smiling. "I'm a lawyer."

The man looked skeptical.

"He's not in trouble," Connolly added. "I just need to ask him some questions. I'm looking for some information. He's not even a witness. I just need him to help me."

Connolly took a handkerchief from his hip pocket and wiped his forehead.

"Wait here," the man said. "You can sit over there." He pointed to the chairs around the stove, then disappeared behind the rows of shelves.

Connolly took a seat and waited. As he did, voices filtered in from outside. A moment later, he heard a car door creak. He jumped to his feet and stepped to the screen door. Outside, two men stood by the Chrysler. One held the driver's door open and looked inside. They glanced at him but seemed unfazed by his presence. The man holding the door slipped inside the car and sat behind the wheel. The other man stood beside him. Connolly watched, unsure what to do.

Suddenly, the man standing beside the car froze. Connolly could see his eyes were wide with fright. The man behind the wheel jumped from the car, pushed the other man aside, and slammed the door closed. Without a word, both men darted around the corner of the building.

"They don't mean any harm," a voice said from behind him.

Startled, Connolly jumped at the sound. He turned to see who spoke.

Behind him stood a man about his own height, but much leaner and much harder. His arms and face were dark and leathery from days in the hot sun. He wore a sleeveless white T-shirt, stained with grease and dirt, stretched tight over a torso of lean muscle. In contrast, his khaki trousers were baggy and loose. Cinched at the waist by a belt too long for his size, the pants flapped and rustled when he moved. His curly dark hair, oily and matted, dangled below his ears. On his feet, he wore white rubber boots.

"Didn't mean to scare you. Justin said you wanted to see me."

Connolly gathered himself.

"Are you Stamm Guidry?"

"Yes, sir."

"I'm Mike Connolly."

They shook hands.

"Don't get many lawyers down here," Guidry said. "You did good just to find us. I hope it's worth the trouble."

Connolly glanced around for the man he had spoken with earlier. He was nowhere in sight.

"I represent a man who's charged with murder," Connolly began. "The police think my client killed a man with a bomb."

Guidry frowned.

"I ain't heard nothing about no bomb."

"He was killed in his garage. Sitting in his car. Scattered him and the garage all over the place."

Connolly paused.

Guidry waited for him to continue.

"I'm trying to find out who around here might have the expertise to do something like that."

"And you think I know something about it?"

"I was told you might," Connolly said.

"Who told you that?"

"David Landry. I grew up in Bayou La Batre."

A faint smile crossed Guidry's face.

"Whoever did this used something called Semtex," Connolly continued. He felt more at ease now, and his voice took a more natural cadence. "Ever hear of it?"

The smile disappeared from Guidry's face.

"I've heard of it." Guidry shook his head. "Mister, you don't want to get into this. The people you're talking about aren't anything like you." Guidry chuckled. "They aren't much like me, either, and that'd make them just about foreigners to you."

"I don't have much choice," Connolly replied.

"I'm telling you, you don't want to know these people. And you don't want them to know you."

Connolly waited. Guidry let out a long, slow sigh.

"There's a guy in Pascagoula named—" He stopped in midsentence. "You're probably better off not knowing his name." His voice was low and hushed. "Runs an army-surplus store off Market Street." He thought for a moment. "I think it's actually in Moss Point. Mississippi Surplus or Gulf

Surplus, something like that. You'll recognize him when you see him. Missing an ear on one side, and one hand only has two fingers. Walks with a limp. Demolition man for the Green Berets in Vietnam. Blew up all kinds of stuff. Got caught short one day. Nearly got himself killed." Guidry paused a moment before continuing, as if debating whether to go further. "He can get that stuff."

Connolly nodded.

"But don't tell him I sent you," Guidry warned.

Connolly shoved his hands in his pockets and looked away for a moment.

"Any idea who would be willing to set a charge like that?"

Guidry dropped his head and stared at the tops of his white rubber boots.

"Ahh ..." He shuffled his feet as he struggled to formulate an answer. "Listen ... you're getting in way over your head."

Connolly shrugged his shoulders. Guidry continued.

"The people you're looking for are pretty rough. I mean, I don't know if they blew up the guy you're talking about or not, but killing ain't a problem for these people. Guy at the surplus store, these guys, they're all the same crowd."

Connolly nodded and waited again. A wry smile spread across Guidry's face.

"You really don't want to know these people."

"I know," Connolly replied.

Guidry sighed once more.

"These guys aren't like anybody you've ever seen before. They ain't nothing like the guys at the country club or even the people you see in jail."

"I understand," Connolly said.

Guidry folded his arms across his chest and dropped his gaze to the floor once again. He rubbed his left foot along the floor as if playing in the dust.

"There's a bunch of guys live up around Hurley." His head

was down. His eyes still focused on the floor. "I don't know their names. They fight dogs for entertainment on weekends."

Guidry glanced up. Connolly looked puzzled.

"Like some folks fight chickens ... roosters," Guidry explained.

The puzzled look passed from Connolly's face.

"Cockfights."

"Yeah," Guidry replied. "Like cockfights. These folks raise dogs. Rottweilers. Bulldogs. Mean dogs. Get together some place at night. Watch the dogs fight each other."

A pained look spread across Connolly's face. Guidry nodded.

"It ain't pretty."

Connolly shook his head in disgust.

"Now that's your crowd," Guidry said.

Connolly ran his hands through his hair and took a deep breath. The hot, stuffy air inside the building filled his lungs. He held it in a moment, then let the air escape as he thought about what Guidry had told him.

The man appeared behind the counter once again. Guidry turned to him.

"Justin, give us a cold drink."

The man reached under the counter and took out two bottles of Coca-Cola. A bottle opener hung from a string tied to a nail on a post behind the counter. He flipped the tops off both bottles with the opener and handed them to Guidry.

"Here." Guidry passed one of the bottles to Connolly. "You look like you could use something cold."

"Thanks," Connolly replied.

Slivers of ice slid down the outside of the bottle onto Connolly's hand. He raised the bottle and took a long, slow drink.

Twenty

From the fish camp at Bayou Heron, Connolly retraced his route to the highway. There, he turned right and drove back toward the state line. This time, he ignored the sinking feeling inside and turned the Chrysler into the parking lot at the Imperial Palace. He steered the car under the portico and brought it to a stop at the front door. A valet dressed in black pants and a gold jacket with black piping on the sleeves opened the car door.

"Hey, Mr. Connolly. Haven't seen you here in a long time."

"It's been a while," Connolly said, as he stepped from the car. He slipped a ten-dollar bill into the attendant's hand. "Be gentle with the car."

The attendant glanced at the bill in his hand and grinned.

"Yes, sir."

As Connolly approached the front entrance, a doorman stepped forward. He wore a long, gold-colored coat with shiny brass buttons buttoned all the way to the top and gray trousers with gold piping down the seams. A gold-colored hat sat atop his head, and he wore white gloves.

"Welcome to the Imperial Palace," he said. He tipped his hat with one hand and opened the door with the other.

Connolly nodded in response and extended his hand. The doorman grasped it. Connolly pressed a five-dollar bill into his palm. The doorman smiled.

"Enjoy yourself."

The front doors opened into a lobby that ran the width of the building. Crystal chandeliers hung from the ceiling twenty feet above on thick brass chains. The floor was covered with dark red carpet. There were no windows, but the walls were covered with mirrors that made the place seem immense.

Across the lobby from the main entrance, six doors ten feet tall and painted metallic gold led into the showroom. Two doors in the center stood open, guarded by still more doormen in uniform accompanied by muscular bouncers dressed in blue jeans and red T-shirts emblazoned in gold with the Imperial Palace logo.

Connolly crossed the lobby. The doorman smiled and nodded. The bouncer glanced at him, then turned away. Connolly paused and looked around, waiting for his eyes to adjust to the dim light inside. Beyond the door, a low wall about waist high separated the entrance from the main floor. A stage extended across the far end of the room with a long runway that stretched toward the entrance.

Along the wall to the left was a carved oak bar. Salvaged from a club in Biloxi following Hurricane Camille, it was brought to the Palace as an afterthought. Dark, heavy, and ornate, it fit well with the rest of the decor. Above the bar was a wooden rack filled with glasses. Tiny spotlights hidden along the front edge of the rack lit the top of the bar. Bottles of liquor lined the shelves behind the bar. In back of the bottles, a mirror ran from one end to the other.

Between the entrance and the bar, tables were arranged in no apparent order from the low wall near the doors to the stage in the back and along both sides of the runway. Most of them were empty. The afternoon crowd was clustered around the runway.

Cigarette smoke stung Connolly's eyes as he scanned the

room. With each breath he felt it burning the inside of his nose. Beneath the laughter of the men gathered along the runway, snatches of conversation drifted across the room. The language was raunchy, base, and dredged with the earthiness that reduced life to its most primal urges. Connolly found it painfully familiar.

"There's a five-dollar cover in the afternoon," the doorman said.

Connolly took a five-dollar bill from his pocket and handed it to the doorman. The doorman shoved the bill into a small box on a stand near the door and tipped his hat.

"Enjoy yourself," he said.

From the doorway, Connolly crossed the showroom to the bar. The bartender saw him coming and greeted him with a smile.

"What could I get you, Mr. Connolly?"

"Ginger ale," Connolly replied.

The bartender gave him a questioning look.

"That all?"

"That's it."

"One ginger ale. Coming right up."

He filled a glass with ice and ginger ale and set it on the bar. Connolly glanced at him.

"How much?"

"Forget it," the bartender said, with the wave of a hand. "On the house."

Connolly gestured to him with the glass.

"Thanks."

The bartender lingered a moment. He picked up a towel and wiped the bar.

"Don't get too many requests for ginger ale."

Connolly was about to respond when the sudden noise of the crowd interrupted him. Catcalls echoed through the room. Loud music burst from speakers at either end of the stage. He glanced over his shoulder in time to see a young woman prancing down the runway, clad in only a g-string.

Connolly turned back to the bar, feeling awkward and out of place. The bartender smiled.

"You'll miss the show."

Connolly gave him a faint smile.

"Is Marisa around?"

The bartender's face turned sober.

"I think she's in the back."

A waitress came to the end of the bar for a drink order. The bartender said something to her. She glanced at Connolly, then stepped away and disappeared through a door near the stage. Connolly took a sip from the ginger ale and stared into the mirror behind the bar.

In a few minutes Marisa appeared behind him. He watched in the mirror as she nuzzled the back of his neck, sending a shudder through his body. As she moved from his neck to his ear, her blond hair brushed across his cheek, and the scent of her perfume enveloped him. She lingered a moment, her lips gently caressing his earlobe. He sat transfixed, unable to resist.

A moment later, she slid around him and leaned against the bar. She smiled, amused at his reaction.

"Hello, Mike."

"Marisa." He cleared his throat and straightened himself. "You're looking well."

"I work at it."

He was silent. She pointed to his glass.

"So you decide to give up and come back to the good life?"

Connolly raised his glass.

"Ginger ale."

She ran her hand over his shoulder and slipped her fingers into his hair.

"You want to reconsider my offer from the other night, or you just passing by?"

"Passing by, I guess."

He took another sip of the ginger ale. She ran her fingers lightly over his hand and nuzzled close to his ear again.

"Miss me?"

"Only when I think about you."

"I'm staying not too far from you." Her voice was low and sultry. "Maybe I'll drop by again."

"Who's the lucky man?"

"You wouldn't know him. He works construction or something like that."

"Somebody with a real job."

"Yeah," she said. "A real job."

He rolled the glass between his fingers and the palm of his hand. In the mirror behind the bar he saw Marisa leaning next to him. His collar was unbuttoned and his tie hung loose. He looked away.

"I shouldn't be here."

His voice was all but inaudible.

Marisa's lips brushed against his ear.

"What did you say? I couldn't hear you."

Connolly turned toward her. She was only inches away. All he had to do was lean forward, and her soft lips would welcome his kiss. Her breasts would press against him. She would revel in the touch of his hands as they wandered across her body. For an instant, he calculated how they could pull it off. They could steal away to her dressing room and lock the door. She had time before her next show. No one would bother them. She was beautiful, alluring, and right in front of him. He wanted her. He would have her.

"You want to ..."

She smiled at him as if she knew what he was going to say. The look in her eye said all he had to do was finish the sentence. It was the same smile he'd seen, the same look he'd said yes to many times before. But this time he knew there was nothing behind it except a moment of physical pleasure, and that wasn't enough anymore.

The tension evaporated. His body relaxed.

"Never mind," he said. "I shouldn't have come here."

She gave him a blank look as he stepped away from the bar. Without looking back, he walked across the showroom floor and out the door to the lobby. At the front door, he handed an attendant the check stub for his car. In a few minutes, the Chrysler rolled to a stop under the portico. The attendant held the door open as Connolly slid in behind the wheel.

"That's a smooth-running car."

"Yes, it is," Connolly replied.

The attendant closed the door.

"You ever think about selling it?"

"Not for a moment."

Connolly touched his foot lightly against the gas pedal. The car started forward.

At the highway, he brought the car to a stop and took a deep breath. His eyes still burned from the cigarette smoke inside the building. He sniffed the sleeve of his jacket. It smelled like an ashtray. He pulled it off and draped it over the back of the seat beside him. Reaching to the opposite side of the car, he rolled down the front passenger window.

A tight band seemed to squeeze his head. A throbbing headache built at the base of his neck. Listening to Guidry, wading through the Palace, talking to Marisa left him feeling heavy, drained, and dirty. He rubbed his hands over his face and stretched his neck.

When he reached Mobile, Connolly turned off Government Street and made his way over to Texas Street and the house where Rachel lived. From the corner, he saw her in the yard with Elizabeth. He brought the car to a stop at the curb across from the house. The door creaked as he got out. Rachel turned around. A frown clouded her face.

Connolly slipped on his jacket as he crossed the street toward her. Rachel picked up the baby and held her close.

"What do you want?"

"Just wanted to see my granddaughter."

He stopped a few feet away. Rachel turned Elizabeth so he could see her, but wrapped both arms around her. Connolly stepped closer.

"I'm not going to hurt her."

Rachel looked suspicious.

"You been drinking?"

"No," Connolly replied, irritated. "Why?"

"You smell like cigarette smoke."

He looked at Rachel, shifting his focus away from Elizabeth.

"Working on a case. Had to go to a couple of places."

"I hate that smell," she said. "You used to smell like that in the morning. I thought it was just you for a long time. Then I realized you'd been out all night and were just coming in. I'd rather forget those memories."

"Me, too," Connolly replied.

She looked at him a moment.

"Take off your jacket," she said.

"What?"

"Take off your jacket."

Connolly slipped off his jacket. Rachel took it from him with one hand and thrust Elizabeth toward him with the other. Connolly took the baby in both arms and snuggled her under his chin.

Rachel spread the jacket over a bush nearby.

"You need to send that thing to the cleaners."

Connolly paid her no attention. His eyes were closed as he softly hummed a tune to Elizabeth and rocked her on his shoulder.

Suddenly, a loud crashing sound came from upstairs. Connolly jerked his head away from Elizabeth and looked around.

"What was that?"

"Craig and Mark," Rachel said.

"What are they doing?"

"Uh ... rearranging the furniture."

Connolly looked alarmed.

"Something wrong?"

"No. Why would anything be wrong?"

Connolly gave her a look.

"It's all right, Dad," she said. "I can handle it."

"What about Elizabeth?"

"She's all right," Rachel replied. She stepped closer and took Elizabeth from his shoulder. "It's not anything we can't handle."

Just then, the front door opened. Mark stepped out. He had an angry look on his face until he noticed Connolly. He managed a smile in their direction.

"Rachel," he called. "Can I speak to you?"

Connolly looked at her.

"You sure about this?"

"It's okay," she said.

She started across the yard with Elizabeth in her arms.

Twenty-one

Connolly awoke the next morning still feeling heavy and tight from his conversation with Guidry and from seeing Marisa at the Imperial Palace. After a shower and a cup of coffee, he left the guest house and drove to St. Pachomius Church. He arrived early. The janitor was unlocking the front door as he stepped from the Chrysler.

Inside, the nave was dark and cool. Just beyond the door, he paused near the last row of pews. Behind him, the door banged shut. He felt safe, protected, cut off from the world outside. He glanced around at the stained-glass windows. The soft morning light made the images in the scenes stand out as though they were three dimensional. After a moment, he made his way down the center aisle and took a seat midway in the sanctuary.

At the front of the church, marble steps led from the nave to the chancel. Beyond the chancel was the altar rail and behind it the altar itself. In the center of the wall, a stained-glass window rose above the altar to within a few feet of the ceiling, almost thirty feet high above the floor. The window depicted Christ, his outstretched arms nailed to a cross. Light from behind the window cast a glow across the altar and chancel.

Connolly stared at the window, then lowered the kneeling pad from the back of the pew in front of him and knelt. In what seemed like only a few moments, he heard Father Scott begin morning prayers.

"Blessed be the name of the Lord, who was, and is, and is to come."

Glancing around, Connolly saw a small crowd had gathered near the front. The morning sun now streamed through the stained-glass windows. The sanctuary was awash with warm, inviting light. He opened the prayer book and followed along with the service. As he did, the tightness in his head eased. The tension in his neck evaporated. Like water washing over his soul, the words of the ancient ritual swept away the oppression from the day before.

Connolly reached the office shortly before nine that morning. Mrs. Gordon was in the break room when he entered. She called to him as he passed the door.

"You want your phone messages?"

He stopped and leaned against the doorframe.

"Anything important?"

"Not really. I can bring them to you."

"You check the—"

"Yes." She cut him off. Her face wrinkled in an irritated scowl. "I checked the pay phone."

Connolly smiled, amused at her reaction. He turned away and walked down the hall to his office. He slipped off his jacket and tossed it across a chair near the door, then took a seat behind the desk. A large brown envelope lay in the center of the desktop. He picked it up to open it. Mrs. Gordon entered the room. He glanced up at her.

"What's this?"

"Photographs," she replied. "From the video."

He tore open the envelope, slid out the photos, and laid them on the desk.

"That was fast."

"Thank you."

He looked at each one carefully, then stacked them neatly to one side. Mrs. Gordon turned away and stepped to the door. He closed his eyes and rested his head on the back of the chair. She started to pull the door closed, then stopped.

"Oh, I almost forgot."

Connolly opened his eyes.

"Hollis called. Wants you to meet him at Bailey's Marina."

"What for?"

"Something about a boat."

Connolly rocked the chair forward to an upright position.

"So much for a nap," he grumbled.

He rose from the chair and stepped to the door. As he slipped on his jacket, he glanced toward the desk. The photographs caught his eye. He snatched them from the desk and shoved them in his pocket.

Bailey's Marina was located south of town on Mobile Bay at the mouth of East Fowl River, not far from Hollis' shack. From his office on Dauphin Street, it took Connolly an hour to reach it. Hollis was propped under a large live oak tree in the parking lot when Connolly's Chrysler rumbled to a stop near the marina bait shop. Hollis roused himself and walked toward the car. Connolly opened the door and stepped out.

"What's up?"

"Fellow in here you need to talk to," Hollis said. "What took you so long? I been down here all morning."

"I was late getting to the office."

Connolly took a legal pad from the car and followed Hollis inside. The bait shop was empty except for a man who stood behind the counter. He spoke to Hollis as he glanced at Connolly.

"This the man you been waiting on?"

"This is him," Hollis replied. "Pete Graham, meet Mike Connolly."

Graham nodded.

"I suppose Hollis told you what we're working on," Connolly began.

"You want to know if I know anything about that big explosion they had over around Fairhope."

"Yes," Connolly replied. "See anything?"

"Couldn't hardly miss it," Graham said. "Nearly knocked the cans off the shelf."

"Did you notice anything suspicious that morning? I mean, other than the explosion."

"Well, like I told your friend, I was sitting over there in that chair about half asleep. All of a sudden I hear this great big boom. Nearly scared me to death. I rolled out of the chair and onto the floor. When nothing else happened, I went over to the window. It was already light. Maybe seven, eight o'clock. Anyway, I could see a big fireball rolling up and a column of black smoke over on the eastern shore. I stood there awhile, just looking. Then I seen a boat coming toward the dock. They was coming like straight at me from where the smoke and all was."

"A boat?"

"Yeah. I figured they were coming for gas or something, so I walked out yonder on the pier toward the pumps to tie 'em up."

"Did you talk to them?"

"No, sir," Graham said. "They didn't come to the pier. They pulled in one of them slips over there and tied up. The one in front jumped out and tied the bow line. They walked straight over to a maroon pickup parked by those trees." He pointed out the window toward a stand of scrubby oaks at the edge of the parking lot. "Got in and drove off. Far as I know they haven't been back."

"Get a tag number off the truck?"

"No. It was one of them big ones, though. Sat up real high. Four-wheel drive. I think it was a Chevrolet."

"Is the boat still here?"

"Yeah. It's out there in the slip. When they didn't come back, I went down there and tied the stern off. It was banging around down there pretty good."

"Is that a rented slip?"

Graham looked uncertain.

"Well, let me check." He pulled a small cardboard box from under the counter and sorted through a stack of note cards. "No," he said. "That one there has been vacant for two months." He squinted and held the card at arm's length, trying to read it. "Huh. I shoulda known that."

Connolly took the photographs from his jacket pocket and handed Graham the ones of the men in the bedroom.

"Recognize either of these two?"

Graham studied the pictures a moment.

"That looks like them. Maybe. I'm not sure. One of them was tall and kind of slim. A real hard-lookin' sort of fella. The other one was shorter. He was in the bow of the boat."

He handed Connolly the pictures.

"Do you mind if I look at the boat?"

"Help yourself."

Connolly started toward the door. Hollis followed close behind. When they reached the door, Connolly turned back to Graham.

"Have the police been by here to see you about this?"

"No." Graham shook his head. "Haven't talked to a soul, except you and your buddy there." He pointed to Hollis as he spoke.

Connolly smiled and stepped outside. He and Hollis walked toward the dock.

"It's that green-and-white Stauter boat over there," Hollis said. "Got a fifty-horse Evinrude on the back."

Connolly was still grinning from Graham's comment.

"You ever think of us as buddies?"

"Don't start getting mushy on me," Hollis smirked. "We got a long way to go on this."

Connolly and Hollis walked onto the dock and made their way to the boat slip.

"You been in the boat?"

"No," Hollis replied. "Thought you'd want to see it first."

Two fishing rods, a tackle box, and a plastic ice chest were still in the boat. The key was in the ignition, and the gas tank appeared to be three-quarters full. Connolly copied down the registration number.

"That number probably ain't no good," Hollis said. "If somebody used this boat to do that job, they probably made up that number. It's a wonder the boat's here at all."

"Might have stolen it," Connolly replied. "Owner might have reported it."

"Yeah. But if they stole it," Hollis argued, "somebody would have found it by now. Been sitting here nearly two weeks. I mean, we don't even know if these guys had anything to do with Ingram."

Connolly stepped into the boat and opened the ice chest. Inside, the bottom was covered in water. An empty plastic ice bag floated in the water. Connolly flipped it aside with his finger.

A candy wrapper floated in the water. Connolly fished it out and held it up with a smile.

"Tootsie Roll," he said.

"You like Tootsie Rolls?"

"I found several of these over at Ingram's house."

Connolly dropped the wrapper in the chest and closed the lid.

"Wouldn't leave my prints there, if I were you," Hollis warned.

Connolly took a handkerchief from his pocket and wiped the edge of the lid. He leaned over the edge of the boat, grabbed a post on the dock for leverage, and hauled himself out of the boat.

"I think your hunch was right," Connolly said. "Whoever killed Ingram was in this boat."

"Based on a candy wrapper?"

"Yeah."

They started down the dock. Connolly reached inside his jacket.

"I have something that will interest you."

"Like what? Lunch?"

Connolly took the photographs from his pocket. They walked toward the Chrysler as they talked.

"Look at these."

He handed the pictures to Hollis.

"What are these supposed to be?"

"They came from the videotape in that camera we found the other night."

Hollis looked through the photographs.

"This what you was showing Graham?"

"Yeah." Connolly tapped the photograph of the two men in the bedroom. "Think you can find them?"

"If I knew where to look," Hollis replied.

"I'd start looking up around Hurley."

"Hurley?"

"Yeah. If I'm right, you'll find them up there at a dogfight Saturday night."

Hollis looked at the pictures and smiled.

"Shouldn't be too much trouble."

They reached the Chrysler. Connolly opened the door and slid behind the steering wheel. Hollis stood by the car, looking at the photographs.

"Well, come on," Connolly urged.

Hollis handed him the photos through the window.

"You buying lunch?"

"Yes," Connolly sighed. "I'm buying lunch. Get in."

Twenty-two

That night, Connolly had dinner with Harvey Bosarge. They met at the Catalina Restaurant in Bayou La Batre. Bosarge was already there and waiting when Connolly arrived. A waitress took him to the table.

"Have a seat, Mike," Bosarge said. "I hope you don't mind. I went ahead and ordered for you."

Connolly took a chair from the table and sat down.

"Long as it's not raw oysters," he replied.

"No," Bosarge laughed. "It's not raw oysters."

A waitress appeared carrying a tray of food.

"Two seafood platters," she announced.

She set the plates in front of them, then glanced at Connolly.

"You want something to drink?"

"Tea," he replied.

"I thought so."

She set a glass of iced tea beside his plate and walked away. Bosarge leaned toward Connolly.

"Seafood platter's my favorite." He pointed to the plate in front of Connolly. "If you don't want your stuffed crab, I'll eat it."

Connolly smiled.

"I think I'll manage to find room for it."

Bosarge began to eat. He spoke with his mouth full.

"What have you found out?"

"A lot," Connolly replied.

He reached in his pocket and took out the photographs of the two men from the video.

"You recognize either of these two guys?"

Bosarge laid his fork on the plate and took the photographs from Connolly. He looked at them, then handed them back to Connolly.

"Yeah. I've seen them." He lowered his voice. His eyes darted around the room. "Don't know their names, but I've seen them."

"Where?"

"They were at the house that morning."

"Ingram's house?"

"Yes. Lower your voice. No telling who's in here." He glanced warily around the room again, then shoved another bite of food into his mouth. "They were in a boat about fifty yards off Ingram's pier."

The statement hit Connolly hard. This was the exact scenario Hollis had suggested the night they went to Steve Ingram's house.

"Why didn't you tell me this before?"

"You didn't ask."

Connolly bristled at the comment. He wanted to grab Bosarge by the collar and scream. Instead, he took a sip of tea and thought of something else to say.

"Is that the only time you've seen them?"

Bosarge nodded his head.

"Yes." He swallowed the food in his mouth and took a drink. "And I don't want to see them again. Even from where I was, they looked like bad news. Where'd you get those pictures?"

Connolly grinned.

"Where do you think?"

Bosarge smiled.

"How'd you find it?"

"Screws holding the vent cover were marred. Cover was scratched."

Bosarge raised his glass of tea in a mock toast.

"Good work." He took another drink. "I wanted to go back for it, but when the police showed up looking for me, I figured I better just leave it alone."

"Why did you put a video camera in the bedroom?"

"Client wanted pictures. I gave him pictures."

"Grafton?"

"Uhh ... yeah."

The question seemed to catch Bosarge off guard. His response was less than spontaneous.

"He wanted pictures of his wife in bed with another man?"

"I guess so," Bosarge shrugged. "How'd you know it was my camera?"

"When I asked you for a photograph of Ann, you gave me a stack of pictures. One of the photographs was made from the same angle."

Bosarge nodded.

"What about Hammond? Did you talk to him after the bond hearing?"

"Yeah."

"He give you the names of those agents he was talking about?"

"Yeah."

"What did they have to say?"

"I don't know," Connolly replied. "Can't talk to them."

"Why not?"

"FBI won't let me."

"This is a murder case," Bosarge retorted. His eyebrows were scrunched down in a scowl. "They've got me charged with capital murder because of some unsubstantiated sham of a search. You've got to talk to them."

Connolly leaned over his plate toward Bosarge.

"It wasn't a sham of a search." This time, his voice was low and quiet. "Hammond says it was an attempt to save your life."

Bosarge stopped chewing. The scowl on his face turned to a puzzled frown.

"Save my life?"

"Yeah," Connolly replied. "They didn't find the explosives on the workbench. They found them under the hood of your car. Wired to the ignition."

Bosarge swallowed and wiped his mouth with a napkin.

"You're out of your mind."

"No." Connolly shook his head. "I think they saw you that morning."

"Who?"

"Those guys in the boat." Connolly tapped the pocket of his jacket. "The guys in those photographs I showed you."

Bosarge leaned away. The frown on his forehead was now a look of concern.

"Hammond told you this?"

"Yeah. And right after I talked to him, Dave Brenner paid me a visit. Told me to forget about trying to talk to those two agents."

Bosarge laid the napkin in his lap.

"That means the FBI has somebody close, giving them information."

Connolly nodded. Bosarge pushed his plate away.

"Think you can find them?"

"I have somebody looking for them," Connolly replied.

Twenty-three

*L*ate in the afternoon, two days later, Connolly's cell phone rang.

"I found them," Hollis said.

"Who?"

"Those two in the video."

"Where?"

"You know where Lee's Minute Stop is, on the highway just below Hurley?"

"I can find it," Connolly replied.

"Meet me there in about an hour."

Connolly switched off the phone and moved around the desk. He took his jacket from the coatrack and walked up the hallway to the door.

"I'm going," he said, as he passed Mrs. Gordon's desk. "I won't be back before you leave."

Mrs. Gordon shook her head.

"Why don't you hire a private investigator? There are plenty of good ones around, you know."

"And none of them will do what he does."

He opened the door to leave.

"What are you going to do when something happens and he thinks he's back in Vietnam?"

"Duck," Connolly quipped.

He closed the door and was gone.

+ + +

Connolly left the office and drove west on Dauphin Street. At Florida Street he cut across to Airport Boulevard. Beyond the airport, the boulevard narrowed to a two-lane road. Ten minutes later, he crossed the state line into Mississippi.

A few miles farther, the road narrowed to a single lane and plunged into the swamp along the Escatawba River. Like the road to Bayou Heron, the pavement rose and dipped, tossing the Chrysler up and down like a bucking horse as it wound its way around the ancient trunks of cypress and pine trees. Finally, it crossed the river, a twisting, lazy stream with water the color of tea.

Once over the river, the road rose from the swamp. Before long, Connolly was surrounded by rolling sandy hills covered with pine forest. He pressed the accelerator. The Chrysler picked up speed and hurried on. Soon, the woods gave way to an occasional farm, houses appeared, and then he was in Hurley.

Ahead was a stop sign at the intersection with the highway to Pascagoula. Connolly lifted his foot from the gas pedal. The Chrysler slowed, and he brought it to a stop at the intersection. To the left was a hardware store. In front, across the highway, a snow-cone stand sat empty in a vacant lot. To the right was an empty gas station. A faded sign dangled from a rusty post that read, "Hurley Used Tires."

Connolly turned left onto the highway and drove south. He found Lee's Minute Stop without any trouble.

The parking lot was empty as he eased the Chrysler off the pavement. He parked to the right of the front door and went inside. In a few minutes, Hollis arrived. He parked his pickup truck next to the Chrysler and waited.

Connolly emerged from the store with two bottles of Coca-Cola, a bag of potato chips, and a Milky Way candy bar. He walked to the pickup and got in on the passenger's side.

"Here." He handed the Coke to Hollis. "You look like you could use a snack."

"Snack? I could use some supper. It's getting late. Be dark before long."

"Eat this," Connolly replied. He handed Hollis the candy bar. "Don't you like Milky Ways?"

Hollis took the candy bar, ripped away the paper wrapper, and took a bite.

"You're not a bad cook."

He swallowed the bite of candy and backed the pickup away from the building.

From Lee's Minute Stop, they traveled south a mile or so, then turned left onto a dirt road. Two miles down the road, they turned left again. The last rays of sunlight faded from the horizon as the pickup truck rattled along the road.

A few miles down the road, Hollis turned the truck onto a trail that led around the edge of a rolling green pasture. He guided the truck into a grove of scrubby oak trees and switched off the engine. Connolly looked puzzled.

"What are we doing?"

"Come on," Hollis replied. "Gotta walk from here."

Connolly gulped the last of the Coca-Cola from the bottle he was holding and laid it on the floor of the pickup. He climbed from the truck and followed Hollis into the woods. He soon found himself deep in a tangle of dense undergrowth. Vines and thorns meshed together around them, forming an impenetrable web. Connolly groped in the dark, stumbling as he tried his best to keep up with Hollis.

"Where are we going?"

Hollis didn't answer but plowed ahead, pushing his way through the undergrowth. Finally, they emerged in a stand of pine trees. The ground beneath was clean except for an occasional bush. Hollis stopped and looked around.

"Let's wait over here," he said, pointing to a spot beside a huge pine tree.

Hollis took a seat on the ground near the base of the tree. Connolly glanced around.

"What are we doing here?"

"Waiting. Won't be nobody over there 'til sometime around nine."

"Nine?"

"Yeah. Late crowd."

"Late for what?"

"You'll see."

Connolly scanned the woods around them. Evening had melded into night as they walked. Tree trunks stood out against the darkness like black columns. Arrayed around them, they all looked the same. He felt disoriented.

"You know the way back to the truck?"

"Yeah." Hollis seemed unconcerned. He glanced down at Connolly's shoes. "You should have wore some different clothes."

Connolly looked down. Bits of leaves were stuck to his thighs. Cockleburs clung to the cuffs of his pants. He glanced over at Hollis.

"You didn't tell me we were going on a hike."

Hollis chuckled. He moved to a spot a few feet away and stretched out on the ground. He pulled his baseball cap over his face and closed his eyes.

"If I was you, I'd take a little nap. Be an hour or two before we go. Might be a long night."

A fallen tree lay nearby, its trunk dried and hardened by the sun. Connolly took a seat on the ground beside it and rested his back against it. He closed his eyes and was soon asleep.

Sometime later, he felt a hand on his shoulder. He opened his eyes to find Hollis squatting beside him.

"Time to go," Hollis whispered. "Follow me, and keep quiet."

Connolly stood. The woods looked darker than when they had arrived. He rubbed his eyes and followed after Hollis.

Twenty yards from where they had napped, they emerged from the woods at the edge of a poorly maintained road. Across the road was a pasture, and beyond it, more woods. In between was a rambling, weathered barn. Twenty-five or thirty pickup trucks were parked around the barn. The sound of shouting and cheering drifted across the pasture toward them.

Hollis tapped Connolly on the chest.

"Come on," he said. "This way."

They moved down the road to the far edge of the pasture, then crossed to the woods on the other side. Keeping the open field to their right, they were obscured against the blackness of the woods to their left. They made their way down the edge of the pasture to a position opposite the barn. Hollis stopped there and knelt. Connolly squatted beside him.

"See that truck over there?"

He pointed to a truck to the right, in front of the barn.

"Yeah," Connolly replied.

"That's their truck. Looks just like what that guy at Fowl River described."

Connolly nodded. The truck was a Chevrolet four-wheel-drive pickup, but in the dim light he couldn't tell if it was the correct color.

"All right," Connolly said. "Now what?"

Hollis motioned for him to follow. They crept across the open pasture to the side of the barn. Connolly's heart pounded against his chest. Hollis crept along the wall, then stopped. His face pressed against a crack as he stared into the barn. In a moment, he stepped away and waved his hand for Connolly to take a look.

Connolly stepped to the wall, pressed his face against the weathered boards, and looked through the crack with one eye. Two men stood in front of him. They were shouting and waving their arms in the air. A terrible, viscous growling sound came from somewhere beyond them. Then one of them moved to the right.

Connolly saw a wooden arena in the middle of the barn. The sides were made of unpainted plywood and formed a circle ten feet in diameter. In the circle were two bulldogs. Both were black and wore collars made of steel chain. Locked in a vicious fight, the dogs stood almost erect on their back paws. Their front paws clutched at each other. Their jaws ripped and tore at the hide around each other's necks.

Stamm Guidry was right, Connolly thought. *These are people you'd rather not know.*

Hollis leaned close, his breath hot against Connolly's ear.

"See those two guys to the right?" He spoke with a whisper so soft Connolly had to strain to hear him. "The one in the red T-shirt and the guy next to him?"

Connolly nodded, glad for the impetus to look away from the dogs. He focused his eye to the right and located the man in the red T-shirt. Connolly recognized him as the taller man in the video. The shorter one stood beside him. As he watched, the shorter one slipped his hand in his shirt pocket and took out a Tootsie Roll. He popped it in his mouth and dropped the wrapper near his feet. Connolly smiled and stepped away from the wall.

"That's them," he whispered. "Do you know where they live?"

"Yeah," Hollis whispered.

"Good. Let's get out of here."

Together, they started across the pasture toward the woods. Minutes later, two men came from the barn and walked toward a pickup truck parked nearby. They got in and started the engine. Headlights from the truck shone across the pasture. Hollis shoved Connolly to the ground.

"Get down."

But it was too late. The truck started toward them, its horn blaring to warn the others inside. Hollis scrambled to his feet and started for the tree line at the far side of the pasture.

"Come on," he yelled.

Connolly gathered himself up and followed. In no time at all, the barn emptied. Men and dogs piled into pickup trucks and joined the chase.

Hollis and Connolly reached the woods just seconds ahead of the first pickup truck. Driver and passenger bailed from the truck and ran into the woods after them. Trucks fanned out in patrol across the pasture and the dirt road. Spotlights used for poaching deer at night were now employed to locate Hollis and Connolly.

"We got 'em cut off," somebody yelled. "Let's turn the dogs on 'em."

With a rattle, a tailgate dropped, followed by a scratching sound as a dog slithered across the metal bed and jumped to the ground.

Hollis and Connolly ran as fast as they could, but the woods were thick with vines and thorns, and there wasn't enough light to see even the largest trees. They stumbled and fell every few steps as they scrambled to get away.

"What about the dogs?" Connolly shouted. "I don't hear them."

"Bulldogs," Hollis replied, between gasps for breath.

"What?"

"These ain't like your neighbor's Chihuahua. They don't bark just to hear themselves make a noise."

A few yards farther, Hollis stopped. Connolly collided with him in the dark. They both fell to the ground.

"We're making way too much noise," Hollis said.

A hundred yards to the left, headlights from the pickup trucks on the dirt road shone through the trees. Connolly looked around.

"We're surrounded," he said. "They're ahead of us on the road. Guys behind us. More of them to the left in trucks."

Hollis slapped a mosquito.

"Stay here much longer, the mosquitoes and flies will eat us before the dogs."

Connolly stood.

"Come on."

He started toward the road. Hollis followed.

"What are you doing?"

"If we can get across the road, we'll be home free."

"How you going to do that? Wave your arm and turn us invisible?"

As they crept closer to the road, the sound of the pickup trucks muffled their approach. They crawled to the edge of the woods and lay on the ground. Trucks patrolled in both directions up and down the narrow road, dodging each other as they met.

Hollis turned to Connolly.

"Okay. Now what?"

Before Connolly could reply, he felt something wet and cold nuzzle his ankle. He froze.

"What's that on my leg?"

Hollis turned to look.

"The biggest dog you've ever seen," Hollis whispered back.

"What do I do?"

"I don't know," Hollis replied. "But whatever you do, do it slow."

Connolly pushed himself around for a look. Behind him, a

large black rottweiler sat on its haunches, tongue hanging from his mouth, panting. Connolly eased himself up to a sitting position. The dog stepped forward. Connolly froze. The dog placed one paw on Connolly's lap, leaned forward, and licked him in the face. Carefully, Connolly laid his hand on the dog's back. The dog didn't flinch. Connolly stroked it gently.

"Good boy," he cooed. "You don't want to take my hand off, do you?"

"Not unless I tell him to," a voice said from the darkness behind them.

Connolly stiffened. Hollis stood. The dog gave a low growl.

"Stay," the voice said, commanding the dog.

A limb cracked as the man behind the voice stepped closer.

"Take the dog. Act like you're one of us. Move across the road."

Connolly squinted, trying to see.

"Who are you?"

"Never mind who I am. Just take the dog and go. Turn him loose when you get across. He'll find me."

Hollis nudged Connolly.

"Do like the man says. We ain't got much choice."

A chain dangled from the dog's neck. Connolly bent down and grasped it. The dog did not budge.

"Go," the man ordered.

Connolly led the dog to the road, timing it so they stepped out of the woods when the trucks were farthest apart. With the dog in hand and Hollis at his side, he hurried across. In the middle of the road, the dog broke into a run. Connolly and Hollis followed.

Truck lights fell on them from the left. The driver leaned out the window.

"Hey, where y'all going?"

Connolly ducked his head to the right, avoiding the glare from the headlights, and concentrated on following the dog.

"Dog struck a scent," Hollis shouted. "Looks like they're over here."

Connolly, the dog, and Hollis disappeared into the woods on the opposite side of the road. Behind them, they heard the sound of doors slamming as men left the pickup trucks to join in the search.

The woods on that side were much cleaner. With little underbrush, they were able to run. Connolly dropped the chain from his hand and ran as fast as he could.

"Which way is your truck?"

"Straight ahead," Hollis replied.

In a few minutes, they reached the thick undergrowth they had fought through that afternoon. Connolly stopped, bewildered. Hollis hurried past him.

"Follow me. I've done this before."

Placing both arms in front of his face, he charged into the brush. Connolly was a step behind. He could hear the vines and thorns ripping into Hollis' arms, tearing first his shirt, then his flesh. Finally, they broke free of the undergrowth. Hollis' truck was fifty yards to the right.

Connolly bent over, hands on his knees, and gulped in fresh air.

"Think we lost them?"

"I don't think they'll come through that brush like we did," Hollis replied. "Let's go while we have the chance."

They hurried to the pickup. When Connolly opened the door, the dome light above the seat came on. In the light, he saw Hollis' shirt sleeves had been ripped to shreds. Blood dripped from scratches and cuts on his arms.

"Shut the door," Hollis ordered.

"Your arms."

"Get in and close the door."

Connolly slid onto the seat and closed the door. Hollis started the truck and turned it around.

"Doesn't it hurt?"

The truck rocked from side to side as they drove away.

"Not as much as what they would have done to us," Hollis replied.

Twenty-four

Minutes later, Hollis and Connolly reached the highway. There, they turned right and drove in silence broken only by the whine of the truck's tires against the pavement. Ahead, Connolly saw the lights of Lee's Minute Stop. As the store came into view, he saw the Chrysler parked out front. He braced his hand against the armrest, anticipating the truck would slow. Thoughts of a warm shower and soft bed waiting at home danced across his mind. But the truck didn't slow. Instead, they drove past the store and into the night. Connolly glanced at Hollis.

"Where we going?"

"Didn't you want to see where they live?"

"You think that's a good idea? Going over there now?"

"We'll go in the morning," Hollis replied.

"So where are we going now? My car's back there at the store."

"Your car will be fine. No point in going all the way back home just to turn around and come back before sunup. I ain't driving all the way back to my place now."

Connolly sighed. He was too tired to argue. The sound of the tires on the pavement made him drowsy. His head sagged forward. His chin rested on his chest as he dozed off.

Sometime later, he felt his head bounce against the door of

the truck. He jerked awake as the truck rumbled off the high-way to the left.

"Where are we?"

"Johnson's Farm Supply," Hollis said. "At least it used to be. A few miles north of Hurley. Not far from Agricola."

In the darkness outside, he saw an abandoned concrete-block building. The windows were gone, and the roof had collapsed at one end. Weeds grew inside.

Hollis drove the truck around the end of the building. Behind the store was a gravel lot. A few pieces of rusted farm equipment were parked there. They drove past the equipment, then turned back toward the building. Hollis parked between a faded green Oliver tractor and an orange Allis Chalmers combine with flat tires. He turned off the engine and switched off the lights. The darkness of the night closed in around them.

Hollis slid down in the seat, bringing his head below the top of the steering wheel. Connolly rested his head against the back of the seat and closed his eyes.

"What are we doing here?"

"Waiting," Hollis replied.

"For what?"

"If you look through the front window of that building, you'll see a dirt road on the far side of the highway."

Connolly opened his eyes. The truck was parked facing the back of the building. A portion of the back wall had collapsed with the roof. From where they sat, they had a clear view through the building to the highway in front.

"They live on that road?"

"Yeah," Hollis replied. "We'll wait here 'til they leave in the morning. When they're gone, I'll take you down to their house."

"How do you know they'll be leaving in the morning?"

"You see where they live, you'd leave too."

Connolly closed his eyes and drifted off to sleep.

After what seemed like only minutes, Connolly felt a slap against his leg. He blinked his eyes open. The sun was already well above the trees and burned through the windshield of the truck. His back was sweaty and stuck to the seat. He squinted and raised his hand to shield his eyes against the glare.

Hollis pointed toward the highway.

"They're leaving."

Connolly looked through the building and saw a maroon pickup truck approaching the highway down the dirt road. Hollis was slouched in the seat. Connolly slid below the dash.

When the truck turned onto the highway, Hollis started the pickup. They drove around the building and across the highway to the dirt road. The road was graded and well maintained. They sped along. Connolly began to think they might pull this off without any problems.

A mile or so down the road, Hollis slowed the truck and turned left onto a dirt road filled with ruts and mud holes. The truck rocked and bounced as they made their way. A few minutes down the road, they came to a house trailer. The trailer had been painted blue, but most of the color had faded away. Dark streaks of rust ran down the sides between the windows and door. A plywood shack had been built along one end. A bright green tarp was draped over the top.

"That it?"

"No," Hollis replied. "That ain't it."

A little farther down the road, they came to a small frame house sitting fifty yards off the road in high weeds. An oak tree stood to the left, its branches sprawled across the roof. The roof was covered in leaves. The last remnants of white paint dangled in thin strips from the wooden siding, peeled away by years of weather and neglect. A chimney ran up the end to the right. The roof around it was covered in green moss. Atop the chimney was a Confederate flag tied to a mop handle that had been secured to the chimney with a rope. The flag was snagged on a branch from the oak tree.

The frame of a screen door hung by one hinge at the front doorway. The screen itself was long since gone. A dirty, torn curtain hung out a window opening to the right. All the windows had been removed.

As they neared the front of the house, Connolly saw the front door propped against a bathtub that sat a few feet beyond the oak tree. On the door, someone had painted the words "Keep Out" with red paint. The house looked abandoned.

A trail led from the road to the house, but Hollis brought the truck to a stop in the road.

"We better get out here," he said. "If we pull in there, they'll know somebody was here."

Connolly looked at Hollis in disbelief.

"This is it?"

"This is it."

Hollis opened the door and stepped from the truck. Connolly followed him. Together, they walked up the trail toward the end of the house near the tree.

The back of the house wasn't any better than the front. Like the front, the back door was gone, leaving an open doorway. Connolly stuck his head inside.

A counter ran from the door along the back wall to the right. A sink sat along the end wall. Connolly noticed the faucet was missing. An electric oven sat next to the sink. The oven door was open. Inside was a smoldering charcoal fire. The place reeked of rotten food and raw feces.

Hollis leaned through the doorway beside him.

"No running water. No electricity."

"They'd be better off outside," Connolly said.

A candy wrapper lay on the counter near the doorway. He leaned inside and picked it up.

"Tootsie Roll," he said, holding the wrapper for Hollis to see.

Hollis chuckled. Connolly tossed the wrapper on the counter.

"Where are the dogs?"

"In a pen near the creek behind us."

Just then, Connolly felt a tap on his shoulder. He jumped to see who touched him.

Behind him stood a slender, muscular black man dressed in blue jeans and a khaki work shirt. His boots were scuffed and muddy, but his hair was cut short, and his scruffy beard wasn't more than three days old.

"What y'all doing here?"

"Uhh ... looking," Connolly replied.

He moved away from the door.

"Biscuit find you poking around in his stuff, he'll feed you to the dogs." The man paused. A smile spread across his face. "Right after that little nut Willie Mizell carves you into bite-size pieces."

Connolly felt uneasy but not threatened.

"Biscuit?"

"Yeah. Biscuit. Herman Fontenot. You know him. Tall, raw-boned fellow."

Something about this man was familiar. Connolly had seen him somewhere. Or heard him.

The man smiled at Connolly.

"If I was you, I'd turn that truck around and get out of here. Right now."

The voice. Connolly recognized the voice.

"I know you," he said.

The man shook his head.

"I doubt it."

"Yes, I do," Connolly insisted. "What's your name?"

The man looked at him a moment, as if deciding whether to answer.

"Folks around here call me Ozzie."

"You were the man in the woods last night," Connolly said. "You gave me your dog. Told us to use him to cross the road."

The smile vanished from the man's face.

"You better go." It was an order, not a suggestion. "They'll be back before long. They haven't gone far. If you leave now, you can get to the highway before they see you."

He turned away and disappeared into the woods behind the house. Hollis nudged Connolly.

"Come on. Let's get out of here."

Twenty-five

Connolly and Hollis reached the highway without incident. They turned south and drove toward Hurley. Not far down the road, they met Fontenot and Mizell coming toward them in the maroon pickup. Connolly slid low in the seat and turned away toward the window.

"They see us?"

"I don't think so," Hollis replied.

Connolly watched in the side mirror. The maroon pickup continued away from them. He sat up straight in the seat.

They drove through town and reached Lee's Minute Stop a few minutes later. Hollis parked beside the Chrysler. Connolly got out.

"You need to have somebody check those places on your arms."

"I'll be all right," Hollis grumbled. "I've had worse."

Connolly closed the door and walked around to the car. As he opened the car door, he glanced back at Hollis.

"Have somebody look at them anyway. Send me the bill."

Hollis nodded. Connolly got inside the Chrysler and started the engine.

The drive from Hurley to Mobile took about an hour. Connolly went home to the guest house for a shower and a change of clothes. Though tired from spending a night in the cab of Hollis' truck, he drove downtown to the office anyway. He arrived after lunch.

Mrs. Gordon sat at her desk to the left of the door as he entered. He expected to hear her usual sarcastic remarks about coming in late. She gave him a concerned look but instead of a wry comment, she glanced past him and gave him a quick nod across the room. He turned in the direction of her nod and found Rachel sitting in a chair to the right. In front of her, Elizabeth lay sound asleep in her stroller. Suitcases and cardboard boxes were stacked to one side.

Connolly hesitated, unsure what it all meant and unsure what to say. It had been years since Rachel had been in his office and even longer since she last sought his help.

Tears came to Rachel's eyes. Connolly turned to Mrs. Gordon.

"Can you look after Elizabeth?"

"Sure," she replied.

He turned toward Rachel.

From somewhere deep in his soul he felt a surge of paternalistic pride and duty. He might not know what to do, but the thought of returning to the role of father filled him with a sense of purpose he hadn't felt in a long time. A tender smile softened his face.

"Come on back to the office."

She gathered herself from the chair, nervous and self-conscious, and stepped past him to the hallway. Connolly followed her. At the office door he laid his hand lightly on her shoulder and guided her toward a chair near his desk. She slouched in the chair and leaned to one side, propping an elbow on the armrest and resting her chin in her hand.

Connolly rummaged through one of the filing cabinets along the far wall and found a box of tissues. He set the box on the desk in front of her, then took a seat beside her.

"What happened?"

She took a tissue from the box and wiped her nose.

"Craig and Mark had a fight."

Connolly tried his best not to scowl. She wiped her nose again. He waited for her to continue.

"Mark went off somewhere yesterday. Craig loaded his stuff in a friend's pickup and moved out. Mark came back and got his stuff. The landlord showed up today. Told me I had to get out. They haven't paid the rent in over three months." She looked at him as if pleading for help. "I don't have anywhere to go."

Tears spilled from her eyes and streaked down her face. He wanted to hug her and tell her everything would be all right, but he held back.

"How'd you get down here?"

She wiped her eyes.

"Lady across the street brought me."

"What did your mother say?"

"I haven't told her." She glanced away. "I don't know what to do. I don't have a job. And now I don't have anywhere to live."

Connolly stood.

"Well, come on, we'll take your stuff to my place. You can stay with me while we figure this out."

Rachel managed to smile, but more tears rolled down her cheeks. She stood to follow him.

"Daddy, I ..."

"I know, Rachel," he interrupted. "I know."

He felt his arm slip around her shoulder. She leaned against him and sobbed.

They loaded her things in the Chrysler and drove to the guest house. In less than an hour, Rachel and Elizabeth were settled in one of the extra bedrooms.

"All right," Connolly said, when they had everything in

place. "I'm going to run down to the grocery store and get a few things. Do you have everything you need for Elizabeth?"

"Yes. She's fine."

"I'll be back in a minute."

Instead of driving to the grocery store, Connolly drove to Barbara's house on Ann Street. He parked the car at the curb in front of the house and started up the sidewalk toward the front door. The door opened as he came up the steps. Barbara leaned against the doorframe, her arms folded across her chest.

"I wish you'd call first."

She smiled playfully, but her eyes told him she meant it.

"We have a problem," Connolly replied.

She gave him a puzzled look.

"We?"

"Yeah. Rachel."

She rolled her eyes and stepped away from the door.

"Come on in. Sounds like this may take a while."

Connolly moved past her into the hall. She closed the door, then led him to the living room. He took a seat on the sofa. She sat in an armchair across from him.

"What's happened now?"

"Her roommates haven't been paying the rent," Connolly explained.

"Why am I not surprised?"

"There's a little more to it. They got in a fight."

Barbara looked horrified.

"Rachel?"

"No. The roommates," Connolly said.

"Over what?"

"I don't know. I didn't ask many questions. At any rate, they moved out. Then, the landlord showed up and threw Rachel and Elizabeth out."

"Threw them out?"

"Yes."

"Anything you can do about that?"

"Probably not."

"Where are they?"

"They're over at my place."

Barbara raised an eyebrow.

"She came to you?"

"Yeah." Connolly found it impossible to suppress a grin. "I was rather surprised myself."

"What's she going to do?"

"I don't know. I think she'd rather stay with you, but she's afraid to come see you about it."

A scowl wrinkled Barbara's brow.

"She should have known better than to get mixed up with those two. The whole thing was a mess from the beginning. No telling what they've been doing. I tried to get her to move in here with me before Elizabeth was born."

Connolly shrugged his shoulders.

"Yeah. Well, no point in arguing over all of that now."

"But what can she do? She can't live with you the rest of her life. Or here, either. She doesn't have a job. She never finished college."

"I don't know." Connolly's voice had a resolute tone. "I have no idea."

Barbara gave a heavy sigh.

"Well, bring her over here. She can stay here for now."

"Okay," Connolly said, nodding.

He stood to leave, then paused.

"Do you mind if I wait and bring her in the morning?"

Barbara looked up at him from the chair. His eyes were moist and soft.

"Sure," she said. "That'll be fine."

Twenty-six

After breakfast the next morning, Connolly moved Rachel and Elizabeth to Barbara's house. Rachel was guarded and defensive at first. Barbara was tense and aloof. But with Elizabeth demanding their attention, it wasn't long before things warmed between them. By the time Connolly unloaded the boxes and suitcases from the Chrysler, they were beginning to talk.

He left them in the kitchen, drinking coffee and entertaining Elizabeth.

From Barbara's, Connolly drove to Irvington. He wanted to ask Ann Grafton about the photographs he made from the video. Something about her answers when they talked the first time left him certain she knew more than she had been willing to tell him.

At the outskirts of town, he steered the Chrysler off the interstate and onto Highway 90 toward Irvington. A few minutes later, he sped past the Handy Pak convenience store. Paul, the man who gave him directions to Jean Weaver's mobile home the first time, was out front, hosing off the parking lot. Connolly didn't bother to stop. At Webster's Motel, he turned right and then left onto the dirt road.

Toys still littered the yard near the front steps of the trailer. The dilapidated pickup truck still slumped against a pine tree, and the clothesline still hung between trees in the backyard.

But the cars that had been there before were gone, and the place seemed unusually quiet. A mint green Chevy Cavalier was parked near the front door.

Connolly brought the Chrysler to a stop behind the Cavalier and got out. As he closed the car door, the door to the trailer opened. A woman appeared in the doorway, dressed in blue jeans and a ragged sweatshirt with the sleeves cut off at the shoulders. She was slender with sandy blond hair and tanned skin. At first glance she appeared to be rather young.

She stood in the door and folded her arms. The look on her face said she expected trouble.

"If you come about the trailer, I'll be out in a week," she grumbled. "The place I'm moving to won't be ready before then."

The tone of her voice sounded dejected and disappointed, but not defeated. Connolly noticed her arms. She was too slender, and her skin was tanned in a way that made it leathery and tough. Wrinkles around her eyes told him the tanned skin came from a hard life.

"I'm not here about the trailer," he replied. "I was looking for Ann Grafton."

The woman dropped her hands to her hips. Her elbows spread wide apart, blocking the door. Her face was suddenly cold.

"She's not here," she snapped.

"Any idea where I could find her?"

"I don't know where she is. She could be in hell for all I care."

"Are you Jean Weaver?"

"Who wants to know?"

Connolly slipped a business card from his pocket and handed it to her.

"Mike Connolly," he said. "I'm an attorney. I need to talk to her."

"This about that Ingram fellow?"

"Yes."

She glanced at the card.

"I run her off a couple of weeks ago." She stepped through the doorway and took a seat on the top step. "Her and that worthless husband of mine. Last I heard, they were living over in Pascagoula. Got an apartment down there on Ingalls Avenue. I can't remember the name of it."

"Any idea where her husband is?"

"No, but I hope he finds them two together. He finds her with Catfish he's liable to give him what he deserves."

"Doesn't seem like anyone has seen him since all this began."

"Doesn't surprise me," she replied.

"Somebody said they thought he worked offshore."

"Used to. He quit that job a week or two before that Ingram guy got killed."

"When's the last time you saw him?"

"Tommy, or Ingram?"

"Tommy."

"A few days before Ingram died."

"Where'd you see him?"

"He come by here looking for Ann."

"Did he know she was seeing Steve Ingram?"

"I don't know. He didn't seem upset, if that's what you're getting at."

"Did you ever see Steve Ingram?"

"Once. He brought Ann over here early one morning. Seemed like a nice-enough guy." She smiled. "I mean, nice for Ann. She wasn't attracted to the real intelligent type, if you know what I mean."

Connolly gave her a polite smile.

"Any idea where Tommy might be staying? Somebody said they have a house in Tillman's Corner."

"Tommy let the bank have that house two or three months ago. I have no idea where he is."

Connolly felt a sudden stab of anger. Bosarge had lied to him about Tommy.

"Who'd he work for offshore?"

"I don't know," she replied. "I think he came and left on a crew boat out of some place the other side of New Orleans. Cameron, I think."

Connolly thought for a moment.

"So you think they're living in Pascagoula?"

"Yeah. Last I heard."

"All right." He stepped away from the trailer. "I appreciate your time," he said. "I'm sorry to bother you."

She nodded in response. Connolly started toward the Chrysler.

"You handle divorce cases?"

"No," he said, turning once again to face her. "Used to, before my wife divorced me."

"Oh," she said. "Well, I need a good lawyer."

"Call Jay York. Tell him I told you to call."

"Okay. I will. Got a number for him?"

"He's in the phone book. If it doesn't work out with him, give me a call. I'll help you find someone else."

Connolly walked to the Chrysler. She rose from the steps and went inside. He heard the door close as he put the key in the ignition.

Twenty-seven

Connolly backed the Chrysler away from Jean Weaver's trailer and turned around in the grass. When he reached the highway at Webster's Motel, he turned left and drove west through Grand Bay. At the state line, he cruised past the Imperial Palace. This time with only a fleeting thought of Marisa. Twenty minutes later he reached Pascagoula.

At Market Street, he turned left and drove to Ingalls Avenue. The avenue ran from one side of town to the other, beginning at Market Street on the east side and ending at Desoto Street near Grant Bayou on the west side. He turned the Chrysler onto the avenue and drove slowly, scanning each block. By the time he reached the bayou, he had seen only two apartment complexes, Blue Vista and Casa Del Mar. He turned around at Desoto Street and drove back to Casa Del Mar. He parked in front of the manager's office and stepped from the car.

Casa Del Mar Apartments was a single two-story building that faced Ingalls Avenue. From the street, it seemed in decent condition, but as Connolly stepped from the car, he noticed the paint was peeling and the doors to many of the units were rotten and splintered. Fast-food wrappers and empty drink cups littered the walkway. A stench wafted from a nearby Dumpster.

He walked to the manager's door and knocked. The door opened and an overweight, middle-aged man appeared, dressed in shorts and a T-shirt. A cigarette dangled from his mouth, and he had a can of beer in his hand.

"Yeah."

"I'm looking for a woman who might live here," Connolly said. "Her name is Ann Grafton."

The man acknowledged Connolly with a nod of his head but did not reply.

"Probably lives with a guy," Connolly continued. "Came over here from Irvington. I can't remember his real name. Everybody calls him Catfish."

"Two-oh-five. Upstairs," the man said.

His voice was flat and lifeless. His face, sullen and disinterested. He closed the door without waiting for a response.

Connolly made his way to the steps and climbed to the second floor. Apartment 205 was located two doors beyond the stairwell. He knocked on the door and waited. When no one answered, he knocked again, louder.

In a few moments, the door eased open an inch or two. He heard someone whisper through the narrow opening.

"Who is it?"

In the darkness beyond the door, he could make out two eyes peering at him.

"Mike Connolly," he said. "I'm looking for Ann Grafton."

"Just a minute."

The door closed. In a minute or two, it opened again and Ann Grafton appeared, wrapped in a robe. It was obvious he had awakened her.

"Sorry about that," she mumbled. "Worked late last night." She pushed the door open farther and stepped away. "Place is a mess, but come on in."

Connolly stepped inside. Ann closed the door and moved across the room. She dropped onto the couch and curled her legs underneath her. He took a seat in a kitchen chair a few feet away.

"I guess you found my sister," she said.

"Yes. I found her."

"She still mad?"

"Yeah," he nodded. "She's still mad."

"Well, she has the trailer all to herself now. I hope she's satisfied."

"Not for long."

"What do you mean?"

"From the looks of things, I'd say she's moving out."

Ann shrugged her shoulders and looked away.

"I wanted to ask you some more questions about Steve Ingram," Connolly said.

She turned toward him.

"You said you went to New Orleans with him. Think you could find the house again?"

She shook her head.

"I'm not going back there. Whatever Steve knew got him killed. I'm still alive. I'd rather stay that way."

"Frank had a friend down there named Perry Loper. Did you ever meet him?"

"No. I don't think so."

"Think that might be the house Steve went to that night?"

"I don't know. I never met anyone named Perry Loper. And Steve never said anything about knowing anybody down there."

Connolly took the picture of Frank and Wu Yi from his pocket. He leaned toward the couch and handed it to her.

"I showed this picture to you once before. Take another look at it."

She looked at the photo.

"Like I told you, I never saw the Oriental guy."

"Man's name is Wu Yi. Ever hear anybody mention him?"

"No."

She handed the picture back to Connolly.

"Any idea what was going on that Steve found so interesting?"

"No. Not really. Like I told you before, it had something to do with his brother Frank."

Connolly returned the photograph to his pocket and took out the pictures from the video. He offered one of them to her.

"You recognize this man?"

Ann held up her hands in a gesture of frustration. She shook her head, refusing to take the picture from him.

"Look, I know you mean well, but I'd really rather not have anything else to do with you or Steve Ingram or this whole thing."

She stood.

"I'm only trying to find out what happened," Connolly explained. "Has someone talked to you?"

"No." Her voice was terse. She held her hands up again as if to ward him off. "Wait a minute. Wait right here."

She brushed past him and disappeared down a short hallway.

Connolly glanced around the apartment. The living room was furnished with a sagging couch, a worn-out recliner, and a small television. Clothes littered the floor. A pile of laundry lay on one end of the couch. To the left, the kitchen was cluttered with dirty pots and dishes. The apartment smelled of stale grease and cigarette smoke. As he looked around, Ann emerged from the hallway.

"Here." She handed him a small white envelope. "Steve gave this to me a few days before he was killed. He said for me to keep it, and if anything happened to him, I should find someone to give it to. I reckon you're it."

Connolly took the envelope.

"What is it?"

"I don't know, and I don't want to know. Just take it and leave."

Connolly slipped it into his pocket.

"That's all I know about Steve Ingram." She opened the door. "And I'd appreciate it if you didn't come around anymore. Like I said, whatever he knew got him killed. I'd just as soon none of them people knew where I was."

Connolly stood and moved across the room. As he reached the door, he hesitated. She glared at him.

"I got nothing else to say."

He stepped outside. She closed the door before he could say good-bye.

When he was seated in the car, Connolly opened the envelope. Inside, he found a single, unmarked computer disk. He stuffed the envelope in the inside pocket of his jacket and started the engine.

Twenty-eight

onnolly drove out of the parking lot at Casa Del Mar Apartments and turned onto Ingalls Avenue. At Market Street he stopped for the traffic light. While he waited, he glanced to the left. A dark blue Ford Crown Victoria sat two cars back on Market Street. Two men sat in the front seat. Dressed in gray suits and white shirts, they looked like carbon copies of each other. Connolly watched as the car moved forward with traffic, then turned toward him onto Ingalls Avenue. They passed within a few feet of the Chrysler but did not seem to notice him.

In the side mirror, he watched as the car moved up the street. In the middle of the next block, it turned into the parking lot at the apartments.

When the traffic light turned green, Connolly turned left onto Market Street. At the next intersection, he made a U-turn and drove back toward the apartments. As he approached the parking lot, he lifted his foot from the gas pedal. The Chrysler slowed.

The blue Ford was parked in front of the apartment building near the steps to the second floor. He scanned the second floor. The walkway was empty, but the door to Ann's apartment was ajar. Connolly let his eyes run along the second floor again, searching for a clue, a sign, an indication of who the men were and why they were there.

While Connolly watched, the Chrysler coasted to a stop in the street. Traffic gathered behind him. Cars began to pass him to the left. He eased his foot against the accelerator. The car started forward. Connolly glanced ahead as the car moved.

Suddenly, Ann Grafton darted from between two cars at the far end of the parking lot and ran down the sidewalk to the left. Connolly pressed the gas pedal. The Chrysler surged forward. To the left, the two men he'd seen in the car at the intersection hurried down the stairs from her apartment. One ran across the parking lot after her; the other sprinted to the Ford. Connolly shoved the gas pedal to the floor.

Ann continued down Ingalls Avenue and crossed Williams Street, running hard. The man chasing her was twenty yards behind, but closing. Connolly raced after them in the Chrysler. As he neared the intersection, the traffic light turned red. He saw it but ignored it and raced past Williams Street. A car horn blared. Tires screeched as a car to the right slid to a stop. The driver had his head out the window, yelling as Connolly shot through the intersection.

By then, Ann was in the middle of the next block. The man chasing her was right behind her. She glanced over her shoulder as he reached for her. His fingers stretched to grab her shirt. She darted into the street in front of the Chrysler, missing the front bumper by inches. Running hard and concentrating only on Ann, the man chasing her didn't see the Chrysler. He slammed into the car, bounced his head off the doorpost beside Connolly, and tumbled to the pavement. Ann reached the sidewalk on the opposite side and continued up the street.

Connolly drew alongside her and sounded the horn, waving for her to get in. He slowed the car, reached across the front seat, and threw open the door. She jumped in the car without waiting for it to stop. Connolly shoved the gas pedal to the floor. The car door banged closed. Ann leaned back in the seat and gasped for breath.

At the next corner Connolly turned right without slowing. The rear tires squealed as the back of the car slid around. A car approaching from the right swerved to one side to avoid them. Two women on the sidewalk jumped for cover in the doorway of a store. Connolly held onto the wheel. The Chrysler made the corner. He glanced across the seat at Ann.

"What was that all about?"

"Said they were FBI," she gasped, still trying to catch her breath. "Wanted to know where Tommy was."

She turned in the seat to look behind them out the rear window. Connolly glanced in the rearview mirror. Ann turned to face forward and slid low in the seat.

"Did you tell them?"

"Tell them what?"

"Where he is."

"Where who is?"

"Your husband."

"No," she replied. "I don't know where he is, but they didn't seem to believe me."

The street came to an end at Highway 90. Connolly turned left and headed west. Ann looked puzzled.

"Where are we going?"

"New Orleans."

"I told you I wasn't going back there," she fumed.

He gave her a broad grin.

"You want me to take you back to your apartment?"

She leaned back in the seat and closed her eyes.

"No," she sighed.

Connolly reached into his pocket and took out the photographs of Fontenot and Mizell, the two men from the video. He nudged her and handed her the pictures.

"Ever see these two guys?"

She studied the photographs.

"Where did you get these?"

"There was a video camera in the air-conditioning duct over the bed."

"Over the bed? What bed?"

"The one in Steve's bedroom."

"What pervert put a video camera over the bed?"

Connolly pointed to one of the photographs.

"The tall one goes by the name Biscuit. Ever hear of him? Ever hear anyone mention his name?"

"No," she replied.

She handed the pictures to Connolly.

"His real name is Herman Fontenot. Other guy is Willie Mizell."

"I've never seen either of them before."

She slid low in the seat and rested her head on the ledge of the door. Connolly loosened his tie and unbuttoned the collar of his shirt. He checked the rearview mirror again.

"Mind if I turn on the radio?"

"Suit yourself," she mumbled.

He turned on the radio and tuned it to an AM station. He turned up the volume loud enough to hear the music over the noise of the wind blowing through the car windows. With the radio blaring, they cruised through Ocean Springs and were soon in Biloxi. The highway became a broad boulevard along the Gulf of Mexico, with white sandy beaches to one side and large summer homes on the other.

In the middle of town, the beaches gave way to a concrete canyon of casinos and high-rise hotels. The street was clogged with traffic. At Delaney Street, Connolly stopped for a traffic light. The afternoon sun beat through the windshield, making the interior of the car hot and stuffy. He rubbed his eyes. Trade Winds Casino was to the left. He watched as people streamed in and out of the front entrance. Ann turned in the seat to look out the rear window.

"Go!" she screamed.

Her shrill shriek startled Connolly. She pounded on his shoulder.

"They're right behind us. Go! Go! Go!"

The traffic light changed. Caught off guard by her outburst, Connolly pressed the accelerator. The Chrysler started forward. He glanced in the rearview mirror. The blue Ford was right behind them.

"I knew we got away too easy," she shouted.

Before they reached the next intersection, Connolly regained his composure. He lifted his foot from the gas pedal. The Chrysler coasted to a stop in the middle of the intersection. He threw the gear shift in park and flung open the car door. Ann screamed at him as he stepped from the car.

"What are you doing?"

Connolly stepped from the car and turned to look the driver of the Ford in the eye. Standing in the middle of the street, he waved at the man, motioning for him to pull around them. The man on the passenger side threw up his hands. The driver grimaced. In a moment, the Crown Victoria pulled around them and sped past.

A truck sounded its horn behind them. Connolly stepped back to the car, slid behind the wheel, and closed the door.

"Are you out of your mind? Let me out," Ann protested. "I'm not going anywhere with you."

"It's the only way to deal with somebody like that," Connolly replied. "Once they know you know who they are, they're useless."

"You're crazy," she repeated.

Connolly laughed.

"Maybe so, but what are they going to do? Shoot me right there in the middle of the intersection?"

An amused grin spread across Ann's face. She leaned against the door again and rested her head on the window.

Twenty-nine

*L*ate that afternoon, Connolly and Ann arrived in New Orleans. Connolly followed the highway down Broad Avenue, then turned left onto Canal Street. He leaned across the seat and gave Ann a nudge.

"We're here," he said.

She raised her head from against the window and rubbed the back of her neck. She was groggy and disoriented from her nap.

"Where are we?"

"New Orleans," Connolly replied. "Canal Street."

Near the French Quarter, he turned off Canal onto St. Charles Avenue and drove west toward the Garden District. Beyond Lee Circle, St. Charles was divided by a wide median filled with large oak trees and lush green grass. Tracks for the St. Charles streetcar line ran down the center of the median. A streetcar rolled by. Its steel wheels made a clacking sound against the rails. A bell rang as it lazily passed over a cross street that cut through the median.

Luxurious old homes lined either side of the avenue, interspersed with apartment buildings and an occasional neighborhood store. Several of the more elegant homes had been converted to restaurants. A few had been turned into professional offices. Connolly moved the Chrysler to the far right lane and slowed.

"We came down here," Ann said, pointing. "I remember the streetcar. I wanted to ride it."

Connolly slowed the car even more, allowing her time to look and remember, hoping she would find something familiar. A few blocks farther, they crossed Jackson Avenue. Connolly glanced around, gesturing with his hand.

"See anything you recognize?"

Ann shook her head. She was trying, but she looked bewildered. Connolly kept driving. They crossed Louisiana Avenue. The houses became somewhat smaller and jumbled. A few were in disrepair. Then, she brightened.

"There." She pointed out the window. "I remember that house."

To the right, a two-story house sat near the street. Its stucco exterior was painted bright blue. The windows and doors were trimmed in red, and the shutters were painted lime green. A small yard in front was separated from the sidewalk by an ornate wrought-iron fence. To the left of the house Connolly caught a glimpse of a small patio on the side with a fountain surrounded by an even smaller garden.

"It was dark when we came by here, but they were having a party. They had a tent over there on the sidewalk, and the yard was full of people. Turn left at the next street." She glanced back at the house as they passed. "I told Steve we could join them. They'd never know we weren't supposed to be there. He didn't pay much attention to me."

Connolly changed to the far left lane and searched for the next street. Ann turned to face forward.

"There." She pointed across the dash out the front windshield. "Turn there."

Connolly turned the car left onto Amelia Street. Narrow but comfortable, the street was lined with turn-of-the-century homes, all with white clapboard siding. On most, gingerbread trim hung from the eaves of deep porches that wrapped around the front and down both sides. Wooden shutters flanked the windows. Oak trees draped with Spanish moss spread like a canopy over the neighborhood. Beneath the trees, azalea bushes thrived in the damp, moldy ground and tangled ivy wrapped around everything.

"Now turn right at that alley up there," she said, pointing once again.

Connolly turned the car to the right into a narrow alley. Houses crowded either side. Under the sprawling oaks, the fading afternoon light all but disappeared.

In the middle of the block, they passed a cluster of garbage cans. Ann nodded her head as if she remembered seeing them before. A little farther, they came to two more houses that sat next to the alley, one on either side facing Taylor Street, the next cross street.

"This is where we stopped," she said. "Right here."

Connolly stopped the car a little way past the garbage cans. Ann glanced around.

"Steve jumped out and took off up that way."

She pointed down the alley toward the house on the right at Taylor Street. Connolly opened the car door and stepped out. He glanced around, unsure what to expect, not real sure why he'd insisted on coming there.

Around them, shadows already hid much of the neighborhood. Twilight was upon them. Evening wasn't far behind. In the background, the muffled sounds of the city slowing down for the night drifted through the trees. He took another look around and started up the alley.

Behind him, the car door opened. Ann got out on the other side.

"I sat here by myself once," she said. "I ain't doing it again."

She closed the car door and started toward him. Together, they moved up the alley. As they came alongside the house, Ann craned her neck to peer through a window. Suddenly, she ducked low and tugged on Connolly's arm. Connolly was startled.

"What's the matter?"

"That's Tommy," she said, her voice a hoarse whisper.

"Where?"

She pointed toward the window. Connolly crept up to the window and peered in from the bottom corner.

Through the window, he saw two men standing in the dining room. One was an older man wearing slacks and a dress shirt. The shirt was starched stiff, the collar points neatly buttoned in place. On his wrist was a gold watch, and he had a single diamond earring in his right ear. Connolly recognized him from the picture made from the negative in Steve's bedroom. He was Perry Loper.

Standing beside Loper was a younger man dressed in blue jeans and a T-shirt. The jeans were faded and dirty. His hair was shaggy and unkempt. His face looked scruffy and unshaven. As Connolly watched, an all-too-familiar feeling crept over him. Grafton might have been many things, but looking at him through the window, Connolly thought he didn't seem the sort to hire a private investigator to find out whether his wife was seeing another man. From what he'd learned about Ann, she probably made little secret of her relationship with Steve Ingram. More than likely, Tommy Grafton knew she was seeing him long before he died and didn't care. Once again, he was certain Bosarge had lied to him, and he was angry with himself for not recognizing it sooner.

As he watched from the corner of the window, a black Chevrolet turned from Taylor Street into the alley up ahead. Connolly dropped below the window, pulling Ann with him. Together, they worked their way along the edge of the house to a bush in back. They ducked behind it and peered through the branches to watch.

The Chevrolet came to a stop beside the house not far from the window where they had been standing. The car door opened and David Daniels stepped out. Connolly groaned. Ann glanced at him.

"You know him?"

"Yeah."

"Who is he?"

"David Daniels. Works for Harry Giles."

"Who?"

"Harry Giles. Ingram Shipbuilding."

Daniels took a briefcase from the car and disappeared around the front of the house.

"Stay here," Connolly ordered.

He worked his way back to the window and raised himself up to look inside. He had a clear view of the dining room and watched as Daniels entered the room carrying the briefcase. He looked serious and determined, but calm. Loper appeared nervous, one moment folding his arms across his chest, the next, shoving his hands into his pockets. Grafton was grinning, cocky, self-assured.

They spoke for a moment, then Daniels laid the briefcase on the dining table and opened it. He took out a package less than the size of a loaf of bread and handed it to Grafton. Grafton smiled, bounced the package once or twice on the palm of his hand as if checking the weight, then grinned even broader.

Daniels said something. Connolly couldn't hear what he said, but he could see the stern look on his face. Grafton's face turned sour. He gave Daniels an angry response. Loper looked apprehensive and retreated toward the opposite end of the table. Daniels dismissed Grafton with a shrug and a wave of the hand, then closed the briefcase. Grafton glared at him as he left the room.

This time, instead of retreating, Connolly hurried past the

Chevrolet parked in the alley and made his way to the corner at the front of the house. Crouched behind a nandina bush for cover, he listened as the front door swung open, then banged closed. Footsteps crossed the porch. He peeked around the corner. Grafton came down the front steps and walked toward the street. A green pickup truck was parked out front. Grafton got in it and drove away.

Connolly moved to the back of the house. He took Ann by the arm and hustled her toward the alley.

"Come on," he said.

Thirty

Connolly and Ann ran up the alley to the Chrysler. Ann sat forward on the edge of the seat and watched the alley anxiously through the front windshield. Connolly started the car and shifted it into reverse.

"Hurry up." She slapped her hand nervously against the dash of the car. "If they come out, they'll see us."

"I'm hurrying as fast as I can," Connolly replied.

He threw one arm across the top of the seat and turned to look out the rear window. He backed the car down the alley toward Amelia Street, steering with one hand, afraid to look around, wondering if Daniels had spotted the car.

At the corner, he turned the steering wheel hard to the right, sending the rear of the car around to the left into the street. In one quick motion, he turned to face forward and jerked the car into gear. He pressed the accelerator and drove down Amelia toward Magazine Street. Ann settled into the seat.

"What happened inside?"

She glanced over her shoulder through the rear window, nervously checking behind them. Connolly checked the mirror.

"I'm not sure," he replied.

"Then why are we still in a hurry?"

"Trying to catch up with your husband. Daniels handed him something before he left. I want to see where he takes it."

At Magazine Street, Connolly turned left.

"What makes you think he went this way?"

"Just a hunch."

They both scanned the street ahead of them, anxiously looking for Grafton's pickup truck. They sped past Lafayette Cemetery and crossed Washington Avenue. As they went through the intersection, Connolly craned his neck to look up Washington as far as possible.

At Second Street, construction crews blocked the street, reducing traffic to one lane. Connolly banged the steering wheel in frustration as they waited to move past. In a few minutes, a workman waved them around.

"He's long gone by now," Ann sighed.

"Maybe not," Connolly replied. A broad grin spread across his face. He pointed ahead out the windshield. "Look there."

At the intersection with Jackson Avenue, the green pickup sat in the left turn lane. Two cars were in the lane behind the pickup. Connolly slowed the Chrysler and changed lanes.

When the traffic light turned green, the pickup moved forward and made a left turn onto Jackson Avenue. He seemed to be in no hurry. Connolly followed the other cars behind the truck, making sure he was well back and out of sight.

At Claiborne Avenue, the pickup turned right. Ann shook her head.

"He has no idea what he's doing. Where's he going?"

"The interstate."

"The interstate?"

"Yeah. It's up here about three blocks. This is the easiest way to get to it from downtown."

The pickup continued up Claiborne. Connolly and Ann followed in the Chrysler. Beyond the Superdome, it gained speed and moved up the entrance ramp. They followed the truck onto Interstate 10, traveling east away from downtown.

+ + +

Evening passed into nighttime before they reached the other side of New Orleans. Overhead lights illuminated the highway, but they were too far behind the pickup for Grafton to notice them. East of the city, the interstate turned north and crossed Lake Pontchartrain. Before they reached the lake's north shore, Ann was fast asleep once again, slumped against the car door.

A few miles beyond the lake bridge, the pickup exited the interstate at Slidell, a growing suburban community on the eastern edge of New Orleans' urban congestion. Connolly slowed the Chrysler, allowing the truck to reach the top of the exit ramp before he steered the car off the highway.

At the top of the ramp, the truck turned left onto the overpass across the interstate. Connolly nudged Ann.

"Wake up," he said.

She raised her head from the door and sat up in the seat.

"What is it?"

She rubbed her eyes.

"He's leaving the interstate," Connolly said.

"Where are we?"

"Slidell."

They followed the truck over the bridge and across the interstate. Beyond the interchange, the truck turned into the parking lot at a Union 76 truck stop. Connolly slowed the Chrysler, letting the truck stay well ahead of them.

They watched from the road as the pickup drove across the parking lot in front of the restaurant to an area on the far side filled with large tractor trailer trucks. Connolly turned into the parking lot and drove behind the gas pumps. The pickup rolled between the trailer trucks toward the edge of the parking lot. Connolly found a spot in front of the restaurant from which he could watch and parked the Chrysler there, obscured from view between a worn-out Ford Galaxie and a truck with a horse trailer. He watched the pickup across the hood of the Galaxie.

At the far side of the truck lot, the pickup came to a stop. Ann was restless.

"What do we do now?"

"Wait," Connolly replied.

A few minutes later, a maroon pickup truck entered the parking lot and passed in front of the Chrysler. A four-wheel-drive truck with tires almost as tall as the car. Connolly recognized it immediately.

"Uh-oh," he moaned.

Ann raised her head. Connolly slid down in the seat. He grabbed her shoulder and pulled her down with him.

"What are you doing?"

Ann struggled to free herself from his grasp.

"Stay down," he said.

"What are you doing?"

Connolly held her down with his arm and raised his head high enough to look through the steering wheel. As the truck rolled by, he could see two men sitting in the front seat. His heart seemed to stick in his throat. Herman Fontenot was driving. Willie Mizell sat on the passenger's side. Connolly slid below the dash and held his breath, hoping they didn't recognize the Chrysler from the night he'd left it parked in Hurley. He listened as the sound of the truck faded.

When the truck passed, Connolly sat up in the seat and released his grip on Ann's shoulder. She pushed herself up and tossed her hair back. They both watched in silence as the maroon truck circled Grafton's pickup, then pulled alongside, driver to driver.

"Have you ever seen that other pickup before?"

"No," she replied. "Why?"

"Those two guys are the ones in the photographs I showed you this afternoon."

"Friends of yours?"

"Not hardly."

Across the parking lot, Grafton leaned out the window of his pickup. Fontenot leaned out of the maroon pickup. They talked a moment, and then Grafton turned aside. His head disappeared inside the cab of the truck. In a moment, he emerged and handed Fontenot the brown package he had received from Daniels. Even from a distance, Connolly could see Fontenot's smile.

Through the rear window of the truck, Connolly saw Fontenot pass the package to Mizell. As he did, he said something to Grafton. Grafton smiled in reply, and both men tucked their heads inside. The maroon truck moved first and started toward the road. Grafton followed them out of the parking lot.

Connolly put the Chrysler in gear and started forward. Ann grabbed his arm.

"What are you doing?"

Connolly did not reply. At the exit from the parking lot, he stopped and watched. The maroon pickup crossed the interstate bridge and turned left onto the entrance ramp. The green pickup continued straight.

"Any idea where he's going?"

"That road goes to a little place called the Rigolets. Kind of a no-man's-land between Lake Pontchartrain and the gulf."

"What's down there?"

"You better head for Mobile. You don't want to go where he's going."

"What's down there?"

"He has some cousins down there. They have a camp near Chef Menteur Pass. It ain't too pretty."

"What do you mean?"

She touched his arm once again, this time with a sense of kindness.

"It ain't got nothing to do with Steve Ingram. You better

drive us toward Mobile."

Connolly turned the Chrysler to the left out of the parking lot and drove across the bridge to the other side of the interstate. He hesitated a moment at the end of the bridge. Ann shook her head.

"Don't even think about it," she said, pointing to the left.

Reluctantly, Connolly turned the car onto the entrance ramp to the interstate. Ann leaned her head against the car door and closed her eyes. Connolly pressed the gas pedal. The Chrysler picked up speed.

"Where can I take you?"

"What time is it?"

Connolly checked his watch.

"Almost ten," he replied.

"Let me out at Johnny's Smokehouse. It's down the road a little from the Imperial Palace. You know where that is?"

"Yeah," Connolly chuckled. "I know where it is."

The Chrysler ran smoothly in the night air. Ann was soon asleep.

Johnny's Smokehouse was a legendary hangout. It sat off the highway in a grove of cypress trees down the road from the Imperial Palace. Originally a house, the building had been expanded, with rooms added in every direction. One end became a nightclub, the other a more pedestrian restaurant. It was a beer drinker's beer joint and a diner's delight. Everyone who came to the state line made it to the Smokehouse at least once before the night was over.

Sometime after midnight, Connolly eased the car off the highway and into the parking lot at the Smokehouse. In spite of the late hour, the lot was full. The sound of music drifted from the building.

He reached across the seat and shook Ann's shoulder.

"We're here."

She raised her head and looked around. She ran her fingers through her hair and checked her eyes in the rearview mirror.

"I'm a mess," she mumbled.

"Think you can find some place to stay tonight?"

She looked at him and smiled.

"Are you making a pass at me?"

"No." Connolly grinned. "I just didn't want to leave you stranded."

She checked the mirror again.

"I'll be all right."

The Chrysler rolled across the parking lot. Neon lights from a sign atop the building lit the night. Connolly brought the car to a stop near the door.

"Thanks for your help," he said.

"I didn't have much of a choice. My options were getting rather slim."

"Think those men will come back to your apartment?"

"I don't know." She reached for the door handle. "Catfish can sort all that out. I'm not going back there."

"Where will you go?"

"I don't know." She opened the door and stepped out. "You found me twice already. If you need me for anything, I imagine you can find me again."

She closed the car door and stepped away. Connolly watched as she crossed the parking lot. At the front door, she turned and gave him a quick wave, then disappeared inside.

Thirty-one

*T*he following morning, Connolly drove to the office before six. He was groggy from the late night, but he wanted to get there before Mrs. Gordon arrived.

He switched on the light and moved around her desk. A computer sat on a small table against the wall. He slid his hand along the side, located the power switch, and flipped it on. The machine began to whir as it booted up the operating program.

Connolly did not care much for computers, but Mrs. Gordon had insisted they get one. She took a class and learned enough to use it for word processing. Connolly disavowed it from the beginning and made a show of avoiding it at all costs. At night, however, when the office was empty, he read the owner's manual and taught himself enough to know how to read the files she created.

When the computer was ready, he took the computer disk Ann gave him the day before from his pocket and slid it into a slot on the front of the computer. Then, he found a word-processing program on the computer's menu screen he thought would allow him to read the files on the disk. He loaded the program and attempted to open the disk.

The directory for the disk indicated it contained three files, each one identified by a number. However, when he tried to open the files, he received an error message telling him the computer was unable to read the information. Again and again he tried to access the disk, but to no avail. Frustrated, he removed the disk from the computer, shoved it into his pocket, and turned off the machine.

He checked his watch. It was six o'clock. He turned off the office lights and stepped into the corridor outside. Downstairs, he walked up the street to the Port City Diner for a doughnut and a cup of coffee.

From downtown, Connolly drove to Peyton Russo's shop in Eight Mile. He parked the Chrysler in front and walked to the door. It was locked. Glancing around, he noticed a light in Peyton's house across the street. He started toward the house. As he moved up the front steps, Peyton opened the door.

"Hello, Mike."

"Hope it's not too early," Connolly replied.

"Getting a slow start today. Come on in."

Connolly stepped inside and followed Peyton to the living room.

"Trouble with your phones again?"

"No," Connolly replied. "I have a disk." He slipped the computer disk from his pocket and handed it to Peyton. "I tried to read it this morning on the computer at the office, but I couldn't get it to open the files. I was wondering if you could make sense of it."

"I'll give it a try," Peyton replied. "Come on back."

Peyton led him down the hall from the living room to an extra bedroom he had converted to an office. A desk sat across from the door. To the right was a small table with stacks of papers and magazines piled on top. A computer sat on a table to the left. More stacks of papers, files, and magazines sat on the floor.

"You'll have to excuse the mess," he said. "I've never been able to work without a lot of clutter."

Connolly smiled as he glanced around the room. Peyton

sat in a chair in front of the computer. He slid the disk into a slot on the computer, then opened a program.

"This is a basic word-processing program," he explained. "A little more sophisticated than what you have at your office, but not much."

The machine whirred, and then a message appeared on the screen. Connolly leaned over Peyton's shoulder.

"What's that mean?"

"The program can't read the disk. Whatever's on it is encrypted."

"Encrypted?"

"Like a code within a code," Peyton replied. "The information on this disk has been encoded, and then the encoded files have been encoded."

Connolly looked puzzled. Peyton gave him a faint smile.

"Don't worry. There are other options."

Peyton opened a second program.

"We ought to get somewhere with this."

The machine hummed as the program worked through the files. Peyton turned his chair to face Connolly.

"You want some coffee? This may take a few minutes."

"Sure," Connolly replied.

They walked to the kitchen. Peyton pointed to the kitchen table.

"Have a seat."

Connolly pulled a chair from the table and sat down. Peyton poured cups of coffee for them. He set a cup in front of Connolly and took a seat. They sipped the coffee in silence. The room became uncomfortably quiet. Finally, Peyton spoke.

"See much of Barbara these days?"

"A little. More than I did."

"Good," Peyton replied. "I always liked her." He took another sip of coffee. "How's Rachel?"

"Rachel is ... Rachel," Connolly sighed. "I don't think she hates me anymore."

"That's something, anyway. I saw her the other day. Had a baby with her. When did that happen?"

"Last year."

"What's her name?"

"Elizabeth."

Conversation lagged. They sipped coffee in silence.

"Come on," Peyton said. "Bring your cup. Let's see what the computer is doing."

When they returned to the office, a message box was displayed on the monitor screen. Peyton took a seat at the computer. Connolly looked over Peyton's shoulder.

"What's that mean?"

Peyton's face was clouded with a frown.

"Whatever program they used, it's not one that's commercially available."

Connolly backed away and leaned against the doorframe. He took a sip from his coffee cup.

"Anything else you can do?"

"Yeah," Peyton replied. "But it gets more difficult."

He opened another program.

"This program analyzes the files and then takes each piece of information and tries to make sense of it by trying different combinations. It's a program I wrote myself."

He seemed proud of it. Connolly had no idea what he was talking about. He did his best to look interested.

"Language follows a pattern," Peyton continued. "Most codes have patterns; they're just more complex. Takes a while to unravel them. This may take a day or two. Where'd you get the disk?"

Peyton seemed energized by the challenge. Already he had said more that morning than Connolly had heard him say in years.

"Picked it up from a witness. Why?"

"Just curious," Peyton shrugged. "Whatever's on here wasn't generated by a program anyone could buy at a local store. These files didn't come from some lawyer's office. My guess is it came from the government. Military probably."

"Military?"

"Yeah. Takes a long time to develop a really safe encryption system. Government's about the only one with enough money to do something like this."

"Any chance you can get into that disk?"

Peyton nodded.

"Probably. But it'll take a day or two."

"If you don't have time for this, I can do something else with it. I didn't mean to get you into some complicated project."

"I don't mind," Peyton smiled. "My curiosity is up now anyway. I'll call you and let you know what I find."

Peyton turned back to the computer. Connolly turned to leave, then paused at the door.

"You think it's safe?"

Peyton was puzzled.

"Huh?"

"The phone. You think it's safe?"

"The pay phone still working?"

"Yeah."

"As long as it's working, you're safe from the amateurs ... and most professionals I've ever known. Only way to tap a phone without anyone knowing is to go through the phone company. Takes a wiretap order to do that."

Connolly found a piece of scrap paper on the desk and jotted down a number.

"That's my cell phone. Call me on that if you need to get in touch with me."

He took his coffee cup to the kitchen and let himself out the front door.

Thirty-two

That afternoon, Connolly drove to Hollis' shack on Fowl River to tell him about the trip to New Orleans and about seeing Fontenot and Mizell. Hollis' pickup was parked out front when he arrived, but Hollis was not in sight. Connolly parked the Chrysler next to the pickup and got out.

The sky above was clear and blue. A breeze rustled through the tops of the pine trees. Seagulls called from the bayou a few yards away. In the distance, he could hear a motorboat farther downstream on the main part of the river. But there at the shack it was quiet—too quiet.

Connolly closed the car door and looked around. Something seemed wrong. It smelled wrong, too. He called out.

"Hollis!"

There was no response. He shouted again.

"Hollis!"

On bright, clear days like this, Hollis often could be found reclining on the pier, mending a net or dozing in the shade. As Connolly rounded the corner of the shack, he expected to find Hollis sitting in his usual spot. Instead, he was surrounded by a swarm of black flies. They darted around his face, bumped against the back of his neck, and tried to land around his mouth. He swatted at them with both hands and circled to the right, his eyes switching from side to side in search of what attracted the flies. He didn't have to look far.

Between the shack and the bayou, Hollis' cooking pot lay on its side on the ground. Scattered around it were uncooked fish, a few potatoes, and a couple of ears of corn. The fish were dried and stiff, their tails curled up in the air. Kernels on the corn were shriveled and dehydrated from lying in the sun.

Now he was worried.

"Hollis!" he shouted. "Hollis! Where are you?"

An ice chest lay in the weeds near the pier. Its lid, torn loose from the chest, was stuck in the branches of a pine sapling at the edge of the marsh grass. The gill net that usually hung from the scrub oaks near the water was gone. Hollis' boat was there, tethered by a single line at the end of the pier.

"Hollis!" he shouted once more.

Again, there was no response. He turned away to check inside the shack. As he did, he heard a faint groaning sound. He stopped and listened. Overhead, a light breeze whispered through the tops of the pines. Two trees behind the shack rubbed against each other, making a faint creaking sound. He did his best to listen past them for what he thought he'd heard. The breeze subsided. After a moment, he took another step toward the shack.

As his foot struck the ground, he heard the groaning sound again. This time, louder. It seemed to be coming from somewhere near the water. He stepped onto the pier. To the left, he saw the gill net rolled and stuffed in a tangled wad lying at the water's edge. Three fingers protruded from between the black strands of netting.

Connolly scrambled off the pier and thrashed through the weeds. Two steps beyond the pier, he mired knee-deep in sticky, black mud. The sharp ends of the stiff marsh weeds jabbed him in the arms as he struggled to keep his balance and lift his feet. He slid one foot free, only to see it buried in the mud a few inches away when he tried to lift the other. A few steps farther he lost a shoe, sucked off by the mucky, thick goo. Finally, he lay on his stomach, pulled his legs free, and crawled the last few yards.

Hollis lay facedown at the edge of the bayou, his head inches from the water. All but one leg was wrapped in the gill net. Though he had managed to work three fingers free, his arms were pinned to his side. Wound tightly around him, layer after layer of net covered his body from head to toe.

Connolly rolled him carefully onto his back. Hollis groaned.

Through the tangled net, Connolly could see his face was little more than a lump of red, bleeding meat. His eyes were swollen shut. His nose, broken and bruised, was buried in his swollen cheeks. His lips were parched and cracked. Strands of net cut deep into his skin. Blood oozed from every part of his face and neck. Connolly swallowed hard and struggled to keep from vomiting.

"Hollis," he whispered, "what happened?"

Hollis moaned in reply. His lips moved, but he was unable to form intelligible words. Connolly touched his shoulder.

"Shhh. Lie still. I'll get you out."

He took hold of the net at Hollis' shoulders and pulled him farther out of the water. Then, he slipped into the bayou and swam over to the pier. He pulled himself out of the water and ran to the shack.

Inside, the room was a mess. Hollis' cot lay on its side to the right of the door. A table that normally sat in the middle of the room stood on its end against the wall to the left. A wooden chair lay in pieces nearby. Clothes, cans, and everything else was scattered about the floor. Connolly stepped across the room to the cot and stripped the sheets off the mattress. He kicked through the debris on the floor and found a butcher knife, then dashed out the door.

From the shack, he ran back to the pier. Holding the sheets above his head to keep them out of the water, he jumped into the bayou and waded back to Hollis. When he reached him, he tossed the sheets onto the marsh grass and moved down to Hollis' feet.

Using the butcher knife, he cut the net away from Hollis' legs and worked up to his waist. He continued up his torso, cutting the net with one hand and peeling it away with the other.

Hollis lay quiet as Connolly worked to free him, but when he reached his chest, he groaned. Connolly laid the knife aside and carefully slipped his hand under Hollis' shirt. Touching him lightly, he felt along the right side of Hollis' rib cage. Near the middle, his fingers moved over a knot along one of the bones.

"It's broken," he whispered. "Good thing it's sticking out and not in."

He took the knife once more, this time working to free the net from Hollis' neck. Blood oozed from his skin as Connolly pulled the strands away.

As slow as the process had been, removing the net from around Hollis' face was even more delicate. Strands of it were buried in his skin. Connolly pulled some free, then decided it was better to leave them in place until help arrived. He cut away the excess but left the worst areas untouched. When he had pulled the last from around Hollis' face, he draped one of the sheets over him. He folded the other for a pillow and slipped it under Hollis' head.

"Okay. I'm going up to my car and call for help. Lay still and don't try to move."

Once again, Connolly waded into the bayou and swam to the pier. As he climbed out of the water, he noticed Hollis' boat. Out of the corner of his eye, he saw something sloshing in the bottom. Flies hovered around it. He took two steps toward the boat, then stopped.

The water sloshing in the boat was dark brown. A foul stench stung his nose and made his stomach rumble. The seats of the boat were stained with smears of blood. In an instant, he realized what had happened.

Whoever attacked Hollis must have beat him senseless and rolled him in the net. They carried him to the boat, bound and unconscious, and used it to dump him in the bayou to drown. Hollis had survived by swimming to shore, wrapped in a fishing net, using only his one free leg. Connolly shook his head at the thought. He turned aside, ran up the pier and around the shack to the car.

When he reached the Chrysler, he jerked open the car door and grabbed his cell phone from the seat. Dripping wet, his fingers trembled as he tried to dial the number to call for help. A breeze blew against his soaked clothes, sending a shiver through his body. Finally, he reached an emergency operator.

An hour passed. Then two. Finally, a sheriff's deputy arrived in a jeep. Not long after that, a rescue squad from Alabama Point showed up in a four-wheel-drive Suburban. They took Hollis to Providence Hospital in Mobile. Connolly remained behind to give the deputy a statement. No one seemed to believe what he had to say.

Thirty-three

Connolly spent the night at the guest house, lying in bed, staring at the ceiling, and trying to think of something besides getting drunk. He finally got to sleep around three the next morning.

When he awakened, the sun was already up. He checked the clock. It was almost ten.

He rolled out of bed and stumbled to the shower. An hour later, he was dressed and ready, but he had no desire to go to the office. He thought about going to see Hollis, but he was in the intensive care unit and still sedated. Instead, he drove to Peyton Russo's house in Eight Mile to check on progress with the computer disk. Peyton hadn't called, but Connolly was curious to know what he had found.

The drive to Russo's house took twenty minutes. He parked the Chrysler in front of the shop and walked to the door. As he reached for the doorknob, he noticed the door was ajar. He pushed it open and stepped inside. The room smelled like burnt popcorn.

"Peyton," he called. "You in here?"

No one answered.

Equipment was stacked along the wall all the way around the room. Several cardboard boxes sat on the floor. Magazines and papers were piled on one of the boxes. The room was cluttered and dusty, but nothing seemed out of place or

changed since he had been there to talk to Peyton about the
office telephones.

Connolly walked across the room and through a doorway to
the back where Peyton had been working before. A fluorescent
shop light glowed over the workbench. The burnt smell was
stronger. In the shadows at the far end of the bench he saw the
red glow of the light on the coffeepot. He lifted the lid. The pot
had boiled dry. Smoke rose from the charred remnants of coffee in the bottom of the pot. Connolly unplugged it and
replaced the lid.

He left the shop and walked across the street to Peyton's
house. At the top of the front steps, he rang the doorbell and
waited. When no one answered, he knocked on the door. As
he rapped on the door with his knuckles, the door came open.
He pushed it back and stuck his head inside.

"Peyton," he called. "You home?"

There was no reply. He eased the door open farther and
stepped inside. Two steps into the living room, a foul odor
enveloped him. His stomach muscles revolted in a visceral
reaction. He bent over, gagging and coughing, and covered his
nose and mouth with one hand. With the other hand, he
pawed at his hip pocket for a handkerchief. He pulled it out
and pressed it against his face. It gave him a moment's relief
but did little to mask the smell.

Still doubled over, he rested his free hand on his knee and
forced himself to relax. After a few moments, he managed to lift
his head to a stooped position. He crossed the room to the hall.

From the corner, he could see the door to Peyton's office
was open. Through the doorway, he saw an overturned chair
lying on the floor. Beside it, he saw someone's arm, visible
almost to the shoulder from where he stood. A dark, thick
stain of dried blood covered the carpet around the arm. He
moved to the far side of the hallway and inched closer. The
stench grew more intense with each step.

Connolly doubled over again in a gut-wrenching heave. He swallowed hard and slumped against the wall. Unwilling to stop, he forced himself closer to the office door.

A few feet farther, he craned his neck to peek around the door for a look inside the office. Peyton lay on the floor, his legs curled close to his body, his knees against his chest in a fetal position. His head rested on his outstretched arm. The handle of an ice pick protruded from his skull behind his right ear. Connolly moved carefully through the doorway.

The room, normally cluttered anyway, was in complete disarray. A computer monitor lay in the far corner, its screen broken, the case in splinters. Books, torn in two at the spine, were strewn about the room. The table on which the computer sat lay on its side to the left of the door. A file cabinet leaned precariously against the window, drawers open, contents scattered. Pieces of a small wooden bookcase lay under Peyton's hip.

Connolly stepped over Peyton's body to the center of the room. To the right was a large, gaping hole in the wall. On the floor beneath it was a pile of papers and file folders, most of it from the filing cabinet.

Using his foot, Connolly raked aside some of the clutter on the floor near the hole in the wall. Underneath the debris, he found the central processing unit for the computer. One corner of its metal case was dented. The top was bent and buckled. He pushed it around with the toe of his shoe and found the slot for the drive on the front of the unit. He squatted beside it and pressed the eject button. There was nothing in the drive.

Still squatting, he turned on his heels toward Peyton's body. Holding the handkerchief to his face, he reached with his free hand toward the hip pocket of Peyton's pants. He gently touched the pocket with the tip of his finger and pressed it against the fabric. As awful as it was, he had to find the computer disk. He felt nothing inside the pocket. Frustrated, he glanced around the room.

"There's no way to find that disk in this mess," he whispered.

The hand holding the handkerchief slid from his face. For a moment, he forgot the smell and took a deep breath. The sour smell of dead flesh rushed into his nostrils. His stomach revolted.

Gagging and coughing, Connolly stumbled over Peyton's body and staggered through the doorway. In the hall, he rested both hands on his knees. Once again, he struggled to keep from vomiting.

With his head bent over, his eyes focused on the carpet. For the first time, he noticed a dark red stain outside the office. Round, and several inches in diameter, it looked like blood. He lifted his eyes and scanned down the hall. A trail of dark stains ran toward the living room. Connolly wiped his mouth with the handkerchief and followed the stains up the hall. At the corner, the stains led him to the left, past the living room and into the kitchen.

At the kitchen door, the carpet ended. White linoleum tile covered the kitchen floor. A round table sat in the middle of the kitchen. Once a pale yellow, the top was now dark red, covered in dried blood. The floor around it was covered as well. Connolly sagged against the wall.

Footprints tracked through the blood and across the floor between the table and the kitchen counter. Outlined in dried blood, the prints led to the back door. Connolly stared in disbelief at the room, overwhelmed by the scene of what had been an unspeakable horror.

As he leaned against the wall outside the kitchen, an image flashed before him. In his mind, he saw Peyton lying on his back across the kitchen table. A man stood behind him, holding Peyton's arms from the back side of the table, pinning them against the table behind his head. Peyton's feet dangled in the air, inches above the floor.

A second man stood near Peyton's feet. He glowered over Peyton, his face twisted and contorted in a snarl. Connolly heard both men shouting. Their words were unintelligible, yet so real and vivid he jumped at the sound.

As the scene played before him, the man standing near Peyton's feet turned aside and jerked open a cabinet drawer. In it, he found an ice pick. With an eerie smile, the man turned toward Peyton. Peyton struggled to get free. The man behind him fought to hold him in place.

The man in front of him stepped to the table and plunged the ice pick into Peyton's thigh all the way to the handle. Peyton's body wrenched to one side. He screamed in pain. The man withdrew the ice pick, then shoved it in his thigh again.

Peyton turned to one side and kicked with his free leg. His foot landed in the crotch of the man with the ice pick. The ice pick slipped from his hand as he staggered backward and crashed into the kitchen counter.

There were more angry shouts. The man standing behind him held his arms tightly against the tabletop and did his best to keep Peyton pinned in place. The man in front grabbed the ice pick from the floor and lunged toward Peyton.

Connolly could stand no more. He squeezed his eyes tightly shut. He shook his head from side to side in an effort to get the images from his mind, but the images wouldn't go away.

As though he was actually present, he saw Peyton lying on his back on the kitchen table, the ice pick planted in his skull behind his ear. Peyton's body slid feet first toward the floor. He watched as Peyton dropped to the floor and flopped on his side near the doorway. Then, with great effort, Peyton pulled himself toward the end of the counter. A few feet from the kitchen door, he slipped his hand in his pants pocket and took out the computer disk. With one final effort, he shoved the disk behind the garbage can that sat at the end of the counter, and then his head dropped to the floor.

When Connolly opened his eyes, his gaze fell on the plastic garbage can that sat a few feet away. A handful of brown paper grocery bags were neatly folded and tucked between the garbage can and the end of the kitchen counter. Stretching from the doorway, he nudged the garbage can aside with his foot. The grocery bags fell to the floor. The computer disk Ann Grafton gave him tumbled out. It landed on the floor near a puddle of dried blood.

Connolly took a step forward into the kitchen and bent over to pick it up. As he did, the fingers of his right hand brushed against the blood stain on the tile. It was tacky to touch. The tips of his fingers were smudged with Peyton's blood. He lifted the computer disk from the floor and stared at his fingers.

Though it seemed like hours, it had taken only seconds to see what happened. As quickly as the image appeared, it vanished. But in that instant, Connolly knew his friend had died an excruciating, lingering death. And he knew it was all because of the computer disk he held in his hand.

He wiped the tips of his fingers with the handkerchief and slid the disk into the pocket of his jacket. From the kitchen, he retreated across the living room to the front door and slipped outside.

At the bottom of the steps, he took a deep breath. Fresh air flushed his lungs. The nausea in his stomach subsided. He took a step toward the Chrysler and stumbled. His knees shook. Beads of sweat formed across his forehead. He staggered to the Chrysler, opened the door, and collapsed on the front seat. After a few more deep breaths, he reached across the seat and picked up the cell phone. A moment later, he was talking to the police dispatcher.

Thirty-four

Within minutes, the street in front of Peyton Russo's house was clogged with emergency vehicles. Police from Mobile cordoned off the area. Detectives questioned Connolly, then began combing through the house for clues. Connolly watched from the front seat of the Chrysler, unable to shake the horrible images from his mind. Finally, as twilight drew near, Ted Morgan, the county coroner, led the way as they carried Russo's body, bundled in a black body bag, toward a waiting ambulance.

Morgan stopped at the Chrysler as they moved past.

"Sorry about your friend."

Connolly nodded.

"When did you get here?"

"Middle of the afternoon."

"You don't look so good. You going to be able to get home?"

"I'll take care of him," a familiar voice said.

Connolly turned to see Toby LeMoyne at the end of the car. Toby was a tall, broad-shouldered man with a sharp chin and an honest smile. His easygoing manner had made him Connolly's favorite among the deputy sheriffs. He stepped toward Connolly. Morgan moved away and climbed in the back of the ambulance. As Toby approached, a city detective passed the car.

"What you doing here?"

"Heard the call," Toby replied. "Wasn't far away. Came to see if I could help."

"You're not supposed to be anywhere near any of our cases," the detective snapped. "Not after what you did last time."

Toby smiled.

"I'm not messing with your case. Go on and do whatever it is you do. I'm not bothering you."

The detective muttered something under his breath and trudged toward the house. For the first time that afternoon, Connolly smiled.

"I guess we made a lot of friends with that Attaway case."

"Yeah. I guess so," Toby chuckled. "How you doing, Mr. Connolly? You need me to take you home?"

"Nah. I'll be all right."

"You've had a busy week."

"What do you mean?"

"Found Hollis Toombs in the nick of time. Came out here and found this." He gestured toward Russo's house. "What's going on?"

Connolly looked away. Toby persisted.

"What you know about the man in the house that you aren't telling?"

"They send you over here to interrogate me?"

"No. But I'm a curious man, and you've got my curiosity up. And besides, I'm your friend. You keep at it like you're going, whoever got Hollis and this man will get you, too."

Connolly sighed and shook his head. Toby brightened and tried a different angle.

"Come on to the house, Mr. Connolly. You can prop your feet on the coffee table. Merris will make you a stiff drink."

Connolly shot him a look.

"Okay," Toby said, waving both hands to acknowledge the look. "We won't have a drink. We'll talk. Maybe a glass of iced tea. Merris makes good tea."

Connolly did not respond. Toby leaned closer and lowered his voice.

"If you don't leave now, while you have the chance, one of these detectives is going to start asking you a bunch of questions you aren't anywhere near ready to answer."

Reluctantly, Connolly got in the Chrysler and closed the door. Toby walked to the street and climbed into a patrol car. Connolly backed the car down the drive and followed Toby away.

Connolly spent a few minutes at Toby's house, then drove downtown to St. Pachomius Church. The sun was setting as he climbed from the Chrysler and started up the steps to the front doors. He wasn't even sure the building would still be open.

At the top of the steps, he grasped the handle of one of the tall doors and pulled. To his surprise, the door swung open.

Inside the sanctuary, fading sunlight glowed through the stained-glass windows. A single light above the altar cast an arc over the altar rail, but the light faded into the shadows near the steps that led from the sanctuary floor to the chancel. The building was quiet and peaceful. The door banged shut behind him. Connolly felt cut off from the world outside, protected from all that had transpired.

He slipped into a pew near the chancel steps and leaned forward, resting his head on the back of the pew in front of him.

"Slide over," a voice said.

Connolly jerked his head up to see Scott Nolan, the rector, standing in the aisle beside him. He slid down the pew. Father Scott took a seat.

"Saw you come in. I was on my way out. Something wrong?"

"Yeah," Connolly replied.

"Tell me about it."

Connolly hesitated, unsure where to begin.

"Went to see my friend Peyton Russo today," Connolly replied. "You know him?"

"No," Father Scott said, shaking his head. "Never met him."

"I found him on the floor in his house. Dead. Been dead for a day or two."

"Um," Father Scott grunted. "What happened to him?"

"You ever ..." Connolly paused a moment, then continued. "You ever see things ... like in your mind. Things that maybe happened some place when you weren't there, but when you see it, it's like it's happening right then?"

"Uhh ... you mean like a vision or something?"

"I guess," Connolly said. He frowned, not quite sure he was able to make Father Scott understand. "But not nice stuff. This was bad."

"What do you mean?"

"I went to this guy's house. He was lying on the floor. Had an ice pick stuck in his skull. Blood every where. Place stunk. Made me sick."

Father Scott shook his head, a pained look on his face. Connolly continued.

"While I was standing there, these scenes started going through my mind. I could see these two guys holding him down on the kitchen table. Stabbing him with that ice pick. Stabbing him in the leg. He was hollering and kicking. He tried to fight. Then the one guy got mad and shoved the ice pick through his skull."

Father Scott grimaced.

"You think that's really what happened?"

"I don't know," Connolly replied. "That's what I'm asking."

"Is that all you saw?"

"No. I kept seeing things. I didn't want to see it. I tried to get it out of my mind. But these scenes kept coming. They left him in the kitchen. I thought he was dead, but while I watched ... I didn't really watch ... I mean ..." Connolly wiped his eyes. "He slid to the floor. Drug himself across the kitchen. Then he reached into his pocket and pulled out a computer disk. One of those little square ones." Connolly glanced at Father Scott. "It was mine. He was working on it for me. I had come there that day to get it from him." Connolly paused again. He took a deep breath and wiped his eyes. "So I see him there. In my mind, I see him lying on the floor. He took the disk out of his pocket and shoved it behind the garbage can. Then I realized that was why those men were there. They were looking for that disk."

"This disk, it was something important?"

"Yeah. I got it from somebody in this case I'm working on. He was trying to read it. Open the files on it."

"So what happened? Did you find the disk? I mean, after you saw it in your mind?"

Connolly slipped the disk from the pocket of his jacket and held it for Father Scott to see.

"Right where I saw him put it. Behind the garbage can."

Father Scott leaned back, resting his head on the back of the pew. He stretched his feet out straight in front of him.

"And I will pray the Father, and he will give you another Counselor, a *parakletos*, to be with you for ever, even the Spirit of truth."

"A *para* what?" Connolly looked puzzled. "What are you talking about?"

"John," Father Scott replied. "The Gospel of John."

Connolly shook his head.

"I guess I haven't read much of John."

"The Spirit of God was given to lead us into all truth."

The more Father Scott said, the more frustrated Connolly became.

"The Spirit of God? What's that got to do with this?"

Father Scott folded his hands in his lap.

"You remember when you came in here that day. And we were looking at the windows?"

Connolly nodded.

"We got to the altar and I prayed for you. You remember that?"

"Yes."

"The Spirit of God met us here that day. He is with you. In you."

"You know that for a fact?"

"I know it for a fact," Father Scott said. "And, more importantly, you do, too."

Connolly sighed and slid low in the pew.

"Look," Father Scott continued. "The Spirit of God was given to us to lead us into truth. Most people think that's just biblical truth. Scripture. But it's more than that. He came to lead us into *all* truth."

"What I saw didn't have much to do with church."

There was more than a hint of sarcasm in Connolly's voice.

"Exactly," Father Scott replied. He sat up straight. "But it had a lot to do with the truth. Sometimes, the truth isn't very pretty."

Connolly gestured with his hands in frustration.

"How do I know if what I saw was really what happened?"

Father Scott glanced at him with a knowing smile.

"Facts are never proved to a mathematic certainty, counselor. You've been a lawyer long enough to know that."

Connolly managed a smile. Father Scott continued.

"You found the disk, didn't you?"

"Yes," Connolly replied.

"Right where you saw it when you saw all this in your mind?"

"Yes."

Father Scott laid his hand on Connolly's shoulder.

"I'd say that's proof enough."

Thirty-five

Connolly pushed open one of the large doors at the rear of the sanctuary and stepped onto the portico outside. The sun was all but gone from the horizon behind him. The last rays of late-afternoon light filtered through the oak trees above the church. Long shadows stretched over the front steps and the sidewalk below. Afternoon was fading into evening. Soon, it would be night. A breeze blew up from the bay a few blocks to the south. It tousled Connolly's hair.

He made his way down the steps toward the Chrysler. In a somber mood, he let his mind wander back over the events of the past few days. Hollis lay in the hospital, unconscious, only beginning to recover. Peyton Russo was dead. Both men had been attacked because of their association with him.

He wondered aloud.

"Why didn't they just come to me?"

His feet plopped down the steps to the sidewalk. Seemingly without any connection to his train of thought, his mind turned to Rachel. Suddenly, a knowing sense of danger swept over him.

He scrambled around the front of the Chrysler and jumped inside, behind the steering wheel. He shoved the key in the ignition. The car came to life. He snatched the car in gear and pressed the accelerator to the floor. The tires squealed as the car shot forward.

He raced up Church Street and turned right. A block farther, he turned left onto Government Street. Weaving through traffic, he reached Ann Street in less than five minutes. The traffic light was red. He cut across the center line and moved into the oncoming lane. He made the turn from Government Street without waiting for the light. Moments later, the car slid to a stop in front of Barbara's house. Connolly leaped from the car and ran up the sidewalk.

He bounded up the front steps and grabbed the doorknob. The door was locked. He pounded it with his fist. Moments later, Barbara opened the door.

"What's the matter?"

"Where's Rachel?"

"Upstairs. With Elizabeth. Why?"

Connolly pushed past her.

"We have to go," he said.

"What do you mean?"

Connolly ignored her and moved down the hall.

"Rachel," he called.

He reached the stairs and started up. Rachel appeared at the top.

"Daddy, what are you doing?"

"We have to go. Get Elizabeth. Grab a few things. We have to leave."

Rachel looked past him to Barbara. Connolly glanced over his shoulder at her. The look on her face made his heart sink. He turned to Barbara.

"I'm not drunk," he argued. "People are coming here to get her. To get Elizabeth." He stepped closer to Barbara. "Look. Smell my breath." He exhaled in her face. "I'm not drunk."

Barbara stepped back.

"Who's coming?"

"I don't have time to explain," Connolly exclaimed.

"You just know they're coming."

Her voice was sharp and cutting.

"Look," he began, frustrated at the delay, frustrated with her lack of belief in him. "They tried to kill Hollis Toombs. He's lying in a bed out at Providence Hospital."

She seemed unfazed.

"Peyton Russo. You remember him?"

Barbara nodded.

"He's lying on a slab in the morgue."

"Peyton Russo," Barbara frowned. "What's he got to do with anything?"

"I'll explain while we drive."

Connolly turned back to Rachel.

"Get moving."

Rachel moved away from the stairs and disappeared down the upstairs hallway. Connolly turned to Barbara.

"You'd better come with us."

"You don't think she's going with you, do you?"

Barbara gave him a wry, sarcastic smile. Connolly felt a dagger slip into his soul.

"You don't believe me."

"I don't ..."

Barbara glanced to the top of the stairs. Connolly turned to see Rachel scurrying down the steps, one arm wrapped around Elizabeth, clutching an overnight bag. Barbara was taken aback. Connolly took the bag from Rachel and turned to Barbara.

"Coming?"

"I ..." Barbara started to reply, then stopped. Rachel glared at her. "Oh, all right." She took her purse from a table in the hall and followed them toward the door.

At the car, Connolly put Rachel and Elizabeth in the back-seat. Barbara sat up front. He started the engine and made a U-turn from the curb.

At Government Street, he brought the car to a stop and

waited for the traffic light. As he waited, he glanced to the right. A maroon pickup truck with oversized tires sat in the turn lane on Government Street. It was third in line behind two cars. In the faint glow of a street light, he saw Fontenot and Mizell sitting in the truck.

When the traffic light turned green, Connolly made a left turn onto Government Street. In the rearview mirror he saw the pickup truck pull out of line in the turn lane. The truck moved around slower traffic and picked up speed.

Connolly pressed the accelerator. The Chrysler responded with a surge of power.

Barbara glanced at him from the opposite side of the front seat.

"I'd rather not die in a wreck."

Connolly nodded over his shoulder. Barbara turned to look out the back window.

"See that pickup?"

Barbara watched for a moment, then turned to face forward.

"What about it?"

"Those are the men who tried to kill Hollis."

She gave him a skeptical frown. Her willingness to believe him had been tested far too many times in the past to give in without good reason now.

"How do you know that?"

"I know them," Connolly replied.

"You know those men?"

"We followed them to a dogfight in Hurley."

"We?"

"Hollis and I."

The frown on Barbara's face disappeared.

"What do we do?"

Connolly glanced in the rearview mirror once again.

"Slide a little lower in your seat," he said. "And hold on."

Suddenly, the pickup hit them from behind. The force of

the collision threw them forward in the seat. Rachel squealed and grabbed for Elizabeth. Barbara caught herself with her hands as she slammed against the dash. Connolly banged his chin against the steering wheel. He pressed the gas pedal closer to the floor. The car sped forward.

They raced out of midtown, moving west through the suburbs. Behind them, the maroon pickup truck was only inches from the Chrysler's bumper.

A few miles farther, the broad avenue that had been Government Street became a two-lane highway. The crowded city gave way to open countryside. Green fields and lush pecan orchards lined both sides of the road. Connolly glanced in the mirror again. The truck was still behind them.

He pressed the gas pedal all the way to the floor. Fences and telephone poles whizzed by in a blur. The dotted yellow line in the center of the road melted into a single yellow stripe, then seemed to disappear altogether. Running at full throttle, the Chrysler felt light, as if it were floating. The pickup truck was still behind them, but they were pulling away.

They passed the Handy Pak in Irvington and moments later blew past Webster's Motel and the racetrack. Just beyond the track was Argyle Road.

"Get a grip on something," Connolly warned.

Barbara clutched the armrest on the door. She looked scared.

"Why? What's happening?"

Connolly glanced over his shoulder. Rachel held Elizabeth against her chest, her arms wrapped tightly around her.

A few yards from Argyle Road, Connolly lifted his foot from the gas pedal. The nose of the Chrysler dropped. The engine rumbled as it backed off. The pickup truck closed on their bumper again. At the last moment, Connolly made the turn onto Argyle Road. As soon as the weight of the car shifted, he pressed the pedal to the floor. The car drifted through the turn. The tires on the right side hit the shoulder of the road. Dirt flew in the air. Just when it seemed the car would slide into the ditch, the tires on the left side gripped the pavement. The Chrysler shot down Argyle Road at full speed.

Fontenot and Mizell tried to follow in the pickup. When the Chrysler turned, Fontenot yanked the steering wheel violently to the left. The Chrysler, built much lower to the ground, made the turn in a cloud of dust and tire smoke. The pickup truck, sitting high above the road on oversized tires, didn't have a chance.

Connolly watched in the mirror as the left side of the truck rose into the air halfway through the turn. The truck made a lazy, slow roll to the right and came to rest in an upright position twenty yards off the road. Steam and smoke billowed from beneath the hood of the truck. Connolly eased his foot from the gas pedal. The Chrysler slowed. He took a deep breath and relaxed his grip on the steering wheel. His right hand began to shake. He wiped his palm on the leg of his trouser and looked across at Barbara. She was turned sideways in the seat, fussing over Elizabeth and still watching behind them. She glanced back at him.

"Where do we go now?"

"Uncle Guy's," he replied.

Thirty-six

By the time they reached Bayou La Batre, darkness had fallen. Connolly turned the Chrysler into the driveway at Guy's and brought it to a stop near the kitchen door at the side of the house. Lights were on in the kitchen. Guy came out to greet them.

"Barbara." He put an arm around her. "It's been a long time." He kissed her on the cheek.

Rachel climbed from the backseat with Elizabeth in her arms. Guy moved past Barbara, grinning. Rachel glanced at Barbara, unsure what to do. Barbara nodded toward the old man. Rachel handed him the baby. He cuddled her in the crook of his arm.

"We ought to get inside," Connolly said.

Guy turned toward the house and started up the steps, still holding Elizabeth. Barbara and Rachel followed him. Connolly lingered near the car.

A few minutes later, Guy emerged from the house. Connolly leaned against the front fender of the car.

"Trouble?"

"Yeah," Connolly replied. "Can they stay here a few days?"

"You know you don't have to ask that, son. Glad to have them. What are you going to do?"

Connolly glanced down the drive toward the road.

"I'm not sure. But I think I'll begin with Harvey Bosarge."

"Harvey Bosarge," Guy snorted. "Not sure I'd want him for a client."

Connolly opened the car door.

"Listen, the guys who are causing the trouble are in a maroon Chevrolet pickup. Big thing. Four-wheel drive. Big knobby tires. If they come around here—"

"I know what to do," Guy said, interrupting. "You just make sure you watch out for yourself."

With Rachel and Barbara settled, Connolly made his way through town. He followed the road around the opposite side of the bayou to Bosarge's house. The front porch light was on when he arrived, but the rest of the house was dark. Connolly parked the Chrysler near the front steps and got out.

Stars dotted the night sky above. Behind him, he heard the gentle sound of waves lapping on the shore of the bay fifty yards away. He turned to the house and made his way to the porch. He banged on the front door with his fist and waited.

In a moment, the door opened a little way. Bosarge peered through the opening. Dressed in a tattered and wrinkled robe, he had a three-day growth of beard, and his hair was disheveled.

"Kind of late for a house call," he grumbled.

Connolly looked at him, trying to decide whether he was sleeping or drunk.

"We need to talk," he said.

Bosarge cleared his throat and wiped his mouth with the back of his hand.

"Can't it wait 'til tomorrow?"

"No," Connolly replied. "We need to talk now."

Bosarge cleared his throat again.

"All right," he said. "Give me a minute."

He closed the door. Connolly moved away and sat in a rocking chair nearby. In a few minutes, Bosarge emerged from the house, wearing the robe over a T-shirt and shorts.

He waddled across the porch and took a seat in a chair next to Connolly.

"What's so important?"

Connolly had to work to control the anger that now boiled inside.

"Mizell and Fontenot came looking for my family today."

"Who?"

"The two men in the pictures," Connolly replied. His tone was short and terse. "The ones I showed you the other day. At the Catalina."

"Oh. That their names? Mizell and Fron—"

"Fontenot."

"Those two are no good," Bosarge grumbled. He took a labored breath before continuing. "Everybody all right?"

"Yeah," Connolly sighed. "They're fine."

"Good."

Bosarge slipped his hand in one of the pockets of his robe and took out a bottle of whiskey. He unscrewed the cap and took a gulp, then offered the bottle to Connolly. Connolly waved him off in disgust.

"What are you doing?"

"Drinking." Bosarge took another drink. "Seems like the thing to do."

He slipped the bottle back in the pocket of his robe. Connolly shifted positions in the chair and leaned against the armrest on the opposite side.

"Who hired you to follow Ann Grafton?"

"Who hired me?"

"Yes."

"I already told you," Bosarge replied. "Tommy Grafton."

Connolly shifted in the chair again and leaned toward Bosarge. His voice was calm but determined.

"Harvey, you wouldn't know Tommy Grafton if he walked up here right now."

Bosarge looked indignant.

"Sure I would."

"Okay," Connolly chided. "Describe him."

"Well, he's ... kind of hard to describe."

"Blond hair?"

"Yeah. Well ... no."

"You don't know him. You've never even seen him." Connolly leaned over the arm of the chair closer. He smelled the liquor on Bosarge's breath. "Now, who hired you?"

Bosarge looked away. Connolly became impatient.

"Hollis Toombs is in the hospital because of Grafton," he argued. "Peyton Russo is dead because of him." His voice grew louder. His finger jabbed the air with each phrase. "My family has been threatened. Now I want to know. Who hired you?"

Bosarge stared ahead into the darkness beyond the porch.

"Frank," he mumbled.

"Who?"

"Frank. Frank Ingram."

The answer caught Connolly by surprise. He took a moment to recover. While Connolly thought about it, Bosarge took a cigar from the pocket of the robe and shoved it in his mouth. He took a match from his pocket and lit the cigar.

"Why did he hire you?"

"Wanted me to follow the woman." Bosarge took a few puffs on the cigar to make sure it was burning well. "Ann. Ann Grafton."

"Why was he interested in her?"

"I don't know. I guess he still had a thing for her."

"Still had a thing for her? He was seeing her?"

"After a fashion," Bosarge said, gesturing with the cigar.

"What do you mean?"

Bosarge took another puff of the cigar.

"He hired me to take pictures. You know. The video camera in the bedroom. That sort of thing."

"Pictures?"

"Yeah. Pictures. You know. Photographs. Videos. Whatever I could get."

"That's why you had the camera in the bedroom?"

"Yeah."

"He hired you to take pictures of her in bed with Steve?"

Bosarge grinned and nodded. He took another puff of the cigar. Connolly was disgusted.

"Pictures of her in bed with his own brother?"

Bosarge nodded once more.

"A weird bunch of folks."

"How long was the camera in there?"

"Couple of months."

"What happened to the videos?"

"Gave a copy to Frank."

"You kept a copy."

"Had a copy of all of them."

"Had? What happened to them?"

"FBI guys took them when they did their search."

Connolly was taken aback once again.

"The videos were in the garage?"

"Yeah."

"How many tapes are we talking about?"

"Boxes."

"Boxes?"

"Boxes."

Connolly rolled his eyes and gave a gesture of frustration with his hands.

"Why didn't you tell me this?"

Bosarge took the cigar from his mouth. He looked Connolly in the eye.

"What was I going to say? I got a garage full of videos, some of them rather explicit, taken with a camera I hid in somebody else's house. They got laws against that kind of thing, you know. Burglary. Eavesdropping."

Connolly glanced away.

"Why did the FBI take them and not list them on their inventory?"

"Who knows?"

"They can't use them now as evidence of anything."

"Maybe they didn't want to use them," Bosarge suggested. "Maybe that's why they came down here in the first place. Maybe they came and got them like that, so nobody could use them."

"What was on them?"

"Steve and Ann in bed, mostly."

"Mostly?"

"Frank was in one or two of them, I think. I don't know. I didn't watch many of them. Kind of gross. I just kept the thing running. Changed the tapes. I only made the copies because it seemed like a good idea at the time."

"Anybody else on the tapes?"

"Nah ... yeah. There was one guy. I don't know him."

"He was with Ann?"

"No. He was in there by himself. Looked like he was just plundering around."

"Daniels."

"No," Bosarge replied. "Not Daniels. I know him. He'd be pretty easy to spot." He took a puff from the cigar and thumped the ashes on the floor. "I'm not too sure those guys with Hammond were FBI. I figure they were guys Frank sent to get the tapes because he was worried about blackmail."

"Nah. He wouldn't have gone to the trouble of doing all that. Hammond said they had an informant. Maybe you had a picture of him."

"Maybe," Bosarge nodded. "Maybe."

Thirty-seven

*C*onnolly left Harvey's house and drove toward Mobile. With the windows down, the damp night air blew through the car. The Chrysler's engine ran smooth and quiet. Outside, the drive seemed peaceful, but inside Connolly's mind there was chaos. What he'd learned from his conversation with Harvey left him confused. Most of what he thought he knew about this case was now up in the air.

For one thing, the players all seemed to be moving in different directions now. Grafton, Fontenot, Mizell, and Frank Ingram couldn't be more different. One, a group of rednecks living in squalor and fighting dogs for entertainment. The other, the wealthy head of a company doing business around the world. And then there was Daniels. Whatever was going on, he was in it to the hilt. Add to all of that Harry Giles, Greg Drummond, Perry Loper, and Anthony Hammond, and the whole thing became unmanageable.

Connolly tugged at his hair.

"I need a diagram to keep it all straight."

Lost in thought, he reached Mobile in no time at all. Streetlights bathed the pavement in soft light. He found himself glancing in the rearview mirror every few minutes, checking to make sure no one was following. At Tuttle Street, he slowed and made a left turn. Two blocks later, he turned into the driveway at the Pleiades. The car came to a stop beside the guest house. Connolly switched off the engine and went inside.

In the living room, he tossed the car keys on the coffee table, threw his jacket across the back of the couch, and collapsed in an overstuffed chair. He propped his feet on the table, closed his eyes, and tried to relax. The day had been long, stressful, and tiring, exactly the kind of day he had always ended with a drink. As he sat there, he remembered an evening not unlike this, before things got out of hand, before he went off the deep end. He'd come home exhausted. Barbara met him in the hall with a drink. Something she called blueberry gin. Sweeter than he normally liked, but cold and refreshing. They sat alone in the den and drank two martini shakers of the ...

He rubbed his hands over his face and did his best to think of something else. Moments later, the thought returned. Aggravated with himself for even thinking of a drink, he stood and kicked off his shoes. Perhaps a long, hot bath would help him unwind.

As he moved toward the hall, he noticed a scent in the room. Not quite sweet, but fresh and alive. He sniffed the air. The fragrance seemed familiar, but he couldn't remember what it was or where he had smelled it before.

Suddenly, headlights washed across the living-room wall. He stepped to the front window. A pickup truck moved up the driveway toward the guest house. Behind it, a second truck entered the drive. The headlights on both went out, but even in the dark he recognized them. The first one was Fontenot and Mizell. The second was Tommy Grafton.

Connolly turned away from the window. Fear rose inside him and threatened to overwhelm him. He pushed it aside as best he could and forced himself to focus on the situation at hand.

The guest house had only one door. It opened to the

parking area outside. The Chrysler was parked a few feet away. He was certain he could reach the car before they reached him, but he knew Fontenot would block him before he could get to the street. He grabbed his shoes and ran down the hall to the bathroom.

A small window was located above the tub. He opened it and hauled himself up and out through it. As he tumbled to the ground outside, he heard someone kick open the front door. He jumped to his feet and ran away from the house into the bushes behind the garden. There, he hid and watched.

A bedroom light came on. Through the window, he saw Mizell and Grafton moving around inside. Even from a distance he could hear them rummaging through the closet and the dresser drawers. Their voices were loud, almost shouting, but he couldn't make out what was said.

Suddenly, he remembered the computer disk. His heart sank. It was in the pocket of his jacket. The jacket was lying on the couch.

Just then, Mizell appeared at the far corner of the house. Fontenot came out a moment later. Connolly slipped through the bushes to the garden and hurried past the fountain to the gardener's shack on the far side of the property. Quietly, he eased open the door and slipped inside. He worked his way into a corner of the building and propped a wheelbarrow in front of him to shield him from view.

Outside, he heard Fontenot and Mizell thrashing through the garden.

"Check in that shack," Grafton called.

Connolly's heart skipped a beat.

Footsteps shuffled closer. His heart pounded against his chest. The door to the building flung open with a bang. Connolly jumped. Someone stepped inside. A moment later, he heard a loud whack, followed by a string of cusswords rolled together in one long biological impossibility. Then he heard Mizell's voice.

"What's wrong with you?"

"I stepped on a rake," Fontenot shouted. "Handle hit me in the head."

Mizell laughed.

"I'm glad you think it's funny," Fontenot retorted.

Connolly peered around the edge of the wheelbarrow in time to see Fontenot break the rake handle across Mizell's shoulder. Mizell continued to laugh. They drifted across the garden, Fontenot rubbing his forehead, Mizell laughing.

After a while, he heard the trucks. From the sound of it, he was sure Fontenot had spun a doughnut in the grass outside the guest house before he left. He waited in the gardener's shack as the sound of the trucks moved down the driveway and faded up the street. When he was certain they were gone, he moved from his hiding place and stepped outside.

The lights were still on in the guest house. As he drew closer, he could see through the window that the bedroom had been torn apart. He walked to the far end of the house. The door dangled from its hinges, splintered at the lock. He glanced to the left. The couch lay upside down against the coffee table in the center of the living room. He stepped through the doorway and lifted the couch to an upright position. To his amazement, his jacket lay on the floor underneath. He picked it up and checked the inside pocket. The computer disk was still inside. He switched off the lights and went outside to the Chrysler.

From the guest house, Connolly headed west, away from town. At the Loop, he turned right onto Airport Boulevard and drove to Providence Hospital. It was almost ten when he turned into the parking lot. Visiting hours had already ended. He drove around back and parked near the emergency room.

Double doors led from a covered entrance outside to a wide hallway that ran past a small waiting room. Connolly entered the building through the double doors. He walked to the hall, avoiding eye contact with nurses and staff in the waiting room. No one paid him any attention. At the end of the hall he turned left and followed the signs to the elevator. He stepped inside and pressed the button for the tenth floor.

When the doors opened, he stepped out of the elevator and found himself standing in front of a nurse's station. No one noticed as he moved past the station. He read the numbers on the doors as he walked down the hall and located room 1005. He pushed the door open and went inside.

Hollis lay in bed to the left of the door. On one side was a stand holding a bag of solution connected to the back of his hand by a long plastic tube. On the other was a monitor with wires running to electrodes affixed to various locations on his torso.

Connolly stared at him. Hollis looked better than when he pulled him from the bayou, but his face still was bruised and swollen. His eyes were thin slits in the middle of his face. Connolly couldn't tell whether they were open or closed.

"You just going to stand there?"

Hollis spoke in a hoarse whisper. The sound of his voice made Connolly smile.

"Thought you were asleep."

"I was, until you showed up." Hollis cleared his throat. "I thought visiting hours were over."

The sight of Hollis lying there in bed struck Connolly in an unexpected way. His eyes became full.

"I ... I never thought they'd ..."

Connolly turned away, on the verge of tears.

Hollis cleared his throat again.

"I ain't mad at you," he said. "If that's what you're worried about."

"You ought to be."

Hollis shrugged his shoulders.

"Stuff happens to everybody."

"Who did this to you?"

"I don't know. I ain't never seen them before."

"Fontenot and Mizell?"

"No. It wasn't them."

"Why?"

"Said they wanted that tape we took out of Ingram's house."

Connolly moved away from the bed and leaned against the wall near the window.

"Mizell and Fontenot paid me a visit tonight," he said.

"What happened?"

"They trashed the house. I saw them coming. Climbed out the window."

The conversation lagged. Neither man spoke for a moment. The room grew quiet. Hollis took a sip of water from a cup on the tray beside his bed. He grimaced as he tried to swallow.

"You all right?"

"Yeah," Hollis replied. "They had that net tied around my throat so tight, doctor said it crushed it inside." He took another sip and set the cup on the tray. "I'll tell you one thing. I think Bosarge is right in the middle of this."

"Nah. I don't think he's that smart." Connolly folded his arms across his chest. "More likely Harry Giles is calling the shots."

"Giles?"

Connolly nodded.

"Those pictures I had of Frank. The ones I made from the negative I found in Steve's bedroom. They were taken at a house in New Orleans. I found the house. Belongs to a guy named Perry Loper. Tommy Grafton was there. While I was watching, David Daniels showed up."

"Daniels?"

"Works for Giles. I followed Grafton to a truck stop in Slidell. Guess who met him there?"

"Our friends from Hurley?"

Connolly nodded.

"With Daniels involved, I figure Giles is right in there with them."

"Not Harry," Hollis said, shaking his head. "At least not the Harry I knew."

Connolly's mouth fell open.

"You know him?"

"Served with him in Vietnam. He was a colonel. Ran our battalion."

Connolly looked puzzled. The further he went with this case, the more he discovered how little he knew about the people around him.

"I never knew you knew him. You think he's one of the good guys?"

"Absolutely."

"Mrs. Gordon sure doesn't care for him."

"I reckon not."

"What do you mean?"

"Because of him and her sister."

"Do what?" Connolly was astounded. "I didn't even know she had a sister."

"For a hotshot lawyer, you sure don't pay close attention."

"What sister?"

"Carol," Hollis replied. "Your Mrs. Gordon's youngest sister. I never really met her. Just knew about her."

"So what about her?"

"Harry was married to Carol. Had two or three kids. Went

to Vietnam. Got involved with a woman in Saigon. I think she had a baby with him, I'm not sure. Very big stink, though. Marine Corps did not like it. Cost him the rest of his career. They let him finish out his time so he could get a pension, but he did it in Vietnam."

Connolly shook his head in disbelief.

"Whole family pretty much hates him," Hollis continued. "But he was a good soldier. That's what caused him all the trouble. If he'd just lied about it, wouldn't have been much to it. But when they asked him about the affair, he owned up to it."

Connolly shook his head.

"I've never heard any of this. I ... I don't know what to say."

"Not much to say," Hollis shrugged. "But if it's a choice between Harvey Bosarge and Harry Giles, I'll take Harry any day, any time."

Connolly moved around the bed to a chair along the far wall. He took off his jacket and sat in the chair. When he pushed against the back, a footrest popped out from underneath.

"You afraid to go home?"

"Yeah," Connolly replied.

"I hope you don't snore. I need to sleep. All this talkin's wore me out."

Connolly folded his jacket across his lap and closed his eyes. The room was quiet. In a few minutes he heard the easy sound of Hollis breathing in his sleep.

With his eyes closed, images of the evening came to Connolly's mind. It seemed like a long time ago now. Headlights on the wall in the guest house. Panic that seized his chest. The fragrance in the—

He sat forward in the chair.

Hollis awakened, startled by the noise of the chair folding up the footrest.

"What's the matter?"

"Cheap perfume," Connolly replied.

"What?"

Connolly stood and fumbled to put on his jacket.

"Cheap perfume. I smelled it in the house. Just before Fontenot showed up." He started toward the door. "She was there."

Thirty-eight

An hour later, Connolly turned the Chrysler off the highway into the parking lot at the Imperial Palace. The lot was almost empty. He glanced at his watch. It was one in the morning.

He parked the car near the front and got out. The parking attendants were gone. So were the doormen who normally greeted guests with a smile and a tip of the hat. Connolly walked across the parking lot to the main entrance, pulled open the door, and went inside. A lone bouncer stood at the doorway to the showroom. Connolly ignored his cold stare and brushed past him.

On the runway, the last dancer for the evening was finishing her routine. The showroom was all but empty. Music blared from speakers at either end of the stage, but with few people left in the room, the sound echoed off the walls, making the dance seem more like the charade it really was.

Connolly crossed the room toward the bar along the wall to the left. The bartender saw him coming and gave him a smile.

"Just like home," he called. "Can't stay away, can you?"

Connolly ignored him and moved down the bar toward the far end of the building. He kept a steady, deliberate pace. A door at the end of the building led to the performers' area behind the stage. A guard stood near the door, watching the dancer on the runway. Unnoticed, Connolly moved past him, opened the door, and stepped inside.

Beyond the door, dancers moved in and out of a long row of dressing rooms in the late-night shuffle that marked the end of their workday. No one paid him any attention. He moved through the crowd to a hallway that ran behind the stage. Doors along the hall led to a second row of dressing rooms. Down the row he came to one with Marisa's name painted on it. He opened the door without knocking.

Marisa sat at a dressing table, wearing a gold and red robe, facing the mirror, her back to the door. Her hair was down, falling about her shoulders. A cotton swab in one hand, she gently removed makeup from her face. She jerked her head around to see who had entered. There was a flash of anger in her eyes at the interruption. It vanished when she saw him.

"How'd you get back here?"

Connolly closed the door behind him.

"Where's Tommy Grafton?"

She turned away and faced the mirror.

"Who?"

He grabbed her arm and turned her toward him.

"Don't think I don't know ..."

He stopped in midsentence as his eyes fell on a bruise that darkened her left cheek. Her countenance fell when she saw the look on his face.

"Pretty, isn't it?"

He released his grip on her arm.

"What happened?"

She turned to the mirror again and continued removing her makeup.

"He hit me."

"Why?"

"'Cause I didn't want to tell him where you lived."

Connolly found a chair and moved it beside her. He sat backward in it, his arms folded along the top of the chair back.

"What were you doing at my house this afternoon?"

She turned on the stool to face him.

"I didn't know they were going to do all this. Okay?"

"Where is he?"

"I don't know. He left this afternoon. Told me he had to go to work."

"To work?"

"Yeah. He tells everybody he works on a rig offshore."

"But?"

She gave him a knowing look, then turned back to the mirror.

"He and his buddies have some big drug operation." She spoke between wipes as she continued to clean her face. "Think it's some big secret. Wonder they ain't been arrested before now." She wiped her face with a towel, then began brushing her hair. "Get the stuff out of Mexico."

"Mexico?"

She gave him an amused smile.

"Crazy, ain't it? Some redneck from Mobile doing business with a bunch of Mexicans."

"He goes to Mexico?"

"No," she laughed. "Tommy'd never do something like that. Too much like work. Mexicans get it to the oil rig. Tommy gets it from there."

"How's he manage that?"

"Got a friend who works for the people who handle the crew boats."

"How'd you find out all this?"

"Never underestimate the power of a woman." She gave him a soft, suggestive smile. "He's usually gone for weeks." She slid her foot up the leg of his trousers. The robe fell away, exposing her thigh. "You want to come over tonight?

I'll be out of here in a few minutes."

Connolly pushed her foot aside. She turned away in a huff.

"What were you doing at my house?"

She ran the brush through her hair. Connolly glared at her in the mirror. She gave him a frustrated sigh.

"He's just a place to stay," she said, exasperated.

He spun her around on the stool to face him again.

"You'd sell me out for just a place to stay?"

"Look. He told me to come over there and keep you occupied. I said no. He hit me a couple times, so I went over there. You weren't there. I left."

"When was the last time you saw him?"

"Tonight. About six. He left when I left for work."

Connolly stood and stepped toward the door. She turned toward the mirror and began brushing her hair.

"You want to ..."

Her voice trailed off behind him as he left the room.

Thirty-nine

*C*onnolly walked out of the Imperial Palace and across the parking lot to the Chrysler. The night air was humid and heavy. By the time he reached the car, his skin was damp. He slipped off his jacket and glanced toward the sky. It felt late. So late it already seemed early. Dawn wasn't far off. It was a time in the night he had always enjoyed. Too late to go home. Too early to worry about tomorrow.

He opened the car door and tossed his jacket on the front seat.

From the Imperial Palace, Connolly drove downtown. At Conception Street he turned right and made his way to Dauphin Street. Outside the Phoenix Club, a man dug through a garbage can, eating bits of food he found there. Someone was asleep on the bench in front of St. Alban Cathedral. Except for them, the streets were deserted.

Connolly parked the Chrysler in front of the office building and got out. With his jacket tucked under his arm, he started toward the lobby door. He stopped cold in the middle of the sidewalk. If Grafton and Fontenot were bold enough to come to his house, they wouldn't hesitate to come to his office. Instead of entering the building, he turned aside and walked up the street.

St. Alban Cathedral faced Cathedral Square, two blocks

past the Port City Diner between Dauphin and St. Francis Streets. Behind it were a courtyard and a garden surrounded by a high brick wall. At the far corner, an oak tree grew between the wall and the sidewalk. Its branches reached almost all the way across the garden. Connolly made his way up the street to the garden wall.

He stood beneath the tree and stared up at the trunk, calculating how he might climb to the first limb that hung over the wall. Assuring himself it wasn't far, he laid his jacket across his shoulder, held the collar between his teeth, and placed his foot against a knot that protruded from the trunk about two feet off the ground. He pushed himself up and dug his fingers into a crack in the bark, then found a place for his other foot. Slowly, he worked his way up to the limb. When he reached it, he wrapped both arms around it and swung his feet free. He dangled above the garden, clinching his jacket with his teeth. As he hung there, the limb now seemed much higher than it had when he thought this was a good idea.

Sooner than he expected, his arms began to ache. He had no choice but to let go of the limb. He felt his stomach rise toward his chest as he plummeted to the ground. Seconds later, he landed in the soft dirt of a flower bed.

He slipped the jacket from his mouth and glanced up at the tree. From the ground, it seemed he could almost touch the branch he'd been holding. He smiled, amused at his fear of heights, and stepped out of the flower bed.

A small bench sat near the back wall, hidden in the shadows. He crossed the garden and took a seat on the bench. He neatly folded his jacket, placed it at one end for a pillow, and lay down on his back. When he stretched out his legs, his feet hung off the end of the bench. He rested his hands on his chest and closed his eyes.

Sometime later, he felt a hand nudging him on the shoulder.

"Sir, are you all right?"

Connolly opened his eyes to see a young priest standing over him. He rubbed his hands across his face and pulled himself into a sitting position. The sun was up. Already the morning was hot. Connolly felt sweaty and dirty. His joints were stiff, and his back ached from the hard bench.

"Yeah," he replied. "Just needed a place to sleep."

"We have an arrangement with the Blue Moon Cafe," the priest said. "On Joachim Street. I can give you a voucher for breakfast and lunch."

Connolly smiled.

"It's all right." He stood and shook the priest's hand. "I appreciate the loan of your bench."

The priest nodded in response but gave him a bewildered look. Connolly slipped on his jacket and started across the garden toward the door at the back of the cathedral.

The Chrysler sat in front of the office building where he'd left it the night before. Connolly stooped beside it and glanced at himself in the side mirror. His white shirt was wrinkled and dirty. He had a scruffy beard, and his hair stood straight up on top of his head. Bags under his eyes made him look like a drunk waking from a three-day binge.

As he turned away from the car, he noticed the pay phone near the front entrance to the building. He paused, considering whether to check it. He took a step toward it, then dismissed the idea and entered the building. He reached the office shortly before seven. The air inside was cool and dry, a welcome relief from the sweaty night. He made his way down the hall to the break room.

The copier sat along the far wall of the room. To the right was a small sink with a mirror above it. To the left was a table with a coffeemaker and a tray of cups. He laid his jacket on the copier and peeled off his shirt. The cool air in the office felt refreshing against his skin. He started a pot of coffee in the coffeemaker.

While the coffee brewed, he washed his face and torso at the sink. By the time he finished, the coffee was ready. He sipped a cup while he shaved. When he finished shaving, he poured himself another cup, picked up his jacket, and walked to his office.

A clean shirt hung behind the door. He hung his jacket on the coatrack and took the shirt from its hanger. He heard Mrs. Gordon enter through the front door as he pulled the knot of his tie against the collar of his shirt. She came down the hall and stood at his office door.

"You get here early or stay late?"

Connolly smiled as he pulled the points of his collar down and buttoned them.

"Just passing through," he replied.

She gave him a suspicious scowl. He leaned toward her.

"Want to check my breath?"

She grimaced and took a step back.

"Probably drinking something I can't smell," she scoffed.

He finished with the tie and slipped on his jacket. She retreated to her desk. He dusted off the jacket sleeves and walked up the hallway.

Mrs. Gordon sat at her desk, trying to look busy. He pulled open the door to step into the corridor, then paused.

"Listen, maybe you should take the day off."

She gave him a puzzled look.

"Huh?"

"Maybe you should go home," he said.

"Home?"

"Yeah. Home."

"What for?"

"Look, some people came to Barbara's house yesterday, looking for her and Rachel."

"What? That landlord?"

"No. Not the landlord."

She looked confused.

"They came to my house last night," he continued. "There isn't anything to keep them from coming here, and I can't hang around with you." He took her by the hand to lead her from the desk. Reluctantly, she followed. He picked up her purse and gave it to her. "Now, just go home, lock the doors, and call the police if you see anything suspicious. Better yet, call Toby."

"Toby?"

"Toby LeMoyne. You call him. He'll come."

He opened the door and pushed her toward the corridor.

"I have things to do," she protested.

"Whatever it is, you can do it later," he replied.

He followed her into the corridor and closed the office door.

"My keys," she exclaimed.

Connolly scowled at her.

"They're right there on the desk," she insisted.

"Get them later."

He took out his key to lock the door.

"Just open the door and get them," she demanded.

Frustrated, he opened the door and stepped into the office. Her office key was lying on the desk, tied to the silver spoon by a ribbon. He picked it up and handed it to her.

"What's so important about a key?"

"Not the key. The key ring." She held up the spoon on the ribbon. "My daughter gave this to me."

Connolly stood transfixed, his mouth gaping open. He stared at her while she opened her purse and put the key inside. She closed the purse and glanced at him.

"What are you staring at?"

"Your daughter gave it to you?"

"Yes. The spoon was hers when she was a little girl. Why?"

"You have a daughter?"

"What do you mean, 'Do I have a daughter?'" A frown wrinkled her forehead. "Are you sure you didn't stay out drinking last night?"

Connolly slumped against the office door.

"I don't believe this."

"What do you mean you don't believe it?"

"First, Hollis tells me you have a sister. Now, you tell me you have a daughter."

"I have two sisters," she said. "What's wrong with you? You act like this is some great revelation."

Connolly stared at her. She shifted positions and gave him an impatient look.

"Are we going or staying?"

He turned around and locked the door.

They rode the elevator to the lobby in silence. Connolly walked with her to the sidewalk outside.

"Where are you parked?"

"Middle of the block," she said. "This way."

She gestured over her shoulder down the street. He could see her car in the middle of the block.

"Go on," he said. "I'll watch you from here."

She turned away and started down the sidewalk, shaking her head and mumbling to herself as she walked. He watched until she reached the car and drove away. When she was gone, he stepped to the Chrysler.

Forty

From the office, Connolly drove to Ingram Shipbuilding. There was nothing left to do but confront Harry Giles. If Hollis was right about him, Harry would point him toward some answers. If Hollis was wrong, Connolly could easily wind up dead. Not much of a choice, but he had no other option. He had exhausted every lead, and so far all he had to show for it was the pain and misery he'd caused his friends and family.

He reached the main gate a little after ten. A guard stepped from the guardhouse as he drove up.

"Yes, sir," the guard said. "May I help you?"

"I'm here to see Harry Giles," Connolly replied.

"Is he expecting you?"

"I don't have an appointment."

"Let me see your driver's license."

The guard held out his hand. Connolly took his license from his wallet and handed it to him. The guard stepped from the street to the guardhouse and picked up the telephone. In a minute or two he returned to the car with a clipboard.

"Sign here," he said, pointing.

Connolly signed his name.

The guard took the clipboard and handed him his license.

"You'll have to surrender your license to the guard in the lobby," he said. "You'll get it back when you leave."

The guard stepped away from the car and waved him past.

Connolly parked the Chrysler in front of the administration building and went inside. A guard at the lobby desk took his driver's license and gave him a building pass. He crossed the lobby to the elevator and rode to the basement.

The door to Harry's office was open. His secretary acknowledged Connolly with a smile as he entered. Connolly moved past her and into the office. Harry was seated at his desk. Connolly pulled the door closed behind him.

"We need to talk."

"I'm kind of busy right now," Harry replied. "You sure this can't wait?"

"No," Connolly replied. "It can't."

Harry stared at him a moment.

"All right," he said. "If you insist. Have a seat."

Connolly took a seat in a chair in front of the desk. Harry slid his chair back and folded his hands in his lap.

"You don't look so good," Harry continued. "Sleep in your clothes last night?"

"Tell me about Tommy Grafton," Connolly said, ignoring the question. His voice was stern, but not demanding.

"What's to tell," Harry replied with a shrug. "He's—"

Connolly sprang from his chair and slapped both hands on the desktop. He leaned toward Harry, their faces inches apart.

"Tommy Grafton and two of his buddies paid Hollis Toombs a visit the other day." His voice was low, but the words hissed out between tightly clinched teeth. "They left him floating in the bayou to die. Then they went to see Peyton Russo. He's lying in the morgue. Then they went after my family." He banged his fist on the desk. "They came looking for me last night." He glared at Harry. "Now, tell me about Tommy Grafton. And don't tell me you don't know about him. I've already seen him with your man Daniels."

Harry's face was emotionless. He appeared unfazed.

"You don't want to know about Grafton," he replied.

"Yeah, well, we're way past that now. He came to my house last night. From the looks of it, he wasn't there to talk. So tell me about him. And while you're at it, tell me why Frank hired Harvey."

Harry grinned.

"Look, if it helps you any, the FBI has been investigating these guys for over a year." Connolly stepped back from the desk. He sat in the chair and waited. Harry turned to one side and crossed his legs. He took a deep breath, then let it out in a long, slow sigh.

"David Daniels and Tommy Grafton were smuggling drugs off a couple of oil rigs in the gulf. Been going on for years."

"What's that got to do with Frank and Harvey?"

"Get to that in a minute." Harry leaned back in his chair. "Grafton used to work on an oil rig. Somehow, he got up with a couple of guys from Mexico who were in the drug business. They cooked up this plan to bring the stuff in on an oil service boat. Mexicans got it to the rig. Grafton made sure it got on the service boat. Most of those boats were never seen by a customs agent or INS or anybody like that. It was a pretty smooth operation, from what I hear."

Connolly was still not sure where this was going, but he nodded for Harry to continue.

"A few years ago, Ingram Shipbuilding bought the company that serviced the rig Grafton was on. When we took over the company, Daniels found out about what they were doing. Instead of blowing the whistle, he joined them."

"And Steve found out about it."

"Looks like it. We haven't tied all that up yet."

"We?"

"After September 11, the Transportation Safety Administration tightened up port security. Started checking all those boats. Somebody caught wind of what Grafton and Daniels were up to. DEA got involved. Then the FBI."

"So what about Frank and Harvey?"

An awkward smile spread across Harry's face. He picked up a pen from the desk and twirled it with his fingers on the desktop.

"Frank and Ann Grafton used to have a ... thing."

"They had an affair."

"Yeah," Harry chuckled. "Kind of twisted, isn't it?"

Connolly shook his head.

"So did Frank know what Daniels and Grafton were doing?"

"Yeah. He knew. That's how he met Ann. Frank took her from Grafton. Steve took her from Frank. Grafton didn't care because it gave him leverage with Frank."

Connolly gave him a knowing look.

"But when Steve took her from Frank ..."

Harry nodded in response.

"That was a different matter," he said, finishing Connolly's thought. "Got into all that brother stuff. They didn't like each other anyway. Just made it worse."

Connolly already knew much of what Giles had told him. Hearing it, though, somehow convinced him Harry wasn't involved. He slipped the computer disk from his pocket and tossed it on the desk. Harry glanced at it.

"What's that?"

"Open it and let's see," Connolly suggested.

"Where'd you get it?"

"A witness. Peyton Russo was trying to read it when he was killed. Said the files on it are encrypted, whatever that means."

"What makes you think I can open it?"

"The person who gave it to me said it came from Steve. If that's correct, I think your computer system has a program that can read it."

Harry let the pen slip from his fingers and picked up the disk. A computer terminal sat on the credenza behind him. He turned toward it and inserted the disk in the drive slot.

Connolly moved around the desk and watched over Harry's shoulder. In a moment, a list of the files from the disk appeared on the monitor screen.

"Looks like you've got three files on here," Harry said.

Using the mouse, he highlighted the file at the top of the list. The computer opened the file and displayed a document. Connolly scanned down the page.

"Looks like a contract."

"Yeah," Harry replied. "It's a copy of the contract between Ingram Shipbuilding and COIC. China Overseas Investment Company. This is an active deal. We just signed this about eight or nine months ago. Who'd you say gave this to you?"

"I didn't," Connolly replied. "What's in the next file?"

Harry returned to the menu and opened the second file. It contained a schematic drawing. Connolly looked bewildered.

"What's that?"

Harry was silent. Connolly glanced at him.

"You know what it is?"

"Yeah," Harry said, finally. "I know what it is. It's classified. You've got to tell me who gave this to you."

"Later. Tell me what it is."

"It's a drawing of an electrical system on a submarine. A nuclear submarine."

"What kind of system?"

"Can't tell you."

Harry closed the document and opened the third file. Another document appeared on the screen. Across the top was the title DefensePac. Down the left side of the page was a list of names. Next to it was a column of dollar amounts. Connolly pointed to the title.

"What is DefensePac?"

"Political action committee. Funded by companies in the defense industry. This looks like a list of the companies who contributed." Harry ran his finger down the list as he spoke.

"These are the companies." He pointed to the column of figures opposite the names. "This is the amount each one gave."

"Ingram Shipbuilding on there?"

Harry scrolled down the list.

"Right there," he said, pointing.

The record indicated Ingram Shipbuilding contributed $500,000 to the committee. Connolly scribbled down the amount.

"Anything else in that file?"

Harry scrolled down the screen. A second document appeared. Like the first, it contained a list of names, along with a corresponding column indicating amounts of money. Connolly pointed to the column.

"This is the money the committee gave?"

"Looks like it," Harry replied.

Connolly scanned the list.

"Scroll down a little farther."

Harry moved down the list. Near the bottom Connolly saw a name that made his heart skip a beat.

"Hogan Smith," he whispered.

"Yeah," Harry said. "He's been pretty good for the industry."

Connolly leaned against the corner of the desk, thinking.

"What was the date of the contribution to Smith?"

Harry glanced at the document on the screen.

"May 24, of this year."

"And the contribution from Ingram to the committee?"

Harry scrolled up the document.

"April 23."

Connolly thought a moment.

"What was the—"

"I'm looking right now," Harry interrupted.

He was already opening the first file. In a moment, the contract appeared on the screen. He scrolled down the document to the signature page.

"Looks like it was signed on March 1."

Connolly's mind raced. He slid around the desk to his chair.

"Frank signed the deal with the Chinese in March." He took his time, thinking as he talked. "Ingram gave the money to the committee in April. The committee passed it to Smith in May."

Harry looked skeptical.

"You think that's what this is all about? A contribution from the Chinese to Smith?"

"I think that disk is a message from Steve," Connolly replied. "He wasn't worried about Tommy Grafton and drug smuggling. He was worried about Frank and this deal. But why did he include the drawing?"

Connolly waited, but Harry did not respond.

"What was that drawing? What kind of system?"

"I can't tell you," Harry replied.

"What do you mean, you can't tell me?" His voice grew louder as he spoke. "Two people are dead. Hollis Toombs is in the hospital. And it's not because some rednecks are smuggling drugs off an oil rig. It's because of what's on that disk." By the time he finished, he was shouting. "Tell me about that drawing!"

Harry stared at Connolly. Again, his face was expression-less, but his eyes seemed to be looking past Connolly to some place far away.

"Hollis going to be all right?"

Connolly crossed his legs.

"They say he'll be fine." His voice was calm. "Going to take a while to recover, though."

Harry nodded thoughtfully. He leaned back in his chair and let out another long, slow sigh.

"Sometime around 1970, the navy decided they had done all they could to make their submarines quiet. Isolated the working parts, redesigned the hull. Whole bunch of stuff. Only thing left to work on was the propeller. Average prop makes a racket churning through the water, especially at high speed. Pockets of air build up on the blade. Big problem."

Harry paused to let Connolly digest what he had said, then continued.

"So the navy came up with a new propeller. Gave it a variable pitch. Complicated thing to manufacture, but it reduced the noise. Made it adjustable." He moved his hands back and forth to demonstrate. "So they could keep the blades at the quietest angle as the speed increased. Then they got an even brighter idea."

He leaned forward and rested his elbows on the desk. He picked up the pen from the desk and began to play with it again.

"They decided to tie the whole thing to the hard drive on the sonar computer and see if they could get the propeller to mimic the sound made by a Soviet submarine. Took a while to figure out the computer programs, but when they did, it worked perfectly."

Connolly's head felt tight again, like it had when he talked to Stamm Guidry. He pressed his fingertips against his temples and closed his eyes. Harry gave him a quizzical look.

"You all right?"

"Yeah," Connolly replied. He opened his eyes. "Pretty impressive accomplishment."

He struggled to find some connection between what he was hearing and Steve Ingram's death.

"It was more than impressive," Harry said. "It was astounding. Put our submarines right on top of the Russians. Never knew it was us."

"Which leaves us with the big question," Connolly sighed.

Harry nodded in agreement.

"Why did Steve have a copy of this drawing?"

"Yeah," Connolly agreed. "And why did he want to make sure someone knew about it?"

"There's another question, too," Harry said. "You have to have a user name and a password to get into our computer system. Steve didn't have either one, and I don't think he would have known how to find these files even if he did. Especially the drawing. It's on a separate server, and he would have needed another security code to get to it."

"So what are you saying?"

"I'm saying, there must have been someone helping him. Where'd you get this disk?"

"Ann Grafton."

Harry leaned back in his chair again.

"You got a lot of loose ends to tie up to get anybody to believe you on this one." He laced his fingers behind his head. "Including me."

Connolly stood and moved around the desk.

"You may be right." He pushed a button on the computer and took the disk from the drive. "But I know someone who has all the answers."

He started toward the door. Harry called after him.

"Where are you going?"

"Frank's office," Connolly replied.

He walked out of Harry's office and strode down the hall toward the elevator. Harry trailed behind him, struggling to put on his jacket as he hurried to catch up.

"You can't just go barging in there without an appointment."

Connolly pressed the button for the elevator.

"Watch me," he replied.

Forty-one

When the doors opened on the top floor, Connolly and Harry stepped from the elevator into chaos. The telephone was ringing. Employees, frantic and confused, scurried about the office suite in every direction, their voices loud and excited. Frank's secretary sat at her desk, frazzled and frustrated.

"We can't find him," she blurted as they stepped toward her desk.

Harry had a pained look on his face.

"Can't find who?"

"Mr. Ingram," the secretary replied.

The noise was so loud Connolly couldn't understand what she said.

"Stop!" he shouted.

Everyone turned to look at him. The office was suddenly quiet. Harry glanced in his direction.

"Thank you." He turned to the secretary. "Are you saying Frank isn't here?"

"Yes, sir." She looked bewildered. "He isn't here, and we can't find him. No one answers the phone at his house. I tried his cell phone. It's been disconnected. His pager won't work. I even tried sending him an e-mail, but our system says he's not an authorized user."

Harry seemed unfazed.

"Why wasn't I informed of this?"

"I called your office. Mr. Daniels came up."

Connolly sensed trouble. He backed away from the desk and started toward the elevator. Harry continued to question the secretary.

"Has anyone been to his house?"

"Sir?"

"Has anyone gone to Frank's house?"

"Mr. Daniels said he was going over there."

Harry turned away and walked toward the elevator. Connolly was already waiting with the door open.

"Your car or mine?"

"Where are you parked?"

"Out front," Connolly replied.

"Let's take yours. Mine's in a lot in back."

They rode to the lobby in silence. When the doors opened, they walked outside to the Chrysler.

Frank lived in a three-story house on Oakland Avenue in the Springhill section of Mobile. Made of brick and stucco, it sat a hundred yards off the street behind a wall of camellias and gardenias. A driveway led from the street along one side of the house to a garage in back. Connolly slowed the car and turned into the drive.

"Looks pretty quiet."

"Yeah," Harry replied. "Too quiet. Supposed to have a lawn service here this morning."

Connolly steered the Chrysler up the driveway and around behind the house. They stopped near the garage and got out.

"Doesn't look like anyone's at home," Connolly said.

Harry did not reply. Connolly followed him across the drive to the back door. He pushed it open and stepped inside.

The door opened to a mudroom. A short hallway led from there to the kitchen. The mudroom was empty, stripped bare to the walls. Harry glanced around, as if taking note of what had been there before, then stepped down the hall to the kitchen. Connolly followed a few steps behind.

When he reached the kitchen, Harry came to an abrupt stop. Connolly came up behind him, curious to see what brought him up short. One look at the counter told him. Like the mudroom, the kitchen was empty. Harry stared at the bare countertops, then opened a cabinet door. The shelves were empty too. Not a cup or a saucer or a plate. Not even a trace of dust or dirty shelf paper. The cabinets had been not only emptied, but also cleaned out, as though someone had taken great pains to make sure not a trace was left behind.

Connolly followed Harry from the kitchen through the butler's pantry to the dining room. It, too, was empty. They moved from the dining room to the living room at the front of the house. Only the curtains remained.

"I don't believe this," Harry whispered in disbelief. He wandered to the far side of the room. "It's all gone." He turned to Connolly, his eyes wide in amazement. "Everything is gone."

Connolly was surprised when they came through the kitchen, but by the time they reached the dining room, he had recovered enough to begin to think again.

"Where's Daniels?"

"I don't—"

"We have him," a voice interrupted from behind them.

Connolly turned to see who spoke. Dave Brenner appeared in the doorway.

"Picked him up this morning."

"What about Grafton?"

"Coast Guard got him and a bunch of Mexicans late last night. Caught them on a platform out in the gulf."

"And Herman Fontenot?"

Brenner shrugged his shoulders and gave Connolly a wry smile.

"Don't worry about Fontenot and Mizell. We'll get to them later."

Harry moved across the room toward Brenner.

"What about Frank?"

"Don't worry about Frank."

Harry looked perturbed.

"You arrested him? You arrested Frank Ingram?"

"No," Brenner said. "We didn't arrest him. He agreed to cooperate. We've ... relocated him."

"Where?"

"I can't tell you." He gave Harry a hard look. "And don't try to find him, either."

"It's not that simple," Harry argued. "We have a multi-billion-dollar company to run."

Joey Ingram appeared in the doorway behind Brenner.

"I have that under control, Harry."

"You?"

"Yeah."

Joey moved toward the middle of the room. Brenner stepped aside to let him pass.

"Before he left, Frank gave me his voting proxy for all his shares in the company. The board met last night and elected me president."

Harry looked confused and angry.

"The board? Why wasn't I informed of this?"

"Couldn't take the risk Daniels would find out." Joey took him by the elbow. "Come on. Let's go back to the office. I'm sure Dave and Mike have plenty to discuss. You and I do, too."

Joey led Harry out of the room. Brenner waited until they heard the back door close, then turned to Connolly.

"You know, you almost cost us a major undercover operation. We'd been working on it for two years."

"Two years?" Connolly snorted. "We made Fontenot and Mizell in two days."

"I'm not talking about those two clowns." Brenner stepped toward him. "I believe you have a computer disk."

"What about it?"

"That disk contains classified information." Brenner held out his hand. "I'd like to have it."

Connolly folded his arms across his chest.

"What are you going to do with it?"

"That's none of your concern."

Connolly moved away.

"There's information on that disk that implicates Hogan Smith."

"I'm sure it does."

"Are you investigating him, too?"

"I couldn't tell you that even if we were."

Connolly stroked his chin.

"If you've been working on this for two years, you must have known Steve Ingram was going to be killed."

Brenner avoided his gaze.

"Steve was a big boy. He knew the risks."

"So you knew someone was going to kill him."

"We ... had our suspicions."

"You let them kill him?"

Brenner looked at him.

"Couldn't be avoided."

"What do you mean?"

"National security."

"National security?" Connolly was irritated by his answer. "That why you let them come to my house last night? National security?"

Brenner gave him a smile. Connolly shook his head.

"You'd have let them have me, too."

"I don't think you know as much about this as you think."

"Enlighten me."

"Can't do it." Brenner stepped forward and thrust out his hand once more. "Give me the disk."

Connolly backed away. He wagged his finger and shook his head.

"Lot of people died because of this disk." He tapped his finger against the pocket of his jacket. "Steve Ingram. Peyton Russo. Tried to kill Hollis Toombs. Would have killed me if they could have found me. My family." He shoved his hands in his pants pockets and glared at Brenner. "You want the disk. Fill in the details."

Brenner sighed and lowered his head as if thinking about what to do next. Finally, he looked at Connolly.

"Frank wanted to build ships for the Chinese. Lucrative deal. Meant a lot to the company. But he had to have approval for it from a number of government agencies. To get it approved, he asked Hogan Smith for help. Halfway through the process, Smith decided he needed some campaign money from the Chinese for all his hard work. The Chinese agreed, but then they wanted something in return."

Connolly lifted an eyebrow.

"Something like ... sonar technology perhaps?"

"Perhaps."

"Did they get it?"

"Almost." Brenner stepped toward him. "That's about all I can tell you. You've probably figured that much out on your own by now anyway. You can wonder about the rest."

He held out his hand.

"You had someone on the inside. Greg Drummond?"

"Can't say."

"How did Steve find out?"

"Overheard a conversation. Pieced it together."

"Where'd he get the stuff on the disk? Harry tells me he didn't have access to the computer system where it was stored."

"Steve wasn't as dumb as people thought." Brenner thrust his hand toward Connolly. "I've told you all I can. Give me the disk."

Connolly hesitated. Brenner looked him in the eye.

"I don't want to get ugly about it."

Connolly slipped the disk from his jacket and handed it to Brenner. Brenner took it and dropped it in his pocket.

"Good," he sighed. "Come on. I'll walk you out."

Connolly followed him through the house and out the back door. Brenner moved across the driveway to his car. Connolly stepped to the Chrysler and opened the car door.

"You driving yourself today? Where's Hammond?"

Brenner opened the car door.

"He's ... having a busy morning."

He slid behind the steering wheel and started the engine. He motioned for Connolly to leave first.

Connolly got into the Chrysler and started down the driveway. In the rearview mirror he could see Brenner in the car behind him, talking on a cell phone as he followed him to the street.

Forty-two

At the end of the driveway, Connolly turned right and drove downtown. He found a parking place on Dauphin Street between the office building and the Port City Diner. As he walked toward the building, he noticed the pay phone. This time, he didn't ignore the urge to check it. He walked across the sidewalk to the phone and lifted the receiver. All he heard was silence.

A wave of panic swept over him. The receiver slipped from his hand and bumped against the side of the phone booth.

Connolly hurried inside the building and across the lobby to the elevator. He jabbed the button with his finger, then pounded it with his fist. In a moment, the doors opened. He darted into the elevator car and hit the button for the third floor. The doors closed. Connolly leaned against the wall.

The ride in the elevator gave him time to think. Fontenot and Mizell were scary enough, but with them in custody, there was no telling who might be waiting for him. Perhaps the men who killed Peyton Russo. Maybe someone worse. By the time the doors opened again, fear gripped his heart. He stood there, staring through the open doors, trying to listen for any sound that someone might be waiting for him in the corridor. After a moment, the doors started to close. He stuck his hand through the opening and pushed them apart. He leaned out, looking up and down the corridor.

The elevator was located on the south side of the building. Connolly's office was down the corridor and around the corner to the right. As far as he could see, there was no one in sight. But they could be lurking just around the corner.

He waited a moment longer, then stepped out. The elevator doors closed behind him. He turned right and walked toward the corner. With each step, his shoes made a clicking sound on the tile floor.

Too much noise, he thought. *I might as well be shouting.*

The corner drew nearer. His heart beat faster. The palms of his hands were sweaty. He loosened the knot on his tie and unbuttoned the top button of his shirt. At the corner, he stopped and listened again. After a moment, he balled his fist tightly and cocked his arm, ready to punch anyone who approached. He took a deep breath and leaped from the corner to the middle of the corridor.

No one was there.

Suddenly self-conscious, he glanced around to see if anyone had noticed him. An embarrassed smile crept across his face. In a few quick steps, he reached the access panel for the telephone system. With one tug, the door came open. Inside, he saw the black crossover wires that had been there before were now missing.

The fear that had gripped him in the elevator melted away. A sense of calm came over him. For a moment, he had a sense that the whole ordeal was finished. Whoever had tapped his phones no longer needed it. They had removed it. A satisfied smile spread across his face.

Then the obvious came to mind. The smile disappeared. No one would put an illegal tap on a phone, then come back to remove it. They wouldn't care. If they were finished, they'd just leave it. They'd never risk being caught taking it off. He closed the access panel and turned to the office door.

The sense of fear rose in him once again. He stared at the

door, wondering what was waiting for him on the other side. He took the key from his pocket and quietly slid it into the lock. Then, in one quick motion, he unlocked the door and shoved it open. As the door swung out of the way, he jumped to the side. The door opened all the way back and banged against a chair, but nothing happened. Connolly leaned his head around the doorframe for a quick look.

Then, from down the corridor, he heard footsteps approaching. He froze. The footsteps drew closer. A woman rounded the corner. She slowed as she approached, a look of concern on her face.

"Are you all right?"

Connolly gave her a sheepish smile. He didn't know her name, but he'd seen her in the building many times.

"Yes," he replied. "Just ... just checking."

She nodded, gave him a hesitant smile, and moved down the corridor. Connolly stepped inside his office and closed the door.

"This is crazy," he mumbled.

Still, he glanced around the room, checking for even the slightest hint someone had been there. Everything on Mrs. Gordon's desk seemed to be in order. Nothing looked out of place. He walked past her desk and down the hall to the break room.

From the doorway, he scanned around the room. The copier was in its place. The coffeemaker looked untouched from when they left earlier that day. He looked over the room once more, then moved on to his office.

The phone sat in its place on the far side of the desk. The pencil holder was next to it. A coffee cup sat on a saucer where he'd left it when he changed shirts. There was still coffee in it. He slipped off his jacket and laid it over a chair by the door, then took a seat behind the desk.

With his hands folded behind his head, he sat there,

listening to the silence of his office. His heart rate slowed. In his mind, he sorted through the case.

All the loose ends had been tied up. Dave Brenner had the computer disk. Fontenot, Mizell, Daniels, and Tommy Grafton were all in custody. Harry Giles had turned out to be a good guy after all. Frank was ... somewhere with the FBI. Nothing was left. But someone had come back to take the tap off his phones.

As he thought through the details of the case, he opened the top drawer of the desk. A brown envelope lay to one side. In it were the pictures Mrs. Gordon made from the videotape he and Hollis took from Steve Ingram's bedroom. A smile lifted one corner of his mouth as he remembered that night. He took the envelope from the drawer and spread the pictures out on the desk.

One of the pictures showed Herman Fontenot standing in front of the nightstand by the bed. A small clock was visible next to him on the stand. Connolly searched through the desk drawer and found a magnifying glass. With his head bent low over the picture, he examined the clock, curious to see what time it showed. He adjusted the distance of the glass from the picture and brought it into focus.

"Six thirty," he whispered, reading the hands on the clock.

Looking through the magnifying glass, he noticed a thin leather strap hanging from the pocket of Fontenot's pants. A knot tied in the end of it held three beads in place.

Beneath the magnifying lens, objects missed by a casual look were now clear and obvious. A pair of shoes in front of the closet was just a pair of shoes, all but lost in the background to the naked eye. But with the magnifying glass he could see a sock was stuffed inside each one. The mirror on the dresser looked like any other mirror, until the magnifying glass showed a pass from a nightclub stuck in the corner between the mirror and the frame. It was an amusing exercise until he moved to a second picture.

Chosen to provide another view of Fontenot, it had been taken from the point in the video where he was about to flip the mattress off the bed. Two seconds later, the mattress would be leaning against the wall. But for this one last instant, everything on the bed was just as Steve and Ann had left it the morning of the explosion.

Connolly panned the magnifying glass over the bed. The man's dress shirt Ann had been wearing lay near the foot, where she'd been when Steve slipped it off of her. Connolly held the magnifying glass over it for a moment. As he did, he noticed the seam across the top of the pocket. Along the edge were the neatly embroidered initials GRD.

A frown wrinkled his forehead. He leaned away and rubbed his eyes.

"Who was GRD?" He whispered to himself. "GRD. GRD."

A knowing look flashed across his face. Greg Drummond. He jumped to his feet and lunged toward his jacket on the chair by the door. Frantic, he checked the pockets for Drummond's business card. When he didn't find it there, he scrounged through the top drawer of the desk. It wasn't there, either. He banged on the desktop with his fist as he tried to recall their one and only meeting.

Drummond had appeared in the hall that day as Connolly and Mrs. Gordon were talking. He walked into the office and took a seat. They talked. He stood as he was about to leave. Connolly stood. Drummond handed him his card. Connolly took it. They shook hands. He walked him to the door. He returned to the desk.

The desk. He looked across the desktop. There was the card, stuck in the pencil holder to the left of the telephone. He took it out and read the name. Gregory R. Drummond.

"GRD," he whispered.

Connolly sank into his chair. He'd solved the riddle of

the initials, but once again everything he thought he understood about this case had evaporated.

Drummond had been at Steve's house. Ann was wearing
his shirt. Steve would have known it was Drummond's shirt.
Which meant Steve knew Drummond was there. Better yet,
was Drummond in the house the morning of the explosion?

"Impossible," he mumbled.

If Drummond had been there, Bosarge would have known
it. Bosarge would have had pictures of it. Surely, he would
have told him by now. But why didn't Ann tell him?

He thought for a few moments, then gathered the pictures
from the desktop. He didn't have time to track down all the
witnesses again and ask them. He didn't have time to drive to
Bosarge's house and grill him one more time about things he
should have been told from the beginning. He laid the photograph of Fontenot aside. The rest he put in the envelope and
returned to the desk drawer.

He grabbed his jacket from the chair by the door, put the
picture in the jacket pocket, and started up the hall. In the
break room, he took a manila envelope from a shelf by the
copier. He slipped on his jacket and started out the door.

Unlike before, the thought that someone might be lurking
around the corner never entered his mind. He charged out of
the building and down the sidewalk to the Chrysler. He didn't
notice the pay phone or the receiver still dangling off the hook
where he'd left it. He started the car and steered it away from
the curb.

A label on the back of the photographs indicated they had
been made from the videotape by Loop Photo and Camera
Supply. Originally a circle of track at the end of the
Government Street trolley line, the Loop was now a trendy
area of shops, restaurants, and galleries. Loop Photo was
located one block off Government Street on Holcombe

Avenue. Connolly parked in front and went inside. A young clerk greeted him.

"May I help you?"

"My secretary brought a video in here a few days ago. You made some pictures from it." He took the photograph of Fontenot from his pocket and handed it to the clerk. "I was wondering if I could get this one enlarged."

The clerk glanced at it.

"We made this for you?"

"Yes," Connolly replied. He pointed to the photo. "I'm really interested in this area down here. The area at the foot of the bed."

The clerk grimaced.

"Can't blow this one up any larger. It would get too fuzzy to do you any good. Could make you another one, though."

"Excuse me?"

"I could make you another one." He pointed to the bottom of the photo. "Just of this area?"

"Yeah, but I don't have the videotape," Connolly replied. "I mean, I have it. Just not with me."

"That's no problem," the clerk shrugged. "We got it all on a CD."

"A CD?"

"Yeah. We digitize the video, then print out the pictures from that. Beats the old way. Used to make a negative and do the prints from that. They never came out too good." He flashed a smile at Connolly. "Wait right here."

The clerk disappeared into the back of the store. Connolly waited. In a few minutes, the clerk returned with a photograph.

"This what you need?"

He handed Connolly an eight by ten. Connolly glanced at it. Enough of the bed was visible to make it identifiable. Drummond's shirt lay at the foot on top of light blue sheets. The letters on the shirt pocket were sharp and legible.

"Perfect," he replied.

He paid the clerk and walked outside to the Chrysler.

Seated in the car, he took a pen from his jacket and drew a circle on the photograph around the pocket of the shirt. He waited for the ink to dry, then slipped the picture into the envelope he'd taken from the break room. He put the envelope on the seat beside him and started the car.

The Essex Hotel was an old downtown landmark. The main entrance opened beneath a large canopy on Royal Street. Brass revolving doors led to a lobby with a ceiling that soared four stories high above a marble floor. In the middle of the lobby, a giant chandelier hung from the ceiling above a large fountain. To the left were the main desk and bell captain's station. To the right was the Brown Pelican, a bar where politicians gathered in years gone by to smoke cigars, drink whiskey, and shape the future.

A second, less opulent entrance was located around the corner on St. Michael Street. Connolly turned the corner and parked the Chrysler in front of the St. Michael Street entrance.

He crossed the lobby to the desk. A clerk greeted him as he approached.

"May I help you?"

"Is Greg Drummond still here?"

The clerk checked the registry.

"Yes, sir. He's here."

"Good. Could I leave him a note?"

"Certainly."

The clerk took a piece of stationery from under the counter and handed it to him. Connolly took the paper and scribbled, "You said to let you know when I found something."

He signed his name and slid the note into the envelope with the picture. He wrote Drummond's name on the outside and handed it to the clerk.

"You'll see that he gets this?"

"Yes, sir. We'll get it to him right away."

Connolly turned to leave. As he started toward the door, a man entered through the Royal Street entrance. Connolly recognized him immediately. He was Mark, Rachel's former roommate. Connolly started across the lobby toward him, angry that they would take his daughter's money and not pay the rent.

Before Connolly could reach him, Mark entered the Brown Pelican. Connolly slowed his pace. He lingered a moment near the fountain, giving Mark time to find a seat, and then he moved casually toward the bar. From the doorway, he saw Mark seated at a corner table with Greg Drummond. They were smiling and laughing.

Connolly backed away and ducked out of sight.

Forty-three

Connolly arrived at the guest house late that afternoon. He parked the Chrysler at the end of the driveway and stepped out. The front door hung precariously from its frame, held only by a single hinge. Through the doorway, he could see the mess inside. The couch sat near the coffee table, where he'd left it when he came back to get his jacket. It was the only piece of furniture in an upright position. Just looking at the mess inside made him tired. He leaned against the fender of the car and let out a long, slow sigh.

The soft orange light of a setting sun filtered through the trees that surrounded the house. The day was almost over. Evening was coming on. Around him, he could hear the sounds of the city as it drifted into twilight. He wanted a drink.

Drinking had been an addiction, but it had also been part of the ritual of his life. Back then, he usually gulped it straight from the bottle throughout the day and most of the night. But at this time of the day, the time between afternoon and evening, he always drank from a glass, his feet propped on something, his tie loosened, his collar open.

He could feel the bite of the gin on his tongue. More than that, he could taste it. He swallowed hard and walked inside.

In the kitchen, he opened the refrigerator and took out a cold bottle of Coca-Cola. He twisted off the top and poured it into a glass. He set the glass on the counter and walked around to the coffee table. He picked it up and set it near the sofa. He retrieved the glass of Coke from the counter and sat on the couch, his feet propped on the coffee table.

Around him, the house was a wreck. Books and papers were strewn about. Pillows and cushions had been ripped open. The contents littered the room. From his seat on the couch, he could see into the bedroom at the end of the hall. It was in bad shape, too.

He sipped on the Coke and waited. Darkness crept across the room.

Before long, he heard the sound of a car coming up the driveway. He swallowed the last of the soft drink and set the empty glass on the coffee table. The car came to a stop behind the Chrysler. He heard the car door close, then the sound of footsteps approaching. Seconds later, Greg Drummond appeared. He stopped to examine the demolished door, then stepped inside.

"Maybe you should think about hiring a maid," Drummond said. He glanced around the room. "A decorator might help, too. What happened?"

"Had some visitors yesterday." Connolly turned on the couch to look at Drummond. "Three of your friends, I believe."

Drummond frowned at the suggestion he knew someone who would do something like that.

"My friends?"

"Yeah. Fontenot, Mizell, and Tommy Grafton."

Drummond's face relaxed, the frown replaced by a sly grin.

"Well, they won't be coming around to bother you anymore. FBI hauled them in this morning." He moved farther into the room, toward Connolly. "I got your message."

"Good."

"You have the last videotape?"

Connolly smiled. *The last tape.* That meant Drummond had the others.

"Yeah," he said. "I have the tape."

"You going to give it to me?"

"Can't really do that."

"Why not?"

"For one thing, it's evidence in a murder investigation."

"You're not going to give it to Hammond."

"I don't have any choice."

"The case is solved," Drummond argued. "The men who killed Steve are in jail. They don't need that video to get a conviction."

Connolly rested his arm on the back of the couch.

"You were in the house when Steve Ingram was killed, weren't you?"

"No," Drummond said. He turned away, his eyes darting around the room. "I left earlier."

"Who tapped my telephones?"

"I have no idea what you're talking about."

"Sure you do. You're the only one left."

"What?"

"The only people who knew about the tap on my office were me and whoever did it. Somebody removed it today. You're the only one left. Everyone else is accounted for."

Drummond looked concerned.

"I ..." He turned to face Connolly once more. "We don't have to get into all of this. Just give me the video and let this case end."

"It's not that easy."

Drummond's look turned angry.

"You can't prove any of what you think you know about this case."

"Maybe so. But like you said, appearance is everything."

Drummond scrunched his shoulders up around his neck. He held them there a moment, then sighed and let them drop.

"Are you going to give me the tape?"

"No."

Drummond nodded thoughtfully, then turned toward the door.

"I'm sorry it's come to this."

He stepped outside. As he moved away, two men appeared in the doorway. About six feet tall, they both wore gray suits with white shirts and red ties. They looked neat, trim, efficient; and they walked straight toward Connolly as if they'd come for only one purpose. Connolly felt his heart jump into his throat. The two men coming toward him were the same two men he'd seen in his mind when he was standing in Peyton Russo's kitchen. The fear he'd felt at his office earlier that day washed over him again.

As the fear crashed down on him like a wave, so also a sudden realization of how all the pieces fit together. Drummond hadn't been Steve's accomplice. He wasn't Steve's friend on the inside helping him. Maybe Steve thought he was, but Drummond had been at Steve's house because Steve was about to blow the lid off the whole deal. If something wasn't done, everyone would know about the contributions back to Hogan Smith's campaign fund and the technology they were willing to swap to get it. Drummond wasn't Steve's accomplice in exposing Frank. He was Steve's murderer.

Connolly forced himself to stand. His legs shook and his hands trembled, but he managed to face the two men. If this was it, he wasn't going to die sitting on the couch.

When they were within a few steps of him, the one on the left slid his hand inside his jacket and drew a pistol from the waistband of his trousers. He took a silencer from his jacket pocket and screwed it onto the end of the barrel. A moment later, he raised the pistol and pointed it toward Connolly.

Connolly looked him in the eye and gave him a calm, self-assured smile.

"You killed Peyton Russo," he said.

The man hesitated.

"Stabbed him in the head with an ice pick," Connolly continued, "while your buddy here held him down on the kitchen table."

The second man grinned.

"He's guessing."

The first man gave him a cold, hard stare.

"There's no way you could know that."

"Believe me. I know."

"Shoot him," the second man growled. "Let's get it over with."

"You had on a gray sweatshirt with the sleeves cut out," Connolly said. He looked at the second man. "You were wearing a white T-shirt with a beer logo on the front."

The two men looked at each other. The first one turned to Connolly.

"All the more reason to kill you."

Behind them, Anthony Hammond stepped into the doorway, pistol drawn and ready.

"Drop the gun," he shouted.

The first man hesitated. Hammond fired a shot. It struck the man on the shoulder. Blood spewed into the air in a fine mist. Connolly felt a piece of shattered bone strike him on the cheek. The man's torso rocked forward, and then he collapsed to the floor. As his head bounced off the tile floor, the pistol slipped from his hand. It landed at Connolly's feet.

In the same instant, the second man turned toward the door. As he came around to face Hammond, he drew a pistol from beneath his jacket.

"Gun!" Connolly shouted. "He's got a gun!"

Connolly dove across the sofa for cover. As he sailed out of the way, a second shot rang out. Behind him, he heard the sound of breaking glass and the noise of people coming down the hall. He landed on the floor in the living room and covered his head with his hands, doing his best to make himself as small as possible. Within seconds, the room was filled with an FBI SWAT team.

"Clear!" someone shouted.

Down the hall, a second voice called out.

"Clear."

Three men emerged from the bedroom and gathered near the dining table. Someone grabbed Connolly by the arm.

"You can get up, sir."

Connolly looked over his shoulder. Men dressed in black uniforms stood around him. Armed with assault rifles, their faces covered with black masks, they looked as scary as the two men who had come to kill him.

"You can get up, sir," the man repeated. "It's over."

Connolly stood and straightened himself. Near the kitchen, the first man lay on the floor, his shoulder and most of his chest blown away. A few feet to the right, the second man lay facedown on the floor between the couch and the door. Blood ran from beneath his body. His legs twitched. Connolly looked away.

"Better step outside," the man beside him said. "You look like you could use some air."

Connolly made his way around the sofa, past the second man's body to the door. One of the men in the room leaned around the corner and stuck his head out the doorway.

"Coming out!"

Connolly walked as far as the Chrysler and collapsed against the rear fender. He laid his head on the trunk lid.

Anthony Hammond stood a few feet away. He moved to the back of the car and propped his foot on the bumper.

"You all right?"

"I don't know," Connolly groaned. "That was really close."

"Yeah."

"So you knew about Drummond?"

"We've been tailing him since he got to town. Caught a break with his friend."

"His friend?"

"Mark something-or-other. He didn't like being part of a murder. You nearly blew the whole thing this afternoon at the hotel. How do you know him?"

Connolly raised his head from the trunk lid and gave him a weak smile.

"Long story."

"Pretty gutsy move," Hammond continued. "You must have known he'd come looking for you when you gave him that picture. What were you going to do if we hadn't showed up?"

The smile on Connolly's face spread to a grin.

"I knew you'd be here."

"How'd you know that?"

"That's an even longer story." Connolly stood. "You need me for anything else here?"

"Not right now," Hammond replied. "We can get a statement from you tomorrow. You got a place to sleep tonight? I don't think you'll be able to use this place, even if you wanted to."

Connolly steadied himself against the car as he took the keys from his pocket.

"Yeah. I got a place," he replied.

He opened the car door and got in the Chrysler. Hammond moved from behind the car. Connolly started the engine and backed away. A patrol car was parked to the left. Drummond sat in the backseat. A police officer stood guard beside the car.

Forty-four

After lunch the following day, Connolly picked up Barbara, Rachel, and Elizabeth from Guy Poiroux's house in Bayou La Batre. Barbara sat sideways in the front seat of the Chrysler, facing Connolly as they drove to Mobile. Her back against the door, she had a perplexed look on her face as they talked about Steve Ingram and the events of the past few weeks.

"So Frank Ingram had his brother killed?"

"Yes," Connolly replied. "I mean, he didn't set the charge and blow him up. But he gave Tommy Grafton and David Daniels enough information to make them believe Steve was about to turn them all in to the DEA. Grafton recruited Fontenot and Mizell."

"But Frank wasn't really involved in their drug deal."

"No. He knew about it, but what he was worried about was that campaign contribution he'd passed from the Chinese to Hogan Smith and what he'd done to get it."

"So what was Greg Drummond doing at Steve's house?"

"He was doing what he always does. Looking out for Hogan Smith. Only this time, he had to clean up after himself, too."

She had a quizzical look on her face as she thought about what he'd said.

"The video."

"Right."

"You think he was in there with Ann?"

Connolly held up his hand as if warding off the question.

"I'd rather not think about what he might have been doing. I figure he knew he was on some of those tapes, one way or the other."

"How'd he find out about the tapes?"

"I don't know. Frank probably told him. But he didn't find out about it until after we removed the camera. Once he learned the camera was missing, he knew someone else knew about the tapes, and that's when things started happening."

"And Peyton Russo? They killed him for the computer disk?"

"No. Hollis said the men who tried to kill him were looking for the video. I don't think Frank or Greg Drummond knew about the computer disk. Drummond never mentioned it, and there was enough stuff on that disk to bury all of them. If he'd known I had it, he would have been after it. I think he thought Peyton had the video."

Connolly glanced at Barbara. She had a puzzled look on her face. He smiled at her.

"You look confused."

"All this over a video?"

"Not just a video. A public image."

"Public image?"

"Drummond's a guy who understands neither he nor Hogan Smith can afford a scandal."

"How is an affair with someone's girlfriend a scandal? Especially someone who's been passed around as much as Ann?"

"Mother," Rachel blurted from the backseat. "You talk about her like she's somebody's property."

"She acted like she was property," Barbara replied.

Connolly glanced over at her.

"He wasn't there with Ann."

Barbara gave him a troubled look and waited for him to finish the thought.

"He was there with Mark."

"Mark?"

Rachel leaned over from the backseat.

"You saw Mark?"

"I saw him with Greg Drummond yesterday. At the Brown Pelican."

"Is he that guy from Washington? Works for some senator?"

"Yeah." Connolly glanced at her over his shoulder. "You knew about him?"

"Came by the house one day."

Connolly gave Barbara an "I told you so" look.

"I was right," he said. "Drummond came down to hide the senator's secrets, but he had his own to hide, too. Only thing was, Mark didn't like being involved with a murderer. He found Anthony Hammond somehow and tipped him off."

She shook her head.

"This is a complicated case."

"It helps to have a diagram."

"How did you know those two men were coming after us the other day?"

"I just knew."

"You just knew."

"I just knew. Deep inside. At a place I've never been before." He smiled at her. "I knew."

She gave him a strange smile.

"Is that how you knew Drummond's men killed Peyton?"

"Sort of."

He turned the car onto Ann Street and brought it to a stop in front of Barbara's house.

"You want to come in?"

"Nah," he said, shaking his head. "I better go on."

"Do you have a place to sleep tonight?"

"Mother!" Rachel blurted before Connolly could answer. Barbara turned in the seat toward her.

"What?"

"You can't just ask him to sleep with you ..." She shoved open the rear door. "I can't believe it. My own mother."

She took Elizabeth from the car and started toward the house in a huff. Barbara turned to Connolly.

"I wasn't talking about that."

"I know you weren't," he replied. He looked over her shoulder at the house as he spoke. "I'd love to stay. But there are too many memories in that house."

"Some of them were pretty good."

"Yes, they were. But the bad ones were pretty bad, too."

She leaned across the seat and kissed him on the cheek. He was lost in thought.

"Did you know Mrs. Gordon had a sister? Carol?"

Barbara gave him a perplexed look.

"Carol? Sure. I knew her. She has another sister, too. Why?"

"I didn't know anything about Carol until a few days ago."

"What do you mean?" She frowned at him. "She's been to our house several times."

There was a blank look on Connolly's face.

"I don't remember her." He stared at her a moment, trying to recall a time when he'd seen her. "Did you know Carol was once married to Harry Giles?"

"Yes."

Connolly shook his head. He looked down at the center of the steering wheel.

"Did you know Mrs. Gordon has a daughter?"

"She had a daughter, but she died."

He glanced up at her.

"Her daughter died?"

"Yes. Four years ago ... I think."

Connolly sighed.

"Where was I?"

"I'm not sure. You didn't attend the funeral. Rachel and I went alone."

Connolly turned away and stared out the window.

"I remember standing on the steps the other day at St. Pachomius, knowing you and Rachel were in trouble. I knew it better than I've known anything. I saw in my mind what happened to Peyton and knew for certain it was the truth. And yet, I didn't even know my secretary had a sister or a daughter." He gave another long, heavy sigh. "I must have been in a coma." He looked at her. "I must have been terrible to live with."

She took his hand.

"It's all right, Mike," she whispered. "It's all right."

Tears filled his eyes. He squeezed her hand.

"I'm sorry," he whispered.

READERS' GUIDE

For Personal Reflection
or Group Discussion

Readers' Guide

A book is supposed to be an experience of discovery, of seeing something unfold in your mind as your eye travels along the page. I saw one thing in my mind as I wrote this story. You saw something else when you read it. That is the beauty of a story. It comes to you when you aren't expecting it and finds a place in your own experience. The following questions are offered as a way to help you think about the story. That's all. They aren't *the* questions of the book, and they certainly aren't the only ones that arise from the text or from your experience in reading it. But perhaps you will find them useful as you think about *Double Take* and the things you've experienced as you read it.

1. Place is important in a novel, often becoming as much a character in the story as any of the people. How many different places does Connolly visit in this story? List them.

2. Of those places to which this story takes Connolly, which are the most significant to the story? To you? Why?

3. St. Pachomius Church is one of the first places encountered in the story. Who was St. Pachomius?

4. Describe Connolly's relationship with his 1959 Chrysler Imperial. Can you think of an object with which you have a similar relationship?

5. What does the car symbolize?

6. While standing in Peyton Russo's kitchen, Connolly sees something that has already happened. Have you ever had a similar experience?

7. Do people have visions today? Are they real? From where do they come?

8. Later in the story, as Connolly leaves St. Pachomius Church, he has an experience in which he "knows" what is about to happen. He doesn't see an image of it in his mind. He simply knows with the assurance of fact that something is about to happen. Describe a similar experience you've had.

9. From where do you think this kind of knowledge comes?

10. Diagram the relationships in this story. Any relationship. Every relationship. Day to night. Twilight and evening. Night to Connolly. Connolly to Hollis. Hollis to the swamp. Diagram the relationships.

11. What is the significance of these relationships?

12. As I wrote this book, I found the relationship between Connolly and Barbara moving in an arc across the story. Something drove them apart. Now, something seems to be bringing them together. What things drive people away from each other? What things bring them together?

13. Mrs. Gordon has been with Connolly since he first became an attorney. Why wasn't she driven away?

14. What role does Mrs. Gordon play in Connolly's life?

15. What role does she play in the structure of the story?

16. I hope you have a Hollis Toombs in your own life. A person who is your friend for no logical reason. When someone asks, "Why are you friends?" your only answer is, "Because we are." You aren't coworkers. You don't share obviously common interests. Your temperaments and experiences are different. What makes for a relationship like that?

17. Have you ever been to a dogfight? A cockfight?

18. Who killed Steve Ingram?

19. Frank, Steve, and Joey Ingram were brothers. Describe their relationship.

20. Which character in the book best describes you? Your role in life? Your role in your family?

21. Connolly attends a service at St. Pachomius described as morning prayers. In what other religious rituals does he participate? How do those rituals influence him? What is the role of ritual in our lives?

22. How are Connolly's parents characters in the story? What is their role?

23. Most of the characters in this story are people Connolly has known for a long time. Yet, as the story unfolds, he seems to know less and less about them. How much do we really know about the people around us?

24. Anthony Hammond plays more than one role in the story. Describe those roles.

25. What happened to Frank Ingram?

These are my questions. What are yours? Visit my Web site and let me know at www.joehilley.com.